THE TASTE OF TREACHERY

EMILY BYBEE

5 PRINCE PUBLISHING

Copyright © 2024 by Emily Bybee, THE TASTE OF TREACHERY

All rights reserved.

This is a fictional work. The names, characters, incidents, and locations are solely the concepts and products of the author's imagination, or are used to create a fictitious story and should not be construed as real. No part of this book may be reproduced in any form or by any electronic or mechanical means, including information storage and retrieval systems, without written permission from the author, except for the use of brief quotations in a book review.

Published by 5 PRINCE PUBLISHING & BOOKS, LLC

PO Box 865, Arvada, CO 80001

www.5PrinceBooks.com

ISBN digital: 978-1-63112-401-3

ISBN print: 978-1-63112-379-5

Cover Credit: Marianne Nowicki

F072324

For Craig.

*You are my rock,
my safe place in this world,
my partner in everything,
and the love of my life.*

ACKNOWLEDGMENTS

First of all, thank you to my readers. You are the reason I keep making stories out of these crazy ideas in my head.

Second, thank you to my mom who reads everything I write and always encourages me to keep going.

Next, thank you to my critique group—Jymn, Christina, Michelle, and Chelsea— who catch me and call me on weak scenes and always find ways to take the story to the next level.

Also, thank you to Bernadette who is an amazing publisher to work with and Cate, who is such a wonderful editor to help make the story shine.

Lastly, thank you to my husband, who with his military service, was able to answer my millions of questions to make this book accurate—as well as being ever so patient.

It takes more than an author to make a great book and I'm so grateful to be surrounded by so many talented people.

ALSO BY EMILY BYBEE

Merry Mix-Ups
The Holiday Rebound
The Taste of Treachery

THE TASTE OF TREACHERY

CHAPTER ONE

US Army Base
Somewhere in the Middle East
March 5th

Dr. Nelson gripped the handle next to his jump seat with one hand while the chopper swayed and dipped in the gusty wind like a roller coaster ride. The folders, clutched to his chest with a white-knuckled grip, flapped and fluttered in the gale-force current the helo's blades created. The soldier next to him leaned out the open door and signaled to someone on the ground.

A wave of nausea swept up the doctor's throat and he swallowed to keep from spewing bile over the metal floor. The sand particles peppering his face signaled they were close to the ground. He said a silent prayer and swore to never venture out of the United States again if he got back home safely.

"Almost there, sir," the desert camo-clad soldier shouted. "Hang on."

This could ruin everything. It has to be stopped. The doctor repeated the mantra in his head and adjusted his sweaty grip on the bar. The helicopter bumped down on the landing pad with a teeth cracking jolt. Dr. Nelson lurched to one side, his body straining against the harness.

"Okay, sir. Off you go," yelled the soldier over the cacophony of the blades and blowing sand while he unbuckled the harness for the panicked doctor.

"Thank you," the doctor said through a dry mouth. He climbed on shaking legs to the edge of the metal floor and gripped both the printouts and his bag while he floundered down the step to the sand. Another tan-clad man stood outside of the danger zone to meet him.

"Where is Mr. Marling?" the doctor yelled. "He is supposed to be here to meet me."

"He's on his way, sir," the soldier answered.

Dr. Nelson glanced at the name on the soldier's uniform—Brooks—then studied the young man's face. He needed to remember the names, follow the data.

Brooks couldn't have been older than eighteen or nineteen. A new wave of nausea washed over him, having nothing to do with the helicopter ride. He firmed his jaw and his resolve. He'd make Marling listen and understand the danger the data showed.

"Any problems around base?" he asked while they walked through the tents.

"Pretty quiet lately, sir. Don't worry, we'll keep you safe," Brooks answered, misunderstanding the doctor's concern.

"I'm sure you will, son," the doctor murmured. "It's imperative I speak to Mr. Marling."

CHAPTER TWO

Chicago, Illinois
March 7th

Nerves twisted my stomach into an origami crane. The gallery owner's nimble hands flipped through my most precious possessions like they were the morning newspaper.

"Hmm." His hands paused. "How would you describe this one?"

I stopped chewing my nail and yanked my finger from my lips, then peered over his shoulder. Red and black paint splashed across the canvas. I'd debated on whether to include the dark painting, which deviated from my artful landscapes. It resulted from a recurring nightmare. I opened my mouth to answer when my phone buzzed in my pocket.

"Sorry," I said as I pulled it out of my pocket and glanced at the display: Will, my brother. I hit decline. He'd pestered me for the last week. I cleared my throat and motioned to the picture. "I painted it after an intense nightmare."

He nodded and pointed to the silver blur racing off the canvas. "Someone was shot?"

I swallowed the lump in my throat. "My dad. He was killed in action in Afghanistan."

"While your landscapes are exceptional, your emotion is vivid here. This is more visceral—piercing, if you will. Reminiscent of Munch's *The Scream*."

I flinched. That painting was the hell I'd been desperate to escape from for years.

"You said you're studying at the Institute?" he asked.

My phone buzzed again. I jumped and nearly dropped the damn thing. Will again. He'd been asking me to check in on his best friend, Caleb, who was in the hospital recovering from surgery to remove shrapnel from his back.

I hit decline again. "I'm really sorry. My brother is serving overseas." My mind battled to remember his question. "Um, the Institute, yes, double major in Computer Science and Art. I'm in my senior year."

It took my professor six months and pulling a lot of strings to get me this interview with the gallery owner. Without her recommendation, I wouldn't have a chance. Getting people to take your art seriously was hard, but it was even harder when you were the size of a twelve-year-old, and a short one at that, with unruly red hair. Most often I got a pat on the shoulder and a *keep up the good work* after they glanced at the results of my blood, sweat, and literal tears.

Damn Will. He was on base. Safe. Not on a mission. When he was, it kept me awake nights worrying. Plus, Caleb had plenty of nurses to keep him company. Knowing him, he probably had every woman in the hospital fighting over who got to give him sponge baths. He didn't need me to check up on him.

I sucked in a breath. The posh gallery even smelled artsy—a

combination of fresh flower arrangements mixed with paint fumes. These white walls launched more art careers than anywhere else in Chicago. A showing here was my dream, when I wasn't having nightmares about Dad getting shot by insurgents.

"Do you have any more along these lines? On the darker side?" the gallery owner asked.

Tender butterfly wings of hope unfurled in my chest. "Yes, I have several," I blurted out. Several more than I cared to admit. I kept the ever-increasing stack of nightmare paintings stuffed away, out of sight. Blood, guts and gore weren't my favorite subjects. I liked to focus on the beauty in the world.

My hands trembled at the thought of getting the intense images out and putting them up for everyone to see. But this was what I'd waited for. What I'd been working so hard for all these years. This chance.

The phone buzzed again, and I suppressed the urge to throw it against the wall.

"Either silence the phone or take the call," the owner said, his gaze darting to my face. His tone made it obvious which he expected. People didn't make him wait.

My finger hovered over the power button, but the tightening in my chest wouldn't let me push it. *What if it's something important?* I swallowed and prepared to end my art career before it even began.

"I am so, so sorry. This will just take a second," I said.

His eyes widened while his mouth tightened.

"If you want to look through the rest, I'll be right back," I said in a cheerleader-esque voice while I smiled so widely my lips practically split. I probably looked like a demented clown. I turned and jogged around a corner—not that it mattered since the walls didn't even go up to the ceiling.

This better be important. I glared at the phone. My finger tapped the green button. "I have better things to do than babysit Caleb," I hissed.

"Harper." The tone of Will's voice stopped the rest of the tirade about to jump off my tongue. "Harper, I'm in trouble."

Anger transformed to fear in a second flat. "What do you mean? What happened?"

Will's heavy breath muffled the sound of his words. "I was trying to get their picture. They know it's me. You're not safe."

"Will, you're not making sense." I squeezed the phone. The blood in my veins hardened into cement, unmovable. Pain spread through my ribs around my straining heart.

Voices sounded in the background. The clamor grew louder, closer. I yelled into the phone. "Will? Will?"

A crash blared over the line, more voices—right on top of him.

The shouts hurt my ears. Will screamed like I'd never heard before. A scream of pain.

The line went dead, cutting off his cries.

I gripped a table to stay upright. The sounds of the city faded. My vision fell away, leaving a pinpoint of white. No tears sprang to my eyes, no sobs from my lips. My hand holding the phone dropped from my face, as though my muscles were paralyzed. Nothing existed. Nothing except the infinite expanse of pain erupting from my chest. My fingers tightened on the table to keep the weight of my fear from dropping me to the floor. One thought trickled through my overloaded neurons. *Not again.*

Images crept back into my vision: flowers, paintings, walls. The pinched face of the owner peered around the corner of the partial wall, his irritation somewhat overshadowed by concern. "Are you finished?"

"I have to go," I gasped, letting out a stagnant breath, then pocketed the phone and started for the door.

His voice stopped me. "What about your portfolio? I might want to see more of your work."

I sped back to the table, stuffed the canvases into the leather portfolio, and then ripped the zipper shut, holding myself together by a shoestring. "I'm sorry, but I'll have to get back to you."

His slight drop-mouthed expression would have been comical under different circumstances. I rushed past him and out the door before he recovered enough to talk.

Goodbye art career.

CHAPTER THREE

On the sidewalk racing toward my apartment, I pulled out my phone and scrolled newsfeeds for stories of any activity where Will was stationed. Nothing. No soldiers killed or MIA in the last few days, just a couple of stories about two soldiers going against orders and shooting insurgents, and the subsequent investigation.

The lack of news did nothing to loosen the tightness in my chest. My phone showed multiple voicemails. I hit play on the first call I'd declined.

"Harper." Will's voice was strained from running. "I'm in trouble. I was trying to send a file to Caleb, and I must have hit the wrong contact. They could come after you. Call me back."

Air swooshed from my lungs like I'd been sucker punched in the gut. I stuffed the guilt away and hit play on the second voicemail.

"Harper. I'm sorry. I never meant to drag you into this. It's life or death. Call me back."

His voice shook. I'd never heard Will scared before, never seen him cry, not even at Dad's funeral. Will reacted differently than me to losing our father ten years before. He wanted to go fight the entire world. I saw enough guns in my nightmares to last me a lifetime.

I rushed up the stairs to my apartment and opened the door. The scent of lavender essential oil washed over me from the diffuser I kept running. The high ceilings and walls, covered with work from artists I admired, usually soothed me, but today it would take a lot more than Renoir, Monet, and an oil diffuser to help my nerves.

I threw the portfolio on my paint-covered table and dropped my bag on the floor. Shaking hands ran through my tangled hair. I ripped through the snags and growled before I yanked the annoyingly red shoulder-length curls into a ponytail.

A furry head and blinking golden eyes popped up from the mounds of blankets, some fuzzy, some weighted, on my unmade bed. Burnt orange stripes graced one cheek while the other bore the black stripes of a tortoise shell tabby. The small cat couldn't weigh over five pounds, but she somehow could lift a world of weight from my shoulders.

"Meow." Luna greeted me in her melodic voice and stretched before she picked her way toward me. I lifted the cat and buried my face in her silky fur. The downy-soft feel under my hand as I petted her allowed me to take a deep breath but did nothing for the turmoil ravaging my insides.

Luna waved her tail. When we'd first gotten her, Will joked her father had been a raccoon because of her extra long, puffy tail. She climbed on my shoulder, purring in my ear as if knowing I needed her—sensing my upset. Absently petting her, I ran through the conversation with Will and paused.

"I was trying to send a file to Caleb," he'd said.

My laptop connected about as fast as a sloth climbing a tree. Damn building wifi. My feet tapped the floor in a Riverdance-like rhythm while Luna contemplated me with her calm expression.

"I've got to find him, Luna."

She responded with a trilling meow.

Will was three years older than me. The day after high school graduation, he'd joined the Army with his best friend, Caleb. Just being in the Army hadn't been enough. He'd joined a Delta Force team so he could *really make a difference*. He was out to fight the entire world for taking our dad away.

I, on the other hand, went from the reigning State Junior Sharp Shooting Champion—something I'd always done with Dad when he was home—to never touching a gun again. The mere sight of any gun, including my former prized Colt revolvers, brought grisly images of Dad, face hardly recognizable, to my mind.

Now something had happened to Will. My eyes struggled to focus as images of another funeral took over my brain. Another flag-clad casket. Another gun salute. Luna pushed her head under my hand and brought me back to earth.

The computer chimed, and my fingers flew over the keys, pounding in my password. I had a ton of email messages, but nothing from Will. I searched everywhere I could think—including social media—nothing. Then I checked my anonymous gmail. The newest addition had numbers in the subject line. It was a video.

I clicked play. The screen showed a desert camp landscape with tents in the background, a typical Army base scene. In front of the tents stood a bunch of camo-clad men in a group. The faces were familiar from the various pictures Will sent home.

"Hey man, quit playing doctor with the nurses and get back here!" barked an enormous dark man in a tan tank top, who I vaguely recognized as part of my brother's squad.

A scruffy looking guy in glasses laughed. "Yeah, man. A little shrapnel in your ass don't get you a free ticket home.

Besides, I need someone to clean out when we play poker, and you're the worst bluffer I know."

Will's voice called from behind the camera. "Okay, guys, they did surgery on his spine, not his ass."

The camera turned, and Will's shoulders and head came into view, up close. Luna held her paw out to the screen, as if saying hello to Will. While we'd adopted her as my therapy pet, she'd loved Will.

My breath hitched at the sight of his smiling face. His brown hair looked lighter than usual, covered with a fine sheen of desert dust. Sunglass cutouts circled his eyes, standing out starkly against his tanned face. His cheeks were leaner, sharper—more like Dad's.

"We miss you, Caleb. Do what the doc says and get back here," Will said.

Off-camera voices came on the recording. Angry voices. "You don't understand. The preliminary tests were wrong, incomplete."

The smile dropped from Will's face. His attention focused to his left, but he kept the recording going and shifted in front of his group. His head disappeared and half the soldiers came into view, in addition to two men behind and off to one side.

Will called, "Okay, let's get a picture. Everyone, give him a salute."

A few soldiers from the unit still visible flipped off the camera, grinning. The two men behind them, oblivious that they were on film, stood facing each other. The suit-clad man, who would have fit in better in a boardroom than an Army base, leaned into a shorter man. "You flew here to tell me that? You should have stayed in your lab, Doctor."

"No one paid attention to the memos. This is important," the shorter man exclaimed, clutching papers and a manilla file to his chest.

"I decide what's important. Do you have any idea how much we spent to get this contract?" the Suit hissed.

"The initial results were promising." The doctor held his ground. "It took time for the problems to develop, so we didn't see them in the preliminary data. I insist we stop the tests, until we can—"

"You fix it. Understand?" The Suit shook his head and thrust a finger into the smaller man's face. "Do what we pay you for and make some additive that stops absorption or some shit. I'm not pulling the plug." With a sneer, he turned and spotted the phone. His eyes narrowed and his sneer flipped to a frown.

Will's voice sounded from behind. "One last picture for Caleb!"

The doctor continued. "No one will listen. I'm telling you DX—"

The Suit cut him off. "Not here." He studied the group of soldiers, his fuzzy brow scrunched into a long caterpillar on his face, then strode into a tent.

The screen went black.

My fingers raced over the keyboard. There had to be something else, something more. Nothing.

I stared at the screen, choking down the thickness in my throat and forcing myself to think. They were after Will over this video. I didn't see anything damning enough that they would go after a decorated American soldier. And who the hell were *they*?

Two more run-throughs revealed no new information. The time stamp showed March 5th, two days ago. He'd waited, then sent it yesterday to the anonymous email account I had from my days as a not-so-honest Computer Science major. I checked the account every so often out of habit, but it usually consisted of memes from hacker friends.

"Meow." Luna's voice made me blink. I'd been petting her

faster and faster as my emotions rose. She nuzzled my cheek and pushed her forehead against mine.

"Thank you, sweet girl." I slowed my frantic strokes. "We'll figure this out, right? We have to. I can't lose him."

With no other choice, I pulled my phone from my pocket. I blew a breath out through clenched teeth before I hit the contact.

My mom picked up on the first ring. "How did the meeting go? Did he love the mountain sunset?" The words tumbled from her mouth like a waterfall. "That's my favorite!"

My neurons fizzled and popped. The meeting with the gallery owner seemed like weeks ago. "It, um, he liked the paintings. But I need to talk to you about something else."

The tremor in my voice tipped her off. "Oh, honey. Did you have another anxiety attack?" Her voice held a massive sigh. "It's okay. You said he liked them?"

"Mom," I gritted out. "Listen, something's happened to Will. Someone hurt him. Has anyone contacted you?"

"Harper, Will is on base. He's fine." The calming air of her voice made me want to bash my phone against the wall. I'd heard that tone enough over the last ten years.

I gripped the phone. "No, he's not fine. They attacked him. I need to know if the military contacted you."

"No one's contacted me because *Will is fine.*" She stressed the last three words.

"He called me. There were screams." The memory of the phone call took my breath away. I clutched Luna as my vision narrowed to pinpoints. "He was in pain. Scared." I struggled to put sentences together. "I should have answered."

"You're not making sense. Listen to my voice, honey," she spoke in almost a whisper. "We'll get through this together. I'll talk you through it. Is Luna with you? Let's get her in your lap."

That was the problem with having several nervous

breakdowns in your teen years: everyone treated you like you'd break. Plus, apparently, no one believed you when something was actually wrong. "Mom," I yelled, interrupting her soothing speech about getting to a doctor to get me the help I needed. "I don't need a fucking doctor. Will's in trouble."

"I knew going off your meds was a bad idea." Her tone went from soothing to in-charge in a second flat. "Those holistic remedies might help a bit, but not for someone with problems as severe as yours. I'm calling your therapist to get you in today."

"You do that," I said and ended the call. I'd found out what I needed. And more. I pushed away the black tar of feelings about my mom's obvious, if well-deserved, views of my mental health and focused on Will.

I rose to my feet and set Luna on the bed before I paced around the cramped loft in my usual path: around the easel, into the tiny bathroom, past the kitchenette, over to the window and computer desk, then back to the easel. The cat, used to my quirks, cocked her head to the side and watched my progress.

The gloss had worn off the floor tiles along the route. I paused at the foot of my bed and rested my eyes on the painting directly opposite while I did my 4-7-8 breathing exercises and refused to fall into the *what-if* spiral.

The first thing I saw each morning when I woke up was my favorite Morisot. The artist's brother and his daughter sat in a lush garden. My gaze followed the visible brushstrokes, the familiar swirl of the tiny pool. I longed to live in that perfect picture. At the count of seven, I breathed out for a count of eight and continued on my route. Then I forced my calmed brain back to reality and the problem at hand.

There was only one other person I could trust. My finger tapped Ren's contact info on the screen and I continued the breathing exercises while the phone rang. Ren was my best friend. My only friend really, if you didn't count my hacker friendsmost of whom I'd never met in the flesh.

Ren's voicemail picked up, and I closed my eyes while I rubbed the skin raw on my forehead. "Ren, it's me. Something bad happened to Will. I don't know who else to call. Please call me when you get this."

The phone immediately dinged, and hope rose in my chest until I saw it was a text from my mom. *You have an appointment in an hour with your therapist.* I resumed my pacing, phone clenched in my palm.

A thunderous knock at the door stopped my progress in front of the window. The only person who ever knocked was my neighbor when she needed tech help, and no way was she strong enough to cause that racket. Each heavy thump sent vibrations up the nerves in my arms and legs.

CHAPTER FOUR

Luna in my arms, I glanced out the window and down the seven stories to the parking lot in front of the building. Normal. No scary men surrounding the area. No signs of anyone chasing me down like they had Will. I reined in the images my anxiety sent flashing through my mind.

"Harper, are you in there?"

I recognized the voice even after seven years and through the two layers of metal that made up my door. Fear melted to relief. Caleb.

My brother's best friend had always been the goofy class clown of the group—all talk and skinny, with feet too big for his size—but sure to make you laugh even on a bad day. The last time I'd seen him was the day of their graduation. The red of the caps and gowns had amplified the myriad of zits on his grinning face.

I shifted my grip on Luna and flipped the lock, then ripped open the door. I had to tilt my head up to meet his gaze. A real-life version of GI Joe stood in my doorway. Broad shoulders tapered down to lean hips. Smooth, toned muscle lay under every inch of his exposed skin. I blinked, then swallowed. Hard.

If it weren't for the tousled waves of dark brown hair, though a bit longer now, and his startlingly blue eyes, I wouldn't even have recognized him. My gaze moved from muscle to muscle, each one more defined than the last.

I snapped my gaping jaw shut. "Caleb? What?" was all that could get past my short-circuited neurons. I lowered my gaze to collect myself but got distracted by the way his T-shirt clung like plastic wrap to his abs. *Nope, that's worse.* I looked back up at his face and busied myself with stroking Luna.

Caleb hadn't been back since he and Will joined up together the day after graduation. Will said something about Caleb taking college classes in their off time, not something his dad would approve of. His mom had moved out of Illinois after the divorce, so Caleb spent his off time in Florida with her.

Considering we'd known each other since I was two, I might have been a tad hurt over his decision. During my worst times, right after Dad was killed, Caleb was the one person who could pull me back from the edge. He was a rock solid part of my life who never made me feel guilty for my problems—one of my best friends. Then he was gone. After sending him Christmas cards for the first few years with no responses, I'd given up. I was never really his friend. I was just Will's kid sister. It stung.

His eyes scanned the room behind me, then the hallway to his sides. He gave the door a shove and walked through with a stilted gait. "Aren't you going to invite an old friend in?" Though his voice hadn't changed, I'd never heard such a grim tone out of him. The deep baritone reverberated off the cement walls.

Covering my shock by stepping aside for him and then closing the door, I turned and took in the changes. Hard angles replaced any trace of softness, from his chiseled features to, in my opinion, overly muscled arms and chest. And there wasn't a pimple in sight. Besides the physical changes, his face just didn't look right without his ever-present smile. I'd never seen him so serious. He knew something.

My teeth gritted together. Luna's hair raised and her tail puffed to full raccoon. I set her on the bed and turned to face him. My voice held more than a touch of the hurt I'd felt over his obvious disregard for our friendship. "Why are you here?"

He raised one eyebrow in my direction before he finished investigating my room and lowered himself to the edge of the sole chair. He sat with one arm on the armrest in an unnatural position. His gaze moved over me, pausing several times as if stuck on a few choice areas while his brows drew ever tighter.

I refused to give into the urge to run a hand through my hair or straighten the blouse I'd worn to the interview. Luna hissed, a sound I hadn't heard from her since a dog chased her up a tree in Mom's front yard.

"I remember you," he said to Luna. "What was your name? Star?"

Luna snarled low in her throat, as if insulted.

"I don't think he likes me." Caleb made kissy noises and put a hand out to the cat.

She hissed again and batted at the air, claws out.

"*She* picks up on my emotions."

His chuckle came out more of a rasp. "So, you don't like me either, huh?"

I shrugged and pulled my attention away from the cat to refocus on Caleb.

His nonchalant voice and attitude contrasted the whiteness around his lips and squinted eyes. He was in serious pain. I put my hands on my hips. "Are you supposed to be up and moving around yet? I thought you were still in the hospital. You just had surgery on your spine."

"What the docs don't know won't hurt 'em," he said, his gaze not quite high enough to meet my gaze—which was saying a lot considering my height, or lack thereof. He jerked his attention up to my face. "I wanted to drop in to check on you."

"So, we're going with the 'you just happened to be in the neighborhood' bullshit." I crossed my arms. "What is going on with Will?"

He straightened, his relaxed features now on full alert. "What do you mean?"

"He called me. But while we were talking, someone attacked him." I choked the words out. My hand snuck into my jeans pocket to wrap around the worn prescription bottle. Two small pills tapped the plastic. The sound loosened the twist-ties of anxiety tightening around my chest.

"This is bad," Caleb said, almost to himself.

"Someone attacked Will, and he's halfway around the world. Start talking," I demanded.

A colossal sigh deflated his bravado. He climbed to his feet, bracing a hand on his knee to push off. "Will wanted to keep you out of this." He paused as if uncertain. "You're just a kid."

"I'm not a kid." My voice came out in a growl. "Do you know who those men on the video are?"

His lips pressed together. "Forward the video to me and erase it. You don't need to be involved."

I walked over and poked a finger in his cast iron pec, looking up, as he stood a good eight inches taller than me. *Damn short genes.* "*My* brother, not yours, is in trouble. Tell me what the hell you know. Right. Now."

"Fine, you won't listen to reason, and I don't have time to argue." He held his hands to the side in surrender. "Will called a couple days ago and said he stumbled onto something. He had a video he wanted me to take up the chain of command here. He didn't know who to trust over there. But the email never came. Then I got a text today saying I needed to keep you safe."

"I don't need you to keep me safe. I watched the video and I don't understand why he's in trouble."

"Will said it should be impossible for them to find out who he sent it to. You can stay out of this."

I shook my head. "No, the app makes it a lot harder to trace, but not impossible. A skilled hacker could track it down in about a day."

He glanced out the window and into the parking lot. "Damn. Then we have to go. Now."

"But who would track it? Those guys on the video were American. On an American Army base. Who is the enemy here?"

"We don't have time right now, Harper."

"What do you think they're going to do? We're in the middle of Chicago, not the Middle East. They can hardly storm in and kidnap me from my apartment," I exclaimed and sat on the bed next to Luna.

"College students never disappear or go missing?"

I stared and scratched behind the cat's ears. "When did you become such a conspiracy nut?"

He grabbed the backpack from my chair and threw it to me. "Let's just say I've seen things. Will's missing and he told me this is serious. Priority one is to get you somewhere safe. Then we can figure out the video."

I held the backpack and contemplated my options. Whoever took Will over this video could track my IP address. I would never admit it, but Caleb was right. It wasn't safe here. "Fine. Just give me a few minutes."

He glanced at his watch. "You have sixty seconds."

"Don't." I pointed a finger. "Do not give me orders."

A wince flashed over his face as he shifted his weight. "Fine." He rolled his hand in a hurry up motion.

I threw some clothes and personal stuff in the backpack

along with my laptop, turning my back to Caleb when I randomly grabbed a few items from my underwear drawer. After a moment's hesitation, I opened my bottom drawer and pulled out a rectangular wooden case. Throwing a small bag of cat food and litter in Luna's spare litter box, I hefted the load and picked up the bristly cat.

"Let's go," I said.

Caleb lifted his brows. "You can't take the cat."

"I'm in danger, but I should leave Luna?" I cradled her. "Absolutely not."

"You can't take a cat on the run, Harper." He lowered his voice. "I know it's your calming pet, or whatever, but we can't take it."

"She's my therapy animal. It's okay to say the words."

He threw his hand out to the side, then stiffened as pain flashed over his face. "Therapy animal, sorry."

I chewed on my lip and stalked past him.

After a million kisses and promises to be back soon, Luna was happily deposited with my neighbor who had taken care of her several times in the past. Well, Luna was happy. I was another story.

CHAPTER FIVE

Caleb pulled his truck into the garage and closed the door behind it. He motioned to the case in my lap. "You still keep them?"

I ran my hand over the engraving. *For my little champion.*

"Why? Don't they upset you?" he asked.

"My dad gave them to me." I kept my gaze on the glossy wood. "He was so proud. I'll always remember his face when I won that last competition."

His voice softened from diamonds to coal, warm and like home. "He'd still be proud of you."

I glanced up to meet his gaze. "We both know that's a lie." I popped the door open and hopped down from the high truck seat before he could embarrass us both by denying it.

He followed as I walked toward the house. "Dad's out of town for a couple weeks. Training mission."

"Too bad he couldn't be here to help you recover." Our fathers had served in the same Special Forces unit, which made our families as good as blood.

"I'm supposed to be in the hospital letting nurses take care of me." He shrugged like a tough guy, but his tone held a hint of disappointment. "Not like he could do anything."

"I'm surprised you came here instead of Florida." Even I heard the hurt in my voice.

Caleb paused at the door, the key in the lock. "Harper, I wanted to come back and see you guys, but getting through a semester of school in our six weeks of off time was kind of demanding."

Something about the blue of his eyes tugged at feelings I thought I'd gotten over long ago. I'd missed him. He'd been Will's friend, but unlike the other guys, he'd always treated me like an actual person instead of just Will's little sister—an annoyance. In my teenage mind, we'd been friends as well. *Guess I was stupid.* I nodded and stared over his shoulder. "No worries. What were you studying?"

He opened the door. "Molecular biology with a minor in biochemistry. Hoping to get into med school when I get out."

I followed him inside and looked around the sparse, clean kitchen. A cast iron pan sat on the counter and a few pots lay in a drying rack on the otherwise bare counter. Caleb's dad had bought this bungalow in the city during Caleb's freshman year, after the divorce. With two bedrooms it was just big enough for him and Caleb.

His mom had moved out of the state before the ink was dry on the divorce papers. She left Caleb with his dad, supposedly to finish high school, but we'd all suspected leaving him behind had more to do with her new boyfriend.

"Does your dad know?" Caleb's dad always had ideas about Caleb's future and wasn't shy about sharing them. In his high school class, Caleb had been voted most likely to join the circus—definitely not military material. Things had changed a lot in a few years.

He snorted a laugh. "No way. He thinks I'm a lifer, like him. He'd flip out."

I nodded. "Your secret is safe with me."

A lopsided grin eased his stone-like features and gave me a glimmer of the Caleb I knew. Only this one was definitely not a young boy. I licked my lips and shifted away from the mess of emotions to take in the rest of the room.

The walls stood naked except for a collage of snapshots on the space next to the fridge. Army guys, mostly, all in camo. One picture in the center of the bunch caught my attention. Caleb, Will, and me smiling at the camera the day of their high school graduation.

My fifteen-year-old cheeks were fuller, while my curves were yet to develop. No circles darkened under my eyes, and I actually looked happy. Everything changed the next day. When Will joined the military, I quit sleeping and the anxiety came back with a vengeance.

I turned away from the memory and paced around the living room, chewing on the ragged nub of my fingernail.

"You're still chewing your nails? What are you, twelve?" Caleb teased, nose wrinkled.

I pulled the finger from my lips and stuffed my hands in my pockets, then cast him a glare. He didn't get to tease me. Not yet. Not after disappearing for seven years.

"Give me five minutes to pack a bag, grab some cash and hardware, then we can get out of here," he said and disappeared around a corner. "You said we have a day before they can track down where Will sent the video?"

"Yeah, depending on how good the techs are." My brain couldn't reconcile the memory of goofy, pimple-faced Caleb with this bossy hulk of a man staring at me from Caleb's eyes. I perched on the couch and listened to him thumping around his room before I pulled my laptop from my backpack.

It wasn't hard to guess his wifi name, *a-couple-fries-short-of-a-happy-meal* stuck out. Guessing the password took three tries—I was losing my touch. The smirk on my lips fell away when I spotted several messages marked urgent from my neighbor. *"What the hell is going on? Are you okay? Someone trashed your apartment!"*

Tremors erupted in my core and radiated out. Luna. I replied to the message asking if she was okay, then tapped my foot waiting for a response.

His green canvas duffle thudded to the floor and Caleb read the message thread over my shoulder. "Looks like they figured it out. That was fast."

Still no answer from the neighbor. I bit my lip to hide my worry from Caleb. "They got someone good on it. Someone really good."

He strode to the front window and peeked through the blinds. "Damn."

I jumped to my feet, grabbed the laptop, and shoved everything in my bag. "What do you see?"

"We've got company. Two guys coming in the front. They look like mercs," he said.

"How can you be sure they're mercenaries?" I demanded.

He dropped the blind and grabbed his duffle from the floor. "They've got bulges in all the right places, and I'm not talking about their dicks. Trust me. You know about computers. I know about this."

We'd taken two steps toward the back door when the front door exploded, kicked in from the outside. Caleb pushed me down behind the breakfast bar and leaned against the kitchen wall, hidden by the refrigerator, his gun drawn. I peered around the bottom of the half wall.

A behemoth of a man strode through the open door, a compact semi-automatic weapon in hand. His bulk made Caleb look like a Boy Scout. Another man followed, hanging out closer to the door while the first searched the rooms. Caleb waited for the behemoth's gun to clear his line of sight, then brought his arm down on the guy's elbow, pointing the weapon to the floor, while bringing his other arm around to aim his own gun at the man covering the door. He fired. Before the second mercenary could react, two bullets pierced his chest, and he fell to the floor, dead.

My gaze locked on the sightless eyes of the dead mercenary, the pooling blood creeping out from his body. Caleb killed him. Skinny, class-clown, everyone's best friend Caleb, had turned into a ruthless machine. I shouldn't have been surprised. I knew what Delta Force entailed—well, at least some of it. I knew how the men were when they came home. How they changed. I tore my gaze away from the dead man.

The behemoth had some tricks of his own. Caleb had disarmed his adversary but before he could fire his own gun, the merc kicked it from his hand. The metal clattered to the kitchen floor and slid to the edge of the tile, coming to rest inches from where I hid. Caleb threw blow after blow, landing punches, blocking and countering faster than I could keep up with. With each blow the merc landed, Caleb grunted, his eyes strained.

I swallowed down my desert-dry throat and forced air into my straining ribcage, my muscles frozen in place. With his injuries, it was amazing Caleb fought this long and hard. It wouldn't last. I couldn't watch Caleb die right in front of me, but not a single muscle in my body worked. I was a useless statue crouched on the floor.

Their hands flew in a quick succession of moves and countermoves. To the untrained observer, it looked like a coordinated dance routine. A deadly one. I gaped, elation and horror warring with each blow Caleb landed or received.

I stared at the gun at my feet. The familiar scent of burnt powder reached my nose.

Pick it up. All you have to do is pick it up and fire. I stood up and stared at the weapon.

Blood seeping from a split lip and bloodied eye, the behemoth grabbed Caleb, picked him up and threw him into the stove like some dramatic wrestling move.

A hoarse cry escaped Caleb's lips when his back contacted the metal of the stove. He fell to the floor and crawled into a crouch, moving slowly. The behemoth, his back to me, straightened and kicked Caleb in the ribs.

I looked down at the gun again, paralyzed. *Come on, Harper. Pick up the damn gun.* Then my gaze rested on the counter. The merc brought his leg back to land another blow to Caleb's chest. Without hesitation, my hand closed around the cold metal handle of a cast iron frying pan. I cocked back, kept my elbow up, just like Dad taught me for little league, and swung with an upward arc, aiming at the base of the merc's skull.

The angle of my swing connected where the merc's close-shaved head met his thick neck. A dull tone rang out and the behemoth slithered to the ground in a boneless puddle of muscle. The room fell into a deafening silence.

The heavy pan dropped from my fingers with a clatter.

Caleb pulled himself to his feet using the refrigerator handle but wheezed and clutched his back. I rushed over and slipped under his arm to bear some of his weight.

"Are you okay?" I gasped.

"There's a gun at your feet and you grab a frying pan?" he asked through gritted teeth, ignoring my question.

"It worked, didn't it?"

He straightened, panting, and held a hand to his lower back. Sweat dripped from his brow and his lips were a stark white against his flushed face. His weight crushed my shoulders. The scent of pine mixed with the saltiness of sweat washed over me.

Releasing me, he shifted to lean on the counter in an awkward pose. A quick lopsided grin crossed his lips. "You've obviously been watching too many movies."

He ambled over to the duffle bag as quickly as his back allowed, hunched like a ninety-year-old, and squatted to pick up the bag. He struggled to stand. Reaching back, he took my hand and pulled me toward the back door.

"You shouldn't be lifting that. Let me carry the bag," I said.

He didn't pause, but pulled me harder. "I got it."

"Okay, and I can walk by myself," I said, not sure where my irritation was coming from, and yanked my hand out of his.

He rolled his eyes and motioned to the gaping doorway. "There're more of them. We have to go." The smirk returned. "Unless you want to get your frying pan out again."

Caleb crouched next to a dumpster behind his dad's house and scanned the alley. One beefy man stood at the end of the block, a couple houses down, obviously the lookout while the other two were supposed to kill us.

"Guess we're ditching the truck," Caleb whispered.

"It would be too easy to track, anyway. They have some serious skill working for them to crack the google drop so fast. Tracing license plates would be no problem," I said.

He checked the rooftops and surrounding houses. Blood oozed from a gash on his eyebrow. "We got lucky this time."

"How do you figure that?"

"They underestimated us. Three guys, no backup. They thought since I'm injured and you're a girl no offense we'd be easy to take out." He took one more look at the guy at the end of the alley. "They won't make the same mistake next time."

I nodded and swallowed, acid creeping up from my knotted stomach. Guns, dead mercenaries, and fighting were far from my normal Saturday of painting and studying. "Okay, so let's put some distance between us and them."

He tensed, ready to run. When the man turned his back again, we sprinted to the other end of the alley and behind the next house. Well, I sprinted. Caleb's stride was more of a grimacing lope. Just as we were about to clear the fence of the next house, my phone blared in my pocket. The Minion Song, my mom's ringtone.

My already increased heartbeat kicked up another notch, or three. The high-pitched noise echoed off the brick walls and concrete of the alley. I glanced back. Sure enough, the mercenary heard.

Caleb grabbed my hand in a viselike grip and pulled me after him in a dead run. My phone shrieked again. At this point, I might as well give the merc arrows on the ground to follow our trail. Mom was probably calling about the doctor's appointment I'd missed. Even though she'd texted me five times already. *I never should have called her.* I fumbled with the phone to silence the repeated calls before my mom's persistence killed us.

We raced down the alley, our pursuer's footsteps pounding behind. Caleb took one turn after another, doubling back and weaving until I was lost in the maze of back streets and alleyways. His intimate knowledge of the area gave us the advantage, which we needed with Caleb in extreme pain. I gasped in a breath, being more used to exercising my artistic ability than my body. Caleb pulled me harder.

We ducked behind a fence, and Caleb pressed my body against his torso. His pine smell washed over me again as I rested against him and I closed my eyes for a second. *This is the closest I've been to a guy in...* No need to go there.

Caleb's breath came in wheezing pants and he blew out a deep breath. The pounding footsteps of our pursuer drowned out even the roar of blood in my ears. I wanted to hold my breath but couldn't. I matched my breath with Caleb's controlled inhale and exhale.

On the other side of the fence, the man ran past, not even stopping. After he turned the corner, we crept out and headed the opposite direction. The houses changed to larger buildings, restaurants, and shops.

The alley spit us out onto a busy street. Cars and pedestrians surrounded us. The plethora of younger people with backpacks slung over their shoulders suggested we were near a school. A high school, by the looks of it.

I pulled my crushed fingers out of Caleb's grip and earned a glare in response. He was in full alpha mode. I got the feeling he'd wrap me in bubble wrap and hide me in his pocket if he could.

We slowed to a walk and blended in with the crowd—well, blended in as much as my flaming red, curly hair would allow, although my height fit in perfectly with the average freshman. But to anyone looking, my blazing locks were bright as a signal flare in the dead of night. I wheezed and a knife-like pain stabbed my side. Caleb scanned the street—no sign of any mercenaries. When he turned, a vivid red blotch spreading across the fabric over his lower back caught my attention.

"Caleb, your incision."

He didn't bother to look. "Yeah, I think I popped a few stitches," he said, as if he'd lost a band-aid. "We need to destroy our phones."

He set out down the street, limping but at least still moving.

"I have a better idea. Give me yours." I held out my hand. I took both phones and waited as a garbage truck lumbered by. In one swift motion, I tossed the phones into the exposed trash in the open back of the truck.

He watched the trash truck moving down the street, then nodded.

I headed in the opposite direction. "Now they have someone to chase."

CHAPTER SIX

Dr. Nelson's research lab
  Nansic Headquarters
  Indianapolis, Indiana

"Doctor?" the voice called over the intercom through the phone on his desk.

He punched a button and answered, "Yes?"

"Mr. Marling is on the line."

Dr. Nelson grabbed the receiver. "Marling? Did you look over the data I left you?"

"You have a bigger problem to worry about than your data," Marling growled over the line.

The doctor scrunched his brow, reaching for the file in his locked drawer. "What? No, you need to listen"

"You listen," screamed Marling. "Someone started poking around after your tantrum over here. They got our conversation on film. Now we have a domestic problem to clean up. I can't run it from the base. You're going to have to coordinate from home."

"I have no idea what you're talking about," the doctor stammered.

"You're the only one stateside right now with clearance. I can't get home for a few more days and my men missed cleaning it up in Chicago. I want three teams on it."

"What do you mean, they missed cleaning it up?" The doctor ran a hand over his face and pinched the bridge of his nose. If this got out, it would end everything he'd worked for over the last thirty years. "I'm a doctor, not one of your mercenaries. I have no idea how to organize a strike team."

"You made the mess. Time to get your hands dirty. One scrawny girl shouldn't be too much trouble. Keep me informed." The line clicked.

Dr. Nelson sat with the phone to his ear for several seconds before he returned it to the cradle. Even one news story and it was all over.

He picked up the phone and punched the button for his secretary. "Get me Dunham from security on the line."

Shrill squeaks drew his attention to the cages of rats on the lab counter. His gaze swept over to the small blood splattered bodies of the victims and the frantic movement of the victor. Droplets of crimson ran down the glass like a morbid rain.

CHAPTER SEVEN

The sting of bleach hit my nose, followed immediately by obnoxious floral air freshener, the mark of a cheap motel. I tossed my bag on one of the eighties-orange bedspreads and set the wooden box on the nightstand, then escaped to the bathroom.

A few days in a confined space with Caleb might be the end of me. Every time I'd even opened my mouth on the walk to the motel, words tumbled out like I was thirteen talking to my Hollywood crush, not a guy I'd known all my life who used to eat dog biscuits to make people laugh.

Maybe it was the adrenaline? Damn, Harper. Quit trying so hard. I had nothing to prove. And some half-assed apology for not keeping in touch was the last thing I needed. Especially now. We had bigger things to worry about.

After checking in and paying in cash, he handed me the key, then walked across the street to the drugstore to get supplies and first aid. I had a few minutes by myself to get my mind straight. I rubbed my thumb over my palm, wishing for Luna's silky fur. The memory of the sound of her motorboat purr, so loud for a small cat, brought tears to my eyes. I hadn't been away from her for more than a night in eight years.

I'd checked my email but there was still no answer from my neighbor. If they hurt Luna... I didn't let my brain finish the thought. I ripped the hair tie out of my curls. They sprang free and settled to my shoulders in a red, frizzy mass. Brushing would only make it worse.

The mirror blurred and swam in front of my face. I closed my eyes and heard the audio from the video, Will's voice and laugh repeatedly mixed with the sound of his screams over the phone. The panic attack took me by surprise, and my organs tightened into knots.

Flashes of images paraded before my tortured mind. The crumpled mercenary I'd brained, the guns, Caleb on the floor, Will's smiling face. This wasn't a joke. But part of me couldn't accept it was real.

The air in my chest thickened and solidified, unmovable, suffocating. I struggled to suck in a breath. Will could die, could be dead already. It must be a nightmare. I couldn't live through this again. I couldn't lose anyone else.

I forced a breath into my starving lungs and fought the blackness creeping into my vision. The mercenaries erased all doubt. Someone wanted us dead.

I turned on the shower. I undressed while steam built up, then climbed in. The water droplets pelted me with a decent amount of pressure. I closed my eyes. Gory images flashed behind my closed lids. Usually, Dad's was the face I saw, broken and gruesome. But this time it was Will's face, eyes dead and staring.

I gasped and pushed the horror aside. Instead, I concentrated on the water, the feel of the droplets hitting my skin and running down my limbs, then concentrated on my other senses, as my therapist taught me. One good thing about a motel: no running out of hot water. I stood under the spray, washing away my anxiety.

"Harper, you okay in there?" Caleb called through the door.

My relatively calm state shattered. "Yeah, I'm coming."

"I picked up some food. Are you hungry?" he asked.

"Not really." I closed my eyes, leaning against the shower wall and wishing he'd leave me alone.

"I got you something anyway. You look anemic."

"Thanks. You look like shit, too," I shot back, falling into the easy verbal dueling of our teen years.

I toweled off and put on my pajama pants, then realized one of the likely many things I'd forgotten in my rushed packing job. An extra bra.

Our escape left the white lace one I'd worn to the gallery about as sweaty and appealing as a gym sock. With no other choice, I threw on a T-shirt and used the sink to wash out my bra, then hung it from the shower rod.

A glance in the mirror confirmed my suspicions. Although I'd been left out when tall genes were handed out, I made up for it in my chest. Going braless wasn't usually an option for my D-cups. I adjusted the shirt as best I could, trying to stretch it so it didn't cling to me—damn spandex, they put it in everything. Finally, I sighed. There was no hiding.

As an afterthought, I dabbed putty in my hair, just so it wouldn't go into its full-blown Bozo effect. Meeting my own gaze in the mirror, I sucked in a breath. Time to be strong. When I opened the door, the smell of spice hit me.

"I got you coconut curry. Hope you still like it," Caleb said.

Actually, I'd always hated curry. But somewhere along the way, someone got it in their head that I liked it. Speaking up for myself wasn't my strong suit in my teen years. It seemed like Dad took all my opinions with him when he died. I couldn't even say what toppings I liked on pizza. I'd found more of my voice in the last few years. We'd have to see how Caleb felt about that.

Caleb sat on the bed, his bare chest angled away from me so he could see the surgical site in the mirror on the wall. I bit my lip to contain an expletive.

Two angry four-inch-long incisions, one on either side, ran parallel to his spine like railroad tracks. Blood oozed from gaping skin on the left side where the stitches had ripped apart. The tissue looked like it had been shredded. A multitude of smaller, less precise, and more healed wounds surrounded the surgical cuts. Will told me two weeks ago Caleb was wounded in an explosion and asked me to check in on him when he'd been transported back to the States for rehab. I'd claimed I was too busy getting ready for the meeting with the gallery owner. Besides, Caleb hadn't come around in seven years. It wasn't like we were friends anymore.

Caleb grunted and froze mid-twist, trying to mop clean gauze over the blood. His hand shook with the effort.

Be strong, I reminded myself. I walked farther into the room. "Let me help."

His eyes met mine in the mirror, but he didn't hand me the gauze. "I got it."

"Give me the damn bandage and let me help you." The words came out of my mouth before I processed the thought. I pressed my lips into a firm line to hide my surprise and held out my hand, hoping I hid the tremor in my muscles. Blood wasn't really my thing.

He turned to face me, his brow creased with the struggle of moving. His gaze shifted to my chest, then bounced back up to my face, his eyes wide. He turned away and cleared his throat. "If you think you can handle it."

Did he just...? No. I stopped the thought.

Purplish-black bruises spread all the way around to the

front of his ribs and chest. He dropped the gauze into my waiting hand without meeting my gaze. *I can do this. Just some blood and ripped skin...* I swallowed a gag and choked, coughing to cover the sound.

"Just pretend it's red paint," he said in a soothing voice. "No big deal."

Sucking in a deep breath to stop the floor from tilting, I sat behind him on the bed and wiped the blood away from his skin like I would wipe spilled paint off one of my canvases. His tense muscles relaxed.

"Is this okay? I'm not hurting you?" The tremble in my arm settled as I forced my mind away from what I was doing.

"No, I can barely feel it," he said, his voice tired. "You just need to clean it up and disinfect it, then we can re-bandage." Caleb served as the medic on his Delta Force unit. He was 18D, meaning he had a year of intensive medical training.

"You need a doctor to restitch it," I said.

"The inner stitches held, so it might leave an ugly scar, but as long as we keep it clean, it'll be fine."

My free hand gripped his shoulder, and I leaned closer to see. His smooth skin under my fingers covered iron bands of muscle. Even relaxed, there was no softness, no more of the boy I'd known. I shifted my hand to his arm. His rough fingers covered my own.

"You doing okay?" he asked.

"I'm good," I quipped, a tad too fast. "No big deal."

I stopped wiping the blood off his back and ran a feather-light touch over the boot-shaped bruise across his ribs. The image of the steel toe colliding with Caleb's chest raced through my mind.

Caleb breathed a soft sigh.

My fingers moved, as if of their own accord, to the gash on his triceps and I saw his body flying through the air to impact the stove, the burner cover slicing the muscle like a razor. I wiped the blood away and cleaned the wound as he instructed.

My fingers traced a path from wound to wound over his torso, cleaning and bandaging the cuts and scrapes. Each time, the memory of the fight appeared in my mind. He'd protected me, getting up over and over despite excruciating pain. Moisture clouded my eyes, and I blinked it away.

Not many people in the world would fight till their last breath to keep me safe. Guilt for not visiting him in the hospital tightened my chest. I could have found time to stop in and see if he needed anything.

"Thank you," he said. "The blood isn't bothering you?"

I pushed the image of the fight from my mind but didn't stop. "No. I'm okay." The tension in the room was almost palpable. "So, what kind of doctor do you want to be?"

"Not sure yet. Maybe a neurosurgeon, but then delivering babies sounds good, too." He shrugged. "I'd just like to put people together instead of taking them apart."

"Wow." My brain fumbled for words at the image of Caleb catching babies. "I remember your uncle's a doctor, but your dad—"

"Yeah, that was a fun fight." Caleb's uncle Dillon was a doctor and his father had been none too pleased about Caleb thinking about following in his uncle's footsteps instead of joining Delta. In the end, his dad had won.

Now Caleb was the epitome of everything his dad wanted. I wondered if he was happy with his son being half blown up. "Have you ever thought of pediatrics?" I asked. He'd been so good with all of us younger kids, especially me. "I mean, the little kids on the block used to chase you around like you were Santa. And Marco's daughter called you *bub*. It was her first word." Marco was another one of Dad's team. One side of my lip crept up at the image of Caleb throwing

Marco's giggling baby in the air and catching her. "Just a thought."

"Actually, I never considered peds, but maybe." He chuckled. "I could tell the preteens to ask their parents where babies come from."

I had to laugh. "Yeah, I don't think parents would appreciate that." I worked my way lower, cleaning away the gore, nearing the waistband of his jeans. Red soaked into the denim. "You're going to need to change your pants. The blood soaked them."

He jerked as if stung and pulled away from me, all the comfort and familiarity of the previous moments gone. "I can get the rest."

My fingers paused and I blinked at his back. "Okay. At least let me finish up."

He sat, stiff as stone, but nodded.

I wiped antibiotic cream over the incisions and taped the bandage in place with precise movements. "Okay, it's as good as I can do here."

The bed shifted as he stood, straightening slowly, and put a clean shirt on, his jaw clenched. I caught myself staring at the muscles as they moved under his skin. The vise around my chest constricted and I coughed instead of breathing.

"What's wrong?" he asked, brows together. "The blood getting to you? Do you need your pills or something?"

Blazing indignation stiffened my spine. I jumped off the bed and turned my back, busying myself with my bag. All the fuzzy feelings evaporated. "I'm fine." I bit the words out. "Not that it's any of your business, but I've been off my meds for a year."

"Is that a good idea?" He waved a hand in the air. "I mean, your episodes got pretty intense."

"Don't worry, I won't go off the deep end." I paused and motioned to his torso. "You can't take a shower, but you might want to at least wash. Those mercenaries can probably track you by scent alone."

His gaze rested on me for a beat, then he shrugged and headed to the bathroom.

I collapsed on the bed and put my hands over my eyes to calm my frazzled nerves. *Since when do I drool over musclebound guys? Especially Caleb?* Unable to stay still on the bed, I paced around the room, then grabbed my computer and pulled the video up. Maybe he'd have some insight into the shit-show Will stumbled into. While I waited for the water to shut off, I grabbed the remote and switched on the five o'clock news.

I spaced out while environmentalists debated global warming and overpopulation with some lawyer from a corporation. Then the political segment came on.

"What are you watching?" Caleb asked and mopped water from his longish curls.

"Same old, same old, some politician telling a bunch of lies." I motioned to the congressman on the screen blathering on about budget and overspending in the government.

"That's Congressman Briarwood. At least he doesn't want to cut the military budget. He sees we need a strong military in this world," he said.

"Yeah, you would think by this time we'd have finished killing all our enemies."

"You think we should stay home and paint pretty pictures of how we wish the world was?" His hands went to his lean hips and his chest puffed. "It doesn't work like that. We can't just hold hands and sing Kumbaya and the problems go away."

"I have no problem with the military defending our country. My problem is with my brother, and—" I caught myself just before I said *you* "—people I care about being in the line of fire. For what exactly? What are we fighting over?"

"It's complicated. But there's a lot of bad out there in the world and Will wants to protect you."

"Don't talk to me like I'm a five-year-old. Give me a reason good enough for him to be in danger," I yelled, then swallowed and finished softly. "My family has sacrificed enough."

He pressed his lips together. "Look, us fighting won't help Will. We need to work together."

The heat drained from my face as fear replaced anger. "Watch the video. Maybe you'll see something I missed."

Much as I wanted to look away, I couldn't tear my eyes off Will's face on the screen. His laugh stuck like a thorn in my heart. Caleb watched the short video several times.

"I know I've seen the guy in the suit around the base once or twice. He sticks out, but I have no clue what or who he is. He took meals with the officers. I've never seen the nerdy lookin' guy before."

He grabbed his duffle bag from the foot of the bed, unzipped it, and took out his gun and kit. He removed the magazine and dismantled the gun, his fingers moving as if of their own accord.

I'd seen my dad do the same routine countless times when he was trying to work some problem out in his mind. The smell of the oil and gunpowder mixed in a distinctive perfume that ripped me back to my parents' kitchen. A ten-year-old me, helping him while we talked about my next shooting competition—so happy to spend time together.

My gaze moved from Caleb's agile fingers to focus on the gun. Blood hammered in my ears. Quivering started in my hands and spread like an earthquake up my body. Red splashed across my vision. My father's face, ripped apart by the exiting bullets, swayed before my eyes.

My breath came in gasps. I wasn't supposed to see him in the casket the day of the funeral. Mom only opened it to put my grandfather's medals in before the service. She didn't know I was there, hiding behind the pew. To this day, she didn't know what I'd seen. What caused my vivid nightmares.

The mercenary I'd hit flashed through my mind. I clung to the table to stay upright.

A strong, warm hand gripped my arm. I blinked away the sight of my dead father and the mercenary and struggled to breathe.

Caleb held the now reassembled gun behind him. His hand still squeezed my arm, as if to help the tremors. "Sorry, I wasn't thinking. I should have remembered guns trigger you."

"It has been a weird day," I croaked, my vocal cords unable to function properly.

After one last squeeze of my arm, he released it and tucked the gun under the pillow on the bed, out of sight. Then he took the Styrofoam containers from the to-go bag and set the plastic silverware and napkins on the table in front of me, motioning for me to sit down.

I shook my head and pushed the container away. "I'm not hungry."

He set down his fork and pushed the container back in front of me. "You need to eat. And what's with the circles under your eyes? You look like you're the one who got punched in the face."

He was trying to distract me by being an ass. I glared and crossed my arms, which helped stop the remaining tremors, but tightened the T-shirt over my breasts.

Caleb blinked and focused his attention on his food. "Is it the nightmares again?" he asked, concern filling his voice.

I shrugged. He wasn't the first person to bring up the circles under my eyes. Lately, it was more the way people greeted me: "Wow, you look terrible." But, much as I missed confiding in him, the huge guy sitting across from me didn't feel like my friend anymore. I swallowed. *How is it possible to miss someone who is sitting right in front of you?*

"I thought you'd gotten rid of the nightmares." He picked up his fork and busied himself with stabbing a piece of meat and each type of vegetable.

Anger heated my face. "I did. Until my brother ran off to fight the entire world."

Caleb ran his tongue over his teeth before he responded. "It's all he ever wanted to do." He paused, and his mouth softened. "He didn't know the problem it would cause you."

"Problem? Yeah, I guess you could call it that." If you call a complete nervous breakdown and hospitalization a problem.

"You tried to convince him to stay when he wanted to protect our country. That's plain selfish."

My hands tightened into fists. "So, it's selfish to want the family you have left safe and not being shot at every day?"

"It is if that's not what they want."

I cocked my head to the side. "How is it different from your dad pushing you into joining up when you wanted to be a doctor?"

He leaned halfway across the table. "That's not the same thing. He knew I'd do well in the teams."

"And be miserable doing it?"

His face turned to stone. "I'm not miserable."

I'd pushed him too far. He was in full alpha mode—all signs of softness or weakness gone. To think how I'd admired the very same strength in my dad. I'd thought he was the greatest man in the world, and he did make it safe for me. Until he didn't.

Caleb's jaw firmed. "You would rather have Will miserable here than making a difference in the world?"

I leaned forward as well. He might be twice, hell, three times my size, but I wasn't about to be intimidated. I was tired of biting my tongue. Ten years was plenty. My voice came out a strangled whisper. "Yeah? Is he making a difference right now? He's probably dead."

A choking sound escaped my lips, and I covered my mouth with a hand, as if I could stuff the words back down my throat. *Will can't be dead. God, please don't let him be dead.*

"Harper," Caleb said. The tension drained out of him like helium from a balloon. He rested a hand over mine. "Don't think like that. We'll get him back."

I blinked away the moisture in my eyes and met his gaze. "He can't die. We can't let him die."

Caleb leaned back in the chair. "I'll do whatever needs to be done to get him back. He's my best friend."

He picked up the plastic fork and started eating again.

"How can you eat?" I asked, waving a hand at the food. Even if it had been something I liked, my stomach would reject it.

"Got to keep strong if I'm going to be any use to you or Will." He nudged the container. "You need to be on your A-game. Won't do Will any good if you're half-starved."

The acid in my stomach burned away at the lining. I took an experimental bite while Caleb shoveled food in and chewed mechanically. Shovel, chew, swallow, repeat. I wondered who this person was that took over the Caleb I'd known.

I forced the bite down, followed by two more before I gave up. "I have an idea about how to figure out who those men are."

Caleb closed the empty container. "How?"

"I go to school with a guy who wrote a facial-recognition program for a project. It's better than what they use in the government," I said. "He's on probation now, but he should be able to help us."

"What did he get put on probation for?"

"The school has strict rules against hacking. He got caught."

His lips creased as if he'd tasted something bitter. "I don't know if we can trust some hacker with the video."

"Some *hacker*? You say it like it's a dirty word. Ren is our best bet at identifying the men on the video fast." *Plus, he's probably been blowing up my phone since I left that message.*

"Ren? What kind of name is that?"

"It's his handle. Short for Renegade. His real name is Jacob. Feel better?"

He shook his head. "Some of the worst threats we fight are these computer geeks who can launch a missile with their laptop."

I rolled my eyes. Slowly. "Are you done? I'm a hacker, so if you have a problem, you can leave, and I'll find my brother myself." I grabbed my laptop. "By the way, most hackers I know are extremely trustworthy and know how to keep their mouths shut. It kind of comes with the territory. Besides, he's a friend. I trust him."

"I thought you went straight after that run-in with the cops in high school."

I laughed. "No, I just got better."

He glared.

I smirked back. *What is wrong with me?* Something about him made it impossible to keep my thoughts to myself.

I typed the email in a few seconds using my anonymous set up. Despite what I'd said, I hadn't used this persona for months. I didn't feel comfortable contacting Ren on my school account, just in case someone was monitoring it. My heartbeat sped up while I waited for a response.

"Will he answer that fast?"

"Trust me, he's plugged in," I said.

A message popped up and I let my breath out in a whoosh. I hit open. *"About time you let me know you're okay. I'm freaking out over here! I was waiting to hear about the gallery, then I got your message, and you go MIA. Meet me at the library. I'll bring the program and you can explain what the hell you've gotten yourself into."*

"You called him?" Caleb demanded.

"He's my friend. Leave it alone."

"What gallery is he talking about?" Caleb asked. "Is your art being exhibited?"

"It's not important." What I'd thought was my dream of an exhibition at the gallery lost its luster the moment I heard Will's fear. Now all I wanted in the world was to have my brother home safe.

"This is why I wanted to keep you out of it. So you can have a life." Something in his voice caught me off guard—like he cared. A lot.

I brushed off the thought. "I was in this the moment Will was." My fingers flew over the keys. *"It's too dangerous. I don't want to pull you into it. Just drop the drive and I'll pick it up."*

His response came back almost immediately. *Not a chance, girlie. If you're in trouble, I'm in. Meet me in the stacks in an hour.*

"Huh," Caleb grumbled over my shoulder. "I don't like this."

I bit my lip. "It's not like we have much choice. He can be stubborn." I turned and met his gaze. "Kind of like some other people I know."

CHAPTER EIGHT

A bus took us back to campus. My brain struggled to comprehend the dual realities. My previously mundane student life of only a few hours before morphed into this cloak-and-dagger, people-trying-to-kill-me reality. It was a lot to absorb.

We wove our way through the aisles of books to the back of the library where only the most serious of students ever ventured. Rounding the last corner, I spotted Ren.

His stance made him recognizable, even more than the dark, tightly spiraled hair he kept short. He looked ready to jump up and run a marathon at a moment's notice. Lean muscle lent to effortless movements that spoke of power just under the skin. Unlike many computer geeks I knew, Ren was also a workout freak and health nut. Most people mistook him for a basketball player, given his athleticism and build.

"Ren," I called quietly.

He turned at my voice, relief evident on his face. Without a word, he loped down the aisle and wrapped his arms around me. Comfortable warmth enveloped me, and my eyes closed. I exhaled a breath I felt I'd been holding since I got Will's call.

"You scared me, girlie," he said into the top of my head. He towered a good foot over me.

"Sorry," I said.

Caleb cleared his throat. Reality crashed in and I stepped away from Ren's hug.

Motioning to Caleb, I said, "This is Caleb, my brother's best friend."

The smile dropped from Ren's face, and his eyes darted to mine. "*The* Caleb?"

I swallowed and looked anywhere but at Caleb. "Yeah."

"Like the only-one-who-could-make-you-laugh-for-years, Caleb?" Ren's voice held an edge I'd never heard before. Jealousy?

I glared what I hoped was a shut up look. Though I couldn't blame him. The new Caleb looked more likely to make someone pee their pants than laugh. But I'd rather he not know I'd mentioned him. More than once.

Ren, though a few inches taller than Caleb, looked like a beanpole beside him. He stared at Caleb's face, which might as well have been made of marble, not a smile in sight. Both men straightened to their full height and some unspoken male pissing contest passed between them as they assessed each other.

"I thought you were shorter." Ren held out a hand, ever the gentleman. "Nice to meet you."

"I grew." Although his eyes told me he'd noticed my unease, Caleb held out his hand and shook Ren's. "We don't have a lot of time. Let's get this program and go."

Ren held my arm. "Hold on." He met my gaze. "I'm not just handing over the program. I'm here to help."

"I can't put you in danger," I insisted.

He released me and lounged against the back of a chair as if he had all the time in the world. "Tell me what's going on or no program."

I'd seen that look before. This was when he turned into a major pain in the ass until I agreed with him. What was it with the men in my life? My lips pressed together. "Fine," I said over Caleb's protests and set my computer on a table to pull up the video while I gave an overview of the situation.

"Can they track us if you open the video again?" Caleb asked.

Ren did his best to stifle a grin. "No, man. If she has it on her computer, she isn't even connected to the net."

Caleb grumbled and crossed his arms, obviously not pleased to be so far out of his element.

"When you said you were in trouble, I was thinking, like, pot or something." Ren shook his head.

Caleb stepped away to *check the perimeter*.

"How are you holding up?" Ren asked. His gaze swept over me.

He was asking about my anxiety. Ren had helped me find natural ways to cope so I could function without my medication. He'd dealt with his share of mental health problems and used exercise and diet, as well as holistic avenues. He was the reason my apartment perpetually smelled like lavender, and he was constantly trying to get me to drink kale smoothies and go running with him.

"I miss Luna, but I'm fine," I said to move off the subject.

"This is some serious stress. Do you have your prescriptions?" he pressed.

"I never got refill orders from the doctor. I've been doing good."

He wrapped his hand around my fingers and pulled them away from my mouth. "Keep this up and you won't have any nails left." There was no judgement in his voice, only concern. "If you call the doctor, I can pick up the scripts for you."

Ren's childhood left him scarred and also taught him to be the most supportive person I knew. But if I ever met his parents, especially his mom, they'd be hospitalized, and I'd be in jail. Good thing he hadn't seen them since he turned eighteen.

"No." I shook my head. "I'll do it. I still have a couple emergency doses left. But I'll be fine. I can do this."

"I worry about you, Harper. I care about you." He rested a hand on my shoulder. "There isn't any shame in getting help."

I tilted my head to meet his gaze and nodded. He was right. All the sunshine and vitamins in the world wouldn't help stress like this. But my meds took days—weeks—to kick in, besides the side effects. I couldn't be foggy. *I can do this. Will needs me on my A-game.*

Ren leaned over my computer and began typing.

"What are you doing?" I slapped the screen shut, but he was too fast.

He finished with a smirk. "Just sent myself a copy of the video."

"This isn't a game. Did you miss the part where I told you people are trying to kill me? Promise me you'll delete it." I grabbed his shirt. "Promise me."

His face sobered. "Okay, I promise." He handed over a simple black flash drive.

Caleb returned from his patrol. "We need to get moving."

"Wait." Ren held me back while one hand dug into his pocket. "I was going to give you this for your birthday, or something, but you might need it now." He held out a small box.

"My birthday isn't for months."

His eyes couldn't hold mine as I took the box and opened it. Inside lay a sterling silver oval locket with swirling cutouts on the face and a small bottle of pure lavender essential oil. The cutouts formed my favorite Celtic symbol for eternity.

"I had it made." He cleared his throat. "I mean, not a big deal. This guy I know makes jewelry. You put a couple drops of the oil on the rock inside and it will hold the scent for days. So, you can have it with you."

My voice came out in a whisper. "It's beautiful, Ren." I replaced the lid, then wrapped my arms around him, looking up into his face. "Thank you."

A bashful grin spread over his lips.

I wanted to say more, wanted to ask him to come with us, but Caleb's scowl stopped me. The longer we were with Ren, the more chance he'd be hurt. "Promise me you won't look into this anymore."

"Promise me you'll stay safe," he shot back. "I'd be lost without my little gingersnap."

The sound of the nickname tugged at my lips and I dove in for one last hug. "I'll see you after this is over."

He released me. "You better."

We rushed out of the library and headed back to the bus stop.

"You know he's into you, right?" Caleb said from beside me, his tone matter-of-fact.

I stayed quiet for a moment. Ren was my best friend. Maybe some part of me knew. And maybe at some point I'd liked him back, but I couldn't let anything happen. I couldn't stand to mess it up and lose him. "He's my best friend. That's all."

As soon as we were back at the motel, I plugged in Ren's flash drive and started the facial recognition software. He'd said it could take anywhere from hours to days to find a match.

The program scrolled through images faster than the eye could follow. After watching for a few minutes, Caleb eased himself onto the bed, a hiss escaping his mouth at the movement. With his bravado and strength, it was easy to forget he was recovering from surgery—and a beating. But his movements stiffened, and pain etched his features when he thought I wasn't looking.

I leaned back in my chair and crossed my arms, willing the program to find a match. Fifteen minutes later, I sighed and took out Ren's gift. The smell of lavender wafted up when I opened the small bottle. I breathed in the relaxing scent and imagined my stress leaving with my exhaled breath, just like Ren taught me.

This was no substitute for Luna and her purr therapy, but it would have to do. I opened the locket and splashed the oil on the black stone inside, then closed the silver clasp. I looped the chain over my neck. The cool metal settled in the space over my heart.

A chime sounded from the computer and I spun in my chair, leaning into the screen in anticipation. A photo lit up the screen, with a ninety-nine percent match probability and a link to the origin of the photo.

A news article popped up with the man in the suit from the video pictured in the top right corner. I scanned the paragraphs. He was Thomas Marling, Vice-President of Research and Development for Nansic, a major biotechnology company producing anything from household chemicals to seeds and herbicides.

I leaned closer to the screen. Based in Indiana, with factories spread across the nation and in several foreign countries, the company had been around for almost a hundred years.

"Caleb."

He lifted his head from the pillow and rolled on his side, then pushed himself up to a sitting position with his arms.

"Ren's program found a match."

He limped over. "That's him. What would a biotech and agricultural company be doing on an Army base?"

"That's my question. The main research and development facility is in Indiana, about four hours from here. It could be worth checking out."

Caleb sat on the bed and sighed. "Actually, we need to talk about what our next step should be."

I pivoted to face him, his tone setting off alarm bells. "Okay."

"Harper, Will never wanted you involved in any of this."

"I'm involved, so get over it. I can't go back to my normal life and pretend nothing happened." Just when I was starting to trust him. The hurt of betrayal colored my words. "Plus, in case you forgot, there seem to be some mercenaries who want me dead."

He leaned forward. "Exactly. I can't keep you safe. Not like this." He motioned up and down his torso. His voice rose with obvious frustration. "I didn't even really handle the one guy at the house. We can't count on there always being a frying pan available." He ran a hand through his hair. "I almost let Will down, let you down."

I stood and put my hands on my hips. "What do you want to do? Leave me hiding in this hotel and hope they don't track me down?"

"No, I called my OIC and asked to bring you in. I set up a meet for the morning."

I stared, just stared.

"They don't know where Will is. He's missing and no one has any idea who took him," he said.

Will's screams sounded in my head again. My voice came out as a strangled whisper. "Is he dead already?"

"They haven't found a body or any evidence. We have to operate on the assumption we can get him back." His lips pressed together, and he shook his head. "Your brother is the toughest guy I know. He won't go down easy."

My hands clenched into fists. "You want to dump me off on some Army stiff and go off to fight by yourself? In your condition?"

"Let me get you somewhere safe," he pleaded, or as close as I'd ever heard a Delta member get to pleading.

"Right, I need to be safe, so you don't have to worry about me," I said, my voice rising an octave. "But it's perfectly fine for you and Will to be in a war zone so I could worry about you both for the last seven years?" I snapped my mouth shut and hoped he'd missed that part about me worrying about him.

"You're an artist. You paint pretty pictures. You just aren't set up for stuff like this." He made the statement as if it were a well-known fact. "You're... fragile."

My eyes narrowed. He was obviously referring to more than my lack of musculature. That was another problem with having several nervous breakdowns—everyone thought they needed to protect you, or you'd lose your shit again.

Before Dad was killed, no one would ever have called me fragile. I was tiny but tough, fierce, even. I regularly wiped the floor with guys twice my size at shooting competitions and didn't blink at the hushed insults they hurled my way.

After a particularly upset jerk got in my face, Dad decided teaching me a little self-defense was in order. He taught me all the dirty moves. He'd say, "You're never going to be as strong or have the size advantage. So, you have to be smarter and fight dirty."

He'd take Will and me out in the garage with old mattresses

on the floor. I learned eye gouging, the delicate parts of an airway, where to kick a knee to break it with the least force, and other things your typical girl didn't know.

After Dad was gone, Will wanted to continue the lessons. I refused. I didn't want to fight anymore—couldn't.

I ran my hands over my face and rubbed my temples. Now, this is what I was—fragile. Deep in my mind, I'd known it was how people saw me, but having Caleb put it into words was different. When did I go from Dad's little champion to this girl who just painted pretty pictures?

"So, I'll just slow you down, is what you're saying."

"We have years of training. I'm not trying to be insulting. We just need to be real here." He reached out a hand to my arm, but I pushed it away. "You've already helped with the computer stuff. Now, I need to take over."

I shook my head and wished I still remembered the moves Dad taught me. Then I got up and walked to the door.

Caleb lurched to his feet, wincing in pain. "Where are you going?"

"To the vending machine. Is that okay, or do I need an armed escort so I don't get lost?"

His calm shell cracked. "Dammit, why can't you see I'm trying to keep you safe?"

"Why can't you see I never asked you to keep me safe?" I paused, my hand on the door handle. "I never asked you to do anything except be my friend."

Shit. I hadn't meant for that last bit to slip out. I let the door slam behind me and stalked to the vending machines at the end of the hallway, the familiar quivers already quaking up my legs. My vision blurred around the edges in response to my constricted chest and airways, and I gripped the side of the machine to steady myself.

Maybe it was true. Maybe I wasn't the person to count on in a crisis.

Everyone, including my mom, still shielded me from upset, even after years of no major problems. My heart and my pride sank into my stomach and dissolved in the overly acidic juices. It was a miracle she'd let me live in the apartment this year. She'd been so worried I wouldn't be able to handle living alone. Pathetic.

I forced air into my lungs, blew it out, then sucked in more. Still trembling hands fumbled with the coins, dropped a couple, but kept going. If I was going to help Will, then I needed to be strong.

I punched in the numbers and a pack of trail mix dropped to the bottom of the machine. I got a bottle of water from the next machine and leaned against the wall while I chewed bite after bite of the nut and fruit mixture until the bag sat empty.

A few gulps of water and I headed back to the room, still shaking, but not in the grips of a full-blown attack.

Caleb opened the door the minute my card slipped into the slot. I raised my eyebrows and walked past him. I refused to let him see my struggle.

The evening passed without any armed men attacking us, so that was a success. I spent most of the time on my computer. The other man in the video, the doctor, turned out to be the head scientist at Nansic, in the research and product development department. His projects were not on the website, so likely were closely guarded corporate secrets.

I googled the doctor: married, two kids, graduated from MIT at the top of his class then went on to get his MD from Harvard, worked at a couple companies including a pharmaceutical company for years before switching to Nansic five years ago, lost his mom two years ago to dementia, father still living. Nothing screamed *involved with mercenary killers*.

Caleb peered over my shoulder a couple times but left me alone. Smart man.

At nine o'clock, Caleb climbed into one of the full-size beds and rolled over to sleep. Against my normal routine, I shut down the computer and got ready for bed. I washed my lone bra again in an attempt to get the fabric white, and hung it on the shower curtain, delaying lying down in the bed. I wasn't looking forward to the nightmares my subconscious had in store for me.

A few hours later, I jolted awake. The sheets were tangled around my legs and drenched in sweat. I gasped for air and coughed while I struggled to break free of the nightmare. My hands searched for Luna before I remembered she wasn't with me.

"Harper, you okay?" Caleb asked from his bed, not a bit of sleep in his voice.

I choked out a response. "I'm fine."

"Another nightmare?"

Now he wanted to act like a friend? I rolled over and let irritation replace my fear. "I said, I'm fine."

I watched the clock at the bedside but didn't let myself get up and pace, like I usually did. The last time I remembered looking at the clock it was four fifty-five. I woke to the sound of the shower turning on. The clock showed six thirty. I added up the hours I'd slept—five. Way better than my typical night.

CHAPTER NINE

Dr. Nelson's research lab
Nansic Headquarters
Indianapolis, Indiana

Ringing interrupted the doctor's thoughts and pulled his attention away from the microscope.

The research assistant glanced toward his desk, then walked over. "Is that your cell phone, Doctor? Do you want me to grab it for you?"

The doctor contemplated the ringing for a moment before realization dawned. "No," he snapped, then rushed to the desk. "No, thank you, Jim," he said in a softer tone. "Could you go grab more of the pentane? We need to run another column."

Jim said nothing at the unusual outburst, but nodded and left.

The phone stopped ringing, then immediately started again while the doctor fumbled with the keys to unlock the drawer. He shoved a cheap phone aside to pull the second burner cell from the depths.

"What?" he hissed into the phone.

"The Senator called." Dunham's deep baritone came over the line. "Something came up the chain of command. We know where they're going to be at eight-thirty AM but it's going to be out in the open. Do we have clearance?"

Dr. Nelson swallowed, unable to give the go-ahead. Then his gaze rested on the picture of his wife and sons on his desk, smiling for the camera on the sailboat trip they'd taken last year. "Yes. You have the clearance, but make it look like an accident."

CHAPTER TEN

I sat and collected my thoughts, doodling an image of Luna sitting on my windowsill on the pad of paper next to the motel phone. My fingers twitched, longing to feel her fur.

Caleb got ready in the bathroom. He wanted to pawn me off on the Army—but that didn't mean I would stay where they put me.

Caleb came out of the bathroom, dressed except for a shirt. My gaze glued to the ridges of his muscled shoulders and arms while my hand continued to move over the paper. I forced my attention away to the bandage on his back and noticed water around the edges.

"Isn't it bad to get your incisions wet?" I couldn't help but ask.

He reached back to feel the gauze. "I tied a trash bag over it. It's fine. What are you drawing?"

I glanced at the pad of paper. The outline of a half-drawn male figure centered the page next to the kitten. My muscles jumped to attention. Ripping the sheet off, I crumpled the page and crossed my arms. "No, the bandage is wet. Turn around and I'll change it."

He eyed me, then handed me the first aid bag. "A little bossy this morning, are we?"

"I just don't want to be responsible for you getting an infection in your spine." My cheeks heated as I reminded myself repeatedly that I was mad at him.

He cleared his throat and squirmed, not meeting my gaze in the reflection of the mirror. "I moved your, uh...bra...so I wouldn't get it wet."

Blinking, my mouth dropped open while I watched this hulk of a man—a Delta Force operator, capable of taking out five men without breaking a sweat—grow uncomfortable because of my bra. I bit my lip to contain a laugh.

"Thanks." I smoothed the tape on the fresh pad and tossed the old one in the trash. "You're good to go, for now." I couldn't help but push his discomfort. "Sorry if my bra was in your way."

He met my gaze and held it and I saw a spark of the Caleb I knew—the sweet, considerate one. "Harper, I'm sorry about all of this. It's not that I don't want your help."

I held up a hand as my humor evaporated. "Don't bother, we haven't been friends for a long time."

He opened his mouth as if to protest.

"It's fine," I cut in. "Let's go to this meeting and move on. We're not the best team and Will needs the best."

GI Joe took over again, and he nodded.

I grabbed my bag and the wooden chest, then decided it would be better to have my hands free. I took out my extra set of clothes and shoved them under the blanket to make room for the chest inside my backpack—looked like I'd be doing more laundry in the sink. The pack felt better. Easier to run with.

"Ready?" Caleb asked, all business, with his hand on the doorknob.

"Let's get this over with. Who are these people you're dumping me on?"

His brow scrunched together. "My squad leader overseas contacted someone stateside to meet us and bring you in. These guys know what they're doing."

"I'm sure they do," I forced myself to say.

As we walked across the blocks of Chicago, Caleb glanced sideways at me several times. After the third glance, I stopped in the middle of the sidewalk and put a hand to my hip. "What is it? Do I have something on my face?"

One side of his lips crept up. "No, I was just thinking."

"And?"

"I was thinking it was nice seeing you again, Harper." He paused and cocked his head to the side. "I didn't realize how much I missed you."

Oh, for fuck's sake. Now he decided to say this. Nails rolled around my churning stomach, but I let genuine emotion into my voice. "I missed you, too."

We traveled in silence the next few blocks across town. A block from the meet, I spotted a coffee shop I recognized and pushed away my guilt so I could move forward with my plan. "What time are we supposed to be there?"

Caleb glanced at his watch. "Eight thirty. We've got plenty of time."

I did my best to appear tired and undernourished, which wasn't too hard. "Do we have time to grab a coffee, maybe some breakfast?"

He smiled, a real smile, like the old days. "Yeah, we can stop for something."

"Great, thanks." I pasted a grin across my face while I wilted inside. He wouldn't be smiling soon.

The bittersweet smell of coffee and baking muffins hit me like a warm wave when we walked through the door. I'd been to this coffee shop before, many times. An art group I liked met here once a month. I made myself go but never shared, just sat in the back and pretended to be sociable. A dozen people stood in line before us, but the baristas knew their stuff and it moved forward steadily.

"If I remember right, you're a caramel latte girl."

I blinked up at him. Seven years and he remembered my favorite coffee.

"I still embarrass Will with the story of him tripping over that chair in front of the entire cheerleading squad and spilling coffee everywhere." Humor glinted in his eyes and I recognized the goofball I knew.

I swallowed the guilt creeping up my throat. "Can you order me a medium caramel latte and a bagel with cream cheese? I need to use the bathroom."

He peered down the hall, then leaned in. "Don't get lost and if you fall in just call. I'll have a cute lifeguard ready to save you."

Shame colored my voice. "I promise."

"But seriously," he said and glanced around. "Just be careful."

Why do you have to stop being a jerk now? I stepped away and fought the urge to turn around for a last look back at Caleb.

A door to the kitchen stood directly across from the door to the women's bathroom. I took a left instead of a right. The back kitchen sat mostly deserted with everyone being up front for the breakfast rush—just a dishwasher remained who didn't give me a second glance. I weaved my way through racks and boxes and straight out the open back door.

Pushing shame down to the pit of my stomach, I adjusted the straps of my backpack and chewed a fingernail while I scanned my options—left or right.

Left took me back toward the hotel. Likely the direction Caleb would expect me to take. Right, down the alley, spit me out on one end of the park where we were supposed to meet up with the Army guys. Right was also the most direct route to the nearest L station.

Right it was. I loped down the alley. It wouldn't take Caleb more than a couple minutes to figure out I ditched him. One good thing about him being injured—for once, I was faster than him.

I'd discarded the idea of calling Ren for help, at least for now, given the danger to anyone around me. Though the thought of his support was like a lure on a line—and I was a hungry fish.

I stepped out onto the sidewalk and merged into the pedestrian traffic. Part one of my plan was accomplished. Now to find a place to hide out and figure out why Nansic wanted us dead.

The crowd on the sidewalk thinned. I increased my step and spotted the stairway to the L platform fifty feet ahead of me.

My feet faltered. I stared at a figure leaning against the side of the stairway entrance, his arms crossed and his eyes trained on the park across the street. The man was familiar, large, and imposing. His head rotated to scan the park. Recognition hit me like a truck running into a brick wall. It was the mercenary who'd chased us from Caleb's father's house.

I ducked into the doorway of an office building and peered around the edge of the glass like a stalker. He surveyed the area where we were supposed to meet up with Caleb's superiors. I turned to appraise the street across from the park. My heart struggled to contract, unable to move my blood through my veins. My gaze settled on another large man with a neck brace.

It was the behemoth I'd clobbered over the head with the frying pan.

Boy, did he look mad. He stood facing the park as well. Both men glued their eyes to a bench on the north side of the gardens.

A man in uniform sat on the bench reading the paper—waiting for Caleb.

From my vantage point, I spotted two more particularly large men blending in with the crowd in a four-point box around the bench. It was a trap.

As if on cue, Caleb rushed out of the side street, his gait stilted but moving fast considering his injuries. My insides turned to liquid as Caleb entered the park. Ten more feet and he'd be boxed in with no chance of escape. I ignored my weak legs and sprang into action.

Caleb slowed, taking in his surroundings. I hoped he might have seen the trap, but I couldn't be sure.

I dashed across the street toward him. Car brakes screeched and a taxi veered left, missing my knees by inches. Not pausing, I jumped over the hood of the stopped taxi while I yelled, "Caleb!"

The commotion attracted attention, lots of attention. Caleb paused and glanced toward the noise. I waved and shouted, "It's a trap!"

I pointed to the other side of the park and the man in a brace. The other mercenary sprang into action, chasing me.

Caleb's eyes widened and he dashed toward me. "Harper, run!"

I dodged around the taxi one more time while the driver screamed about stupid teenagers, motioning in my direction. With the L station blocked by one mercenary, and at least three on my trail from the other side of the park, there was only one direction that held any possibility of escape.

A metallic ping sounded off the car to my right. I hadn't heard a shot, but I knew the sound of a bullet ricocheting. I ducked my head but kept running. They were shooting at me. In the middle of the city. With people around to see me die. *What the hell did Will get us into?*

Caleb dodged a car and made it to the sidewalk. Bullets whizzed through the air and shattered glass, sending pedestrians running for cover.

Another bullet collided with the brick of the storefront behind me, missing me by inches. I ducked around the corner and pressed my back to the wall. Caleb joined me moments later, clutching his side.

"You okay?" he gasped.

I chanced a peek around the brick edge. Five large men with guns converged on our doorway, only fifty feet away. "Um, yeah, I've been better."

Caleb nudged me aside and glanced around the corner, then pulled back in. Two bullets impacted the brick where his head had just been. His eyes flicked over the doorway to a bookstore, by the looks of it.

"I'll distract them. You head out the back door of this shop and meet me at your spot. Understand?" he demanded.

I shook my head. "You can't possibly hold off five armed men. It's suicide."

"For once, just listen!" He pulled me to face him, our faces only inches apart.

A bead of sweat dripped down his forehead. My gaze met the liquid blue of his eyes.

"You have to get out of here. Promise me you'll wait at your spot. If I don't show in three hours, get out of town," he said.

I swallowed and nodded, unable to speak around the boulder in my throat. He pushed me toward the door and pulled his handgun from his hip. Two quick shots sent the mercenaries ducking for cover and bought us a few seconds.

The sound of the gun reverberated in our confined space, too loud. My already tight muscles clamped down a notch or three.

With my hand on the shop handle, I paused. "I'm sorry I ditched you."

"I'm not," he said without looking back, still in a crouch, his back pressed against the wall. "If you hadn't, we'd be dead."

Sirens echoed down the streets.

I gripped the handle and pulled. A man and woman cowered behind the counter. I wanted to apologize for picking their doorway to hide in. Without a word, I rushed past the shelves of books to the back of the shop and found the loading dock in the alleyway.

The sirens grew louder while I dashed down yet another alley. Two more shots from Caleb's gun echoed, along with a strangled scream. The sound brought me to a dead stop.

Caleb.

CHAPTER ELEVEN

Sheer will forced my legs to move forward—to follow Caleb's plan. A silent prayer that he wasn't the one hit was the only help I could offer. My feet pounded against the concrete in rhythm with my pack beating against my spine.

He'd said to meet him at my spot. My frazzled brain didn't need to give my feet directions. They moved all on their own on the right course. The blinking lights of a police car slowed my pace to a walk when they came into view, racing to the park. Once the caravan of three cars with blaring sirens passed, I picked up the pace and pounded to the next L station.

It'd been a while since I'd visited. Respect slowed my jog to a walk. My gaze followed my boots through the dormant grass and fallen leaves. I picked my way to my favorite tree and leaned against the trunk. My eyes closed and I imagined being as solid and strong as the tree to fight back the shaking panic threatening to consume me. My fingers closed around the plastic prescription bottle in my pocket.

I can take one if I need to. I'd weaned myself off my daily prescription anxiety medications over a year ago. Not an easy feat. But I still carried the emergency medication for an acute panic attack. I hadn't needed one in six months, and to prove to myself I was doing well, I hadn't refilled the prescription. Two lonely pills rattled around in the plastic bottle.

Most of the time, just reaching into my pocket to hold the bottle and knowing it was there if I needed it was enough to diminish the threat of the attack to a doable level. But most problems didn't involve people trying to kill me, Caleb, and my brother.

My knees buckled and I slid down the rough bark to sit on the grass. My hands struggled to grip my backpack as they rattled like dead leaves in the wind. I set the pack beside me and buried my face in my arms.

The terror crept through my mind, pushing logical thought out in front of it. I could see myself as if I was floating outside my body—pathetic, crushed to the ground, fighting to even breathe and stave off the dizziness sweeping over me. Anxiety had ruled my existence for ten years. Too long.

I reached for my phone to call Ren only to find my pocket empty, not that it mattered. Ren couldn't talk me through it when I was this far down the rabbit hole. No amount of lavender or kale or sunshine, not even through an IV into a vein, would do any good.

I held on while the world tilted, gripped the grass in my hands, squeezed, and battled the dizziness. Will needed me. Caleb needed me. Blindly, I reached into my pocket and popped the top off the prescription bottle. I swallowed the tablet and clung to my sanity while I waited for the medication to take effect, mentally berating myself for giving in.

Sometime later, the blackness faded from my vision, and I sat up against the tree. The panic was still there, but some logic and reason returned. I stared at the stone in front of me and blinked my heavy eyelids. One irritating side effect of the medication was sleepiness. The headstone's white polished surface protruded from the groundbeautiful and horrible at the same time.

"Hi, Daddy," I said. "Sorry to fall apart in front of you again. I know I promised last time I'd do better."

This had been my spot for the last ten years, especially when I was younger. Anytime my mom couldn't find me, she knew I'd be here. Sitting with Dad, talking for hours until she came and dragged me home. They'd started calling it Harper's Spot because I guess that sounded less depressing than Dad's grave or the cemetery.

I liked to sit and think of him the way he was when he was alive—so handsome, laughing, and full of life. Not like the images from my nightmares. Not like the last time I'd seen him with his face half gone, ripped apart by the hollow point round.

Even bad weather couldn't keep me away. I'd sit, soaked in rain, shivering in the snow, and sweating in the sun. I hated to think of him all by himself, cold and alone, with no one to keep him company. So, I'd tell him about everyone and anything I could think of that he'd missed. When I was fourteen, my therapist suggested keeping my visits to a limited time, but when Mom tried, I just came on my own. Five miles only took a couple of hours. She gave up and started driving me when I asked.

At one point, they even considered exhuming the body and having him cremated so I could keep him near me at home, but they discarded the idea when I asked if I could put the urn on my bedside table. Over the years, I came less frequently to see him and tried to move on. It worked, kind of.

The sun caught the reflective surfaces on the gravestone and cast a shimmer. I read the script for the millionth time. William

Henry Bradley the Third, Loving Husband and Father. Brave Soldier who gave his life to save others. August 24, 1962 - February 22, 2014

"Remember when you used to tell me how brave I was, Daddy?" The tears I'd been holding in spilled over with a vengeance. My throat choked on the words as the hot drops poured down my cheeks. "I let you down. I'm not brave anymore. I don't know if I ever really was. But now Will's in trouble and I don't know how to save him."

I wiped away the moisture only to have fresh rivulets take their place. Drops fell from my chin to splash on the ground. I gave up trying to hide the tears and let them fall, my breath coming in ragged gasps. At least in a cemetery, no one thought you were crazy for breaking down.

"I wish you were here. You'd know what to do. But all I have is Caleb and maybe not even him now. I don't know how they found us. They couldn't have tracked us. We got rid of everything."

I sat up straighter, the drowsy feeling of the meds fading. We'd ditched our phones and used cash. They'd been at the meet first—ahead of us. They knew where we'd be. Someone betrayed us. Someone Caleb trusted.

Anger burned up the tears and sped my slow-moving blood through my veins. He'd called his superior in the Army—someone he'd risked his life for. If I ever found the traitor... Well, I still couldn't handle a gun, but I'd kill him with my bare hands.

I used my sleeve to clean up my face. I had a choice—lie here and drown in my sadness or fight until it was over. One way or another, I'd promised myself I'd do better for Will. Time to fulfill that promise.

I pushed up from the ground and ran my hand over the

smooth marble of the gravestone. "Thank you, Daddy. I'm not giving up. I'll make you proud."

Footsteps thudded against the ground behind me. I spun and pressed my back against the tree, my pack gripped against my chest.

"Harper?" Caleb called, out of breath.

I leapt from my hiding spot. "Here."

He charged my way, gripping his side where blood soaked through the fabric.

I stumbled toward him and threw my arms around him. The coil deep in my chest relaxed a fraction feeling him alive and breathing. "Are you okay?" I asked, my voice shaking. "I heard a scream."

His arms crushed me against him, and we stood silent, holding each other. Our breathing fell into sync.

Finally, I looked up to his face. "If I'd lost you," I croaked, the meds loosening my tongue.

Shaking his head, he held me at arm's length and met my gaze. "I'm kind of like gum on your shoe—not that easy to get rid of." He leaned against the tree, beads of sweat on his brow. "I got two of them, then the cops distracted the last three long enough for me to scram."

Aware of his closeness and the warmth spreading through my belly, I stepped away. "Should we have just waited for the cops? I mean, they would have to help us, right?"

He shook his head. "I'm not sure who the hell we can trust now. They were tipped off where we would be. Someone up the chain of command told them."

"What are we going to do?"

He pushed off the tree. "Find out what they're trying to hide and who has the most to lose. That may help us figure out who has Will."

I nodded. "I had an idea. Before you wanted to get rid of me."

"I didn't want to get rid of you."

"Swear we're in this together and I'll tell you my idea."

He shook his head. "Fine."

"Okay, how do you feel about visiting Indiana?"

The bell above the door clattered, announcing our arrival. Caleb pushed the glass door open farther and held it. My grip on the backpack tightened.

Glass showcases lined either side of the shop, and the neon sign in the front window flashed *Pawn*.

"Are you sure you want to do this?" Caleb asked as he pulled his jacket to cover the bloodstain on his shirt. "I can see how much my watch and knife would get us."

Caleb had his military-issued watch from Special Forces and his Spiderco knife that had lived in his pocket since his dad gave it to him for his sixteenth birthday.

"They wouldn't get us enough." I licked my lips with a dry tongue. "Besides, most likely I'll be dead in a couple days, so I guess I won't care then."

His eyes narrowed. "Nice thought."

A clean-shaven man in a polo walked through the doorway from the back of the shop. Hardly the sleazy image of a pawnshop owner. "Can I help you?"

I strode forward past Caleb. "Yes, I have something I'd like to pawn."

He settled a pair of reading glasses on his nose. "Let's have a look."

I unzipped the backpack and pulled out the engraved wooden case. For one last time, I ran my fingers over the inscription: *For my Little Champion.* With a deep breath, I unlatched the metal clasps and eased the cover open. Nestled inside the worn velvet lay two intricately engraved antique Colt revolvers. The pearl handles gleamed white with an iridescent glow.

I'd thought they were more beautiful than the crown jewels when Dad had opened the case for the first time. It wasn't my birthday, or any special day. He'd come home saying he got a surprise for me. Boy, was Mom angry. Her reaction told me he'd spent a ridiculous amount of money on the guns.

At the next sharp shooting championship, I'd insisted upon using them, even though antiques didn't have the ease or accuracy of my modern custom-made Ruger GPs. I took first place.

Dad's face beamed brighter than a lighthouse when I accepted my medal. The next month, he was killed in action. I never touched the pistols again. But I kept them with me, always.

A whistle escaped the shopkeeper's lips. "You sure you want to part with these?"

"Yes," I said and pushed the case across the counter. "What can you give me for them?"

"The first question is do you want to sell, or do you need a loan?" he asked, his eyes still on the guns.

"Sell," I said.

"Loan," Caleb answered at the same time.

I shifted and whispered. "We'll get more if we sell them."

"No way. Just a loan," he growled back.

I turned back to the shopkeeper's raised eyebrows. "A loan."

"Alright, let me do a little research," he said and took the case to a side table to examine the guns under a light.

"The certificate is in the bottom of the case," I added.

Ten minutes later he came back and set the case in front of

me. "Since there was some discussion about selling them, I can offer sixty-five hundred if you want to sell or three thousand for a loan."

Caleb held up a hand. "We aren't selling."

I opened my mouth to protest. This was our only means of getting cash and who knew how long we'd need to be on the run? Meeting Caleb's gaze, I knew he'd dug his stubborn heels in. Arguing was pointless.

Instead, I focused my attention where it could make a difference and turned to the shop owner. "These are 1892 Colt Specials, engraved and certified to have belonged to Annie Oakley. We both know they are worth over thirty thousand at any auction house. Give us an even five for the loan and you got a deal."

The shop owner's eyes widened. Caleb smiled and leaned against the counter. We waited while the shopkeeper assessed his options.

His mouth scrunched up. "Fine, five thousand. I'll write up a ticket."

With the wad of cash stuffed in my backpack, we left the shop. In the doorway, I glanced back once at the case. My pack was way too light and my heart too heavy.

"You okay?" Caleb asked.

I blinked and turned away from the guns. "Yeah, now we just need a car."

CHAPTER TWELVE

"Hit the release for the hood, would you?" Caleb called from the front of the car.

I searched around for the lever under the dash and finally found the release. I gripped the plastic and pulled. The hood popped up and the lever broke off in my hand. I glanced at the salesman. Luckily, his attention was focused solely on Caleb under the hood.

"As you can see, she's in pretty good shape for a car of this age," the salesman said, leaning in.

Caleb poked and prodded. "Yeah, if you say so."

"This Pontiac is really solid, for this price"

"No, thanks. How about we check out the Blazer over there?" Caleb slammed the hood and motioned to the ugliest car on the lot.

I glanced at the plastic lever still in my hand then dropped it on the floorboard. "Good idea."

"I've got a great Explorer I can show you." The salesman scurried after Caleb, completely ignoring me.

Rust spotted the hood of the once metallic hunter green SUV. The sun damage had faded the color to more of a puke green with flecks of sparkle. With the dents in the front fender and driver's door, it had seen better days.

Ten minutes later and a hushed conversation with the salesman after Caleb checked out the engine, I settled into the faded, stained fabric seat of the Chevy Blazer and rested my head on my hands while Caleb threw his bag in the back. The salesman taped a temp tag in the back window.

I pulled out the burner phones we'd bought and sent a quick text to Ren to give him my new number. As an afterthought, I sent one more text. *I took one of the emergency meds. I'm sorry.* It felt like confessing a sin to a priest, or at least what I imagined confession felt like, never having done it myself.

The driver's door groaned in protest, misshapen from the dent. I stuffed the phone back into my backpack as Caleb eased into the seat, the dried blood showing from under his jacket.

"Are you sure you don't want me to drive?" I asked.

"I'm good. Besides, the driver's seat always has the best lumbar support," he said and forced a grin.

I raised my eyebrows. "You want pressure on your ripped-open incisions? I didn't know you were a masochist."

"There's a lot you don't know about me." He shifted the SUV into drive. "Besides, I need you to navigate."

"The navigation should be pretty easy, take the Kennedy east to sixty-five and head south until you see signs for Indianapolis," I said.

Caleb grunted in response.

I pulled a pencil out of my bag and sketched scrolling vines along the outside edge of the map to pass the time. Keeping my fingers busy stopped the hamster wheel of thoughts in my head. And the hamsters were multiplying like rabbits.

The drive to Indianapolis would take just under four hours going the speed limit to avoid any run-ins with the law. Specifically, to avoid having our IDs run and tipping the bad guys off to our location. Any hacker good enough to crack the google account in a couple hours would be easily able to set up a search to let them know when our IDs were run. That made getting a speeding ticket deadly.

The head researcher from Will's video, Dr. Michael Nelson, ran the Nansic lab. Whatever information they were trying to cover up was in that lab somewhere.

With the Blazer's radio broken, I filled the silence before my mind spiraled out of control. "So, dog or cat?"

"What?"

"Are you a dog person or a cat person?"

Caleb glanced my way. "We're back to small talk, huh?"

"You said I didn't know a lot about you."

"We have a Belgian Malinois on the team. He's saved my ass more than once. So, I'd have to say dog." He adjusted in the seat gingerly. "I'm guessing you're a cat person."

Luna's multicolored face flashed in my mind and I closed my eyes to let the pain of her absence, nearly physical at this point, wash over me. When I opened my eyes, Caleb was eyeing me. "I'm both."

He scrunched his nose. "Cheater. You have to pick one. That's the entire point."

"Nope. I would pretty much say I'm an animal person."

"What does that mean?"

"I'd take an animal over a person any day."

"Really," he said, his forehead scrunched.

"Yeah, they're good listeners. And they don't judge." The words came out before I realized what I was saying. I glanced out the window—the small talk suddenly not feeling so small.

Caleb spoke quietly. "I never tried to judge you, Harper."

"No one tries. Ren says it's just human nature."

"He has experience with...this stuff, as well?"

"You could say that."

"I'm glad you have someone who understands." He cleared his throat. "Maybe you should give him a chance."

"No," I shook my head. It was even harder to think of Ren that way now. I glanced over to meet Caleb's gaze. "But he'll always be my best friend."

We fell into silence and I went back to my doodling. An hour in, and with an intricately sketched boarder of ivy with kittens peeking out circling the map, I set my pencil aside. "You still okay driving?"

"Yeah, I'm all good."

"Then I'm going to take a nap. Wake me if you want me to drive." I lowered the seat as far back as it would go.

With my arm over my eyes to block the evening sun coming through the windows, I fell into exhausted oblivion.

The sound of the door slamming shut brought me bolting up in my seat. I gripped the *oh-shit* bar and the door handle in a ready stance, prepared to do—what, I didn't know.

Caleb chuckled and eyed me. He gestured to my raised leg and one hand on the door handle. "You going to kick me or jump out of the car?"

I glanced at my cocked leg and lowered it to the floorboard.

He held out a drink and a bag from the burger joint we were parked in front of. "I was hungry. I figured you might be as well, seeing as how you skipped out on breakfast."

I glared, ready to refuse the burger out of habit, but the scent hit my nose and my stomach gurgled.

Caleb's grin grew wider. "By the way, you might want to check out your phone. Your wannabe boyfriend has been blowing it up."

Grumbling about him being nosey around the bite in my mouth, I scrolled through Ren's texts. My eyes stung with tears at his first text. *Don't ever apologize for taking care of yourself. Did you get your scripts filled??*

How are you doing? How are things going with Caleb? Is he being supportive? Is he being respectful?

Respectful? Maybe Caleb was right about Ren's feelings.

I typed a response. *Didn't have time for the scripts. Had to get out of town.*

He responded immediately. *I can pick them up for you.*

NO! Anything with my name attached can be deadly. I'll figure something out. I typed furiously.

I can get something under my name and bring them to you.

A sad grin spread over my lips. *Thank you. But I'm okay.*

He asked where we were going. I kept it general, no specifics.

His last text stopped me midchew. *I think I may be on to something with the video.*

My fingers raced over the keys to type my response. *You promised me you'd stay out of this. I don't want you hurt.*

I am staying out if it. Just a little research. He responded with a wink emoji. *Miss you, gingersnap.*

With a frustrated sigh, I typed, *Miss you too. Please, Ren, stay out of it.* Then I tossed the phone into the console and ignored Caleb's raised eyebrow.

The piping hot fries hit the spot and I actually finished the entire cheeseburger, to my surprise. I tossed my trash in the back seat. "Thanks. I guess I was hungry."

"There's a trash can five feet away. This car doesn't need any more funk." He grabbed his own trash, opened the back door and took mine and threw it in the can.

I held back my snarky comment.

"We've got about half an hour to Indianapolis, you want to find a good place to hole up for the night?"

I searched nearby hotels that likely wouldn't be too picky about ID.

"Look for motels with an hourly rate," Caleb said from the driver's seat.

A shiver ran up my spine. "And hopefully no bedbugs."

The room wasn't as bad as I'd feared. It appeared clean and for forty-nine bucks a night, I couldn't complain.

Caleb set his bag on the full bed nearest the door and immediately checked all the exits. We were on the ground level, with the door leading directly to the parking lot and a window in the bathroom that could serve as an escape route if needed.

He took off his jacket. The blood, mostly dry, crusted his shirt in a near foot-wide circle over his back and side. A rip in the fabric showed crimson-smeared skin underneath. I swallowed the bile that clawed its way up my throat at the sight of the blood. *It's just red paint.*

"We need to get you cleaned up," I managed, motioning to the stain.

"Yeah, guess it wouldn't hurt."

"If this keeps up, I'm going to have to charge you for my medical services."

"Do you charge by the wound or by the hour?" he said in what I would have sworn was a flirtatious tone—except the words came out of Caleb's mouth.

He pulled the one chair in the room close to the bed and sat down while I opened our bag of first aid supplies. The incision next to his spine oozed blood.

"Watch for any pus or overly angry looking tissue," Caleb instructed.

The word pus almost brought the burger up for an encore performance. "No pus but the tissue sure doesn't look happy."

"It isn't any more painful than normal, so it's probably fine," he assured me. "You good?"

"Yep." I mopped dried blood from his skin but paused when I got to his side.

"How did you get this?" I asked and pointed to a four-inch horizontal gash just above his hip.

"One of those guys was a decent shot. A couple inches to the left, and I'd have been in trouble," he said.

I remembered the rip in his shirt, then closed my eyes and forced myself to breathe. If Caleb was shot...my throat tightened. A mixture of emotions washed over me, surprisingly strong emotions. I slowed my rapid breathing, counting the 4-7-8, slow and steady, until my hands stabilized.

"I might be able to stitch it up, but let's see what you can do with the butterfly bandages first," he said.

Nodding, I leaned to the side and tilted my head to get a better view. The scent of his skin hit my nose, spicy pine with a little musk mixed in. I cleared my throat—and my head—and closed the wound.

"Thank you. You're really good at this. Gentle, you know?" he said.

I moved to the side so I could check the injuries from the fight and glanced up to his face. His gaze held mine. The intensity stopped my hand.

"No problem, it probably comes from working on canvases." My voice sounded odd to my ears. The way he looked at me sent strange tingles to some very interesting places. I'd never thought of Caleb *that way*, never considered...

He reached down a hand and held mine. "Those canvases don't know how good they have it."

My lips parted slightly. I leaned in closer, almost hypnotized, to get more of his spicy scent.

His head bent, only inches from mine. The rigidness of his features softened to resemble the boy I'd known.

I resisted the urge to run my fingers over the ridges and valleys of his muscled back, to explore. If only I'd brought my paints and canvas.

He blinked, his face resuming its stone façade, and jerked away, breaking the moment. "About done?"

Jolted back to reality, I nodded. "Yeah, just about." I focused on cleaning him up while inside me, temptation battled logic. "Okay, that's the best I can do with what we've got. We'll need to get more supplies tomorrow."

He grabbed a clean shirt from his bag and slowly pulled it over his head.

I cleared my throat and stared at my hands.

"I'm going to go grab some ice. You want anything from the vending machine?" he asked.

"No, I'm good. I think I'll just get ready for bed," I said without meeting his gaze.

He closed the door behind him. I fell back onto the bed and threw my hands over my face. *Caleb? What the hell? I don't even like muscle-bound guys.*

My last couple boyfriends—if you could call going out for a few months, then breaking up, a boyfriend—were more of the artistic type. My twiggy arms were probably stronger than theirs. I stayed away from hotheaded, adrenaline junkies. Ren thoroughly enjoyed making pointed comments about the lack of muscle on the last guy I'd gone out with, on top of complimenting him on his beard, which consisted of about ten hairs.

Girls hadn't necessarily drooled over Caleb in high school, but his humor had got him a long way. And certainly, all my friends had swooned over his eyes to the point of nausea.

Forcing myself into action, I did a lightning quick clean up and jumped under the covers, burying my face, before he got back from the ice machines.

CHAPTER THIRTEEN

Nelson family home
Indianapolis, Indiana

Dr. Nelson slammed the burner phone into the wooden surface of his desk and barely resisted the urge to throw the damn thing across the room. Not only did the special security team cause a scene, but they'd also missed the mark. Again.

"Honey? What's the matter?" his wife said from the doorway.

Nelson dropped the burner into his open briefcase and turned, a mask of calm falling over his features. "Nothing to worry about, sweetie. Just a setback at work."

She walked in and ran her nails through his hair, over his scalp. "You'll figure whatever it is out. You always do."

"What would I do without you?" He leaned his head into the massage.

"Probably never eat or leave your lab," she chuckled. "By the way, we got an invitation to tour MIT for Matthew. I'm going to schedule a flight probably next Friday."

"Wonderful. I'm sure he'll love it." The doctor caught her hands and kissed her fingers before releasing them.

She sighed. "Don't stay up too late."

He nodded and settled behind the desk, going over the most recent faxes he'd received from the prison. He scanned the numbers, then went over them again, slower.

Unable to accept what his eyes were telling him, he ran a finger down the columns a third time, clenching the paper in a tight fist. Finally, he set the papers aside, poured himself three fingers of gin and made a note on his pad. "Call Warden".

He pulled out his notes on the chemical reactions and studied them. Something wasn't right. No matter what he tried, he couldn't set the structure to hold longer than a few hours before it broke apart into organic compounds the animal cells could absorb. And once absorbed, a chain reaction of bad to worse started that was the exact opposite of his desired results.

An image of the mice ripping each other to shreds flashed in his mind. That kind of violence was getting in the way of the goal of this research. Though the more pressing issue was that his superiors wouldn't wait forever to see results from their investments.

A burner cell in his briefcase chimed. He picked it up and read the text. *Someone is snooping around looking into you and Marling.*

Who? The girl? Nelson sent back, wishing he could order Marling's assassination. That buffoon was quickly becoming the bane of his existence.

No, an associate of hers. We have an address.

Nelson tossed the phone back into the silver briefcase. He was a researcher, a doctor, not an assassin. With a deep breath, he focused on the chemical structures on the pages in his hand. Work out the science, he told himself, and swirled the alcohol in his glass. *We have to stop absorption of the primary component so the secondary can do its job.* Inspiration struck, and he leapt to his feet.

Briefcase in hand, he headed out the door and called to his wife. "I'll be home late."

CHAPTER FOURTEEN

The lobby of Nansic's headquarters and production facility sported polished concrete floors and a modern industrial vibe. We stood in line with the crowd of people waiting for the ten o'clock tour. I rubbed my sandpaper eyes and sipped coffee. It'd been a rough night but not because of nightmares. No, this time it was other dreams keeping me up. Dreams about Caleb. And me. And not many clothes.

We'd signed waivers to take the tour, with fake names of course. I couldn't stop twitching, like someone was watching me. Caleb lounged in a chair, relaxed, at least to the casual eye.

"If you all are ready, we can begin the tour," said a woman with *Michelle* on her nametag.

The crowd shuffled forward to the door, filtering through one by one.

When I got to the front of the line, she held up a hand to stop me.

They've spotted me. Damn recognizable hair. I should have worn a wig. My muscles tensed, ready to run, hit, fight. My hand tightened around the paper coffee cup, ready to throw steaming coffee in someone's face.

"I'm sorry, miss, but you can't bring any food or beverages on the tour. We do offer snacks and water at the end," Michelle said with a sugary smile.

Straining to breathe, I loosened my grip on the offending cup. With a nod, I stepped to the side while I recovered my wits. Caleb waited. I dumped the cup in the trash before re-entering the line.

He put a hand on my elbow. "Calm down," he hissed. "You looked like you were going to have a heart attack."

Warmth seeped into my skin where his hand touched. I pulled my arm from his grasp and walked faster.

Most of our fellow tourists consisted of farmers—landowners looking to investigate products for their farms. A smaller portion looked like college students, notepads at the ready to jot things down. I grabbed one of the free notepads and pens from a table. The Nansic brand blazed down the side of the pen. While we walked, I sketched out several blocks of a Zentangle, an exercise to sooth my nerves.

"If you'll bear with me, I'm not typically a tour guide but someone called in sick this morning. I'm usually in the research department but I should be able to answer questions," she said.

I sent Caleb a glance and mouthed, *Score*. Maybe she'd be some help.

"We're going to start out in the production portion of the factory. Please don't touch anything." The guide's voice was way too excited for talking about chemicals.

Enormous vats of liquid churned below us while we walked across the catwalk forty feet in the air. Tight metal lids kept the noxious chemicals from spilling, but the vapors threatened to burn off my nose hairs.

I forced a breath in over the stinging sensation in my throat. That explained the waiver and the disclaimer about people with asthma.

We exited the catwalk to a cement hallway. Caleb nudged my side. I looked back. He thrust his chin to the right—a sign up ahead read, *Research.*

Below the sign was a thick metal door with a keypad to the left. While I watched, a slender woman in a lab coat, files in hand, slid a card through then punched an eight-digit code into the pad. With a metallic *thunk,* the door swung open. A glimpse through the closing door showed a long corridor with glass panels on both sides and various lab equipment inside the rooms.

The group moved into view of a security camera trained at the hallway. I pictured security guards on the other side of that feed, watching us. Caleb and I skirted the edge of the group, doing our best to keep from facing the camera head on. With a pounding heart, I noted the brand for future research on security weaknesses.

The group moved to the railing and our guide spouted about the miraculous advancements in pest control, mostly aimed at the farmers in the tour.

"What about the research showing the creation of superbugs because of overuse of these pesticides?" a woman about my age asked, pen in hand and ready to write.

I made notes of my own, placing myself near the keypad and writing down the model number, then noticed the wiring running up the cement wall to the door.

The smile on our fill-in guide's face tightened. "There is no reliable research that supports the so-called superbugs."

The student pressed to the front of the group. "What about the research showing the nitrogen-fixing bacteria in the soil are being killed by your herbicides and pesticides? All life on earth depends on those bacteria."

The smile disappeared altogether. "If you have questions, I

am going to have to insist you save them for the end of the tour and then I can direct you to the appropriate personnel."

"Look who's here," Caleb whispered in my ear.

I followed his gaze. The doctor from the video walked directly toward us. His attention focused on the printouts in his hand. With his frizzy, thinning hair standing up and the way he scurried down the hallway, he reminded me of a terrier going after a toy.

"Ah, and here is our head researcher, Dr. Nelson," the guide said. "Do you have a moment to stop and answer a few questions from these landowners?"

So much for holding your questions to the end. I guess she only wanted the right questions.

Dr. Nelson ripped his attention from the sheet in front of him. The circles under his eyes spoke of a late night, possibly an all-nighter. He forced an obviously strained smile to his face. "Michelle, you're giving tours today? Well, you all lucked out. She's one of our best lab assistants."

The farmers dominated the Q&A with the help of our guide. Most questions centered on the cost and number of recommended sprays of the pesticides.

"I can assure you our products are the cutting edge of control and are the most effective on the market today." The doctor paused and wiped a hand over his brow.

I watched the man from the video, one of the men involved in Will's disappearance, and barely controlled the urge to bash my fists into him and demand he tell me where my brother was. Though, he might not even know anything. He didn't fit the image I'd built up in my head of the enemy.

Michelle piped up. "Dr. Nelson is a genius in the research department. He has something in the works going out for FDA approval shortly that will give you another option when dealing with persistent pests."

"Now, we can't get ahead of ourselves." The doctor fidgeted with the papers, rolling them and unrolling them in his hands. "We don't have a timeline yet and are working to perfect the product."

"Working the bugs out, so to speak." Michelle flashed her obviously bleached teeth at her pun.

The bland stare from the doctor spoke volumes. "Yes, you could say that."

He gave us a final wave and scurried away to the research department.

"This is a waste of time," I whispered to Caleb. "Learning about how much a vat of this stuff costs and superbugs isn't getting us any closer to finding Will or what this company has to do with it. We should get out of here before someone recognizes us." I smoothed down my hair and glanced over my shoulder, half-expecting to see security charging toward us.

"They aren't going to just hand us the information. Keep taking notes on security and I'll find out what I can from our perky guide." He straightened his shirt, sending me a wink.

I glared as understanding dawned and glanced pointedly at the rock on her ring finger. "She's married."

He shrugged. "Shouldn't matter."

"You can't just use people," I hissed.

"I'm not using her. I'm just showing her a good time," he said and wiggled his eyebrows.

What a pig. I glared after him. To think I almost kissed him.

Cocky wasn't attractive on him. I glanced at his retreating form. *And who would want all that muscle, anyway?* I tore my gaze away from his ass, defined beautifully by his jeans.

I'd seen Caleb with girls before—even helped take prom pictures with Will and his dates. I'd never been remotely jealous. Nothing had changed, I told myself.

I kept my distance from Caleb the rest of the tour, avoiding the cameras and hanging out by the windows. Acres of test fields surrounded the factory where they sprayed their newest pest control solutions on crops. Most of the fields were already harvested and only bare mounded rows of soil remained while the winter crops of kale and broccoli still thrived.

We stopped at the final point of our tour in a large white kitchen. Platters of vegetables took up most of the long counters next to bottles of water.

"Feel free to grab a tasty sample of our fresh-from-the-garden veggies and homemade dressing," the guide waved a hand at the food. "Also, don't forget to take a brochure. Inside, you'll find all our bulk pricing, which may especially interest our landowning clients."

The group moved forward and milled around the snacks. With the chemicals still in my nose, I couldn't stomach eating food sprayed with the stuff.

Caleb sidled over to our guide, his chest out, with no sign of the pain he felt. I stared, barely remembering to shut my dropped jaw, as her body language went from helpful-professional to lean-in-and-whisper-in-your-ear flirty in three seconds flat.

My grip tightened around the pen in my hand. I rolled my shoulders to relieve the tense muscles and sat with my back to them, so I didn't have to watch.

Ten minutes later he strolled over. "Ready to head out?"

I refused to look up from my notepad. "Done already?"

"Yep, I got her number and we're meeting up later to talk about a possible security job, and maybe get a quote for my little sister's research paper."

I glared from under my drawn brows and whispered. "Are you kidding? Let me guess, I'm the little sister."

He grinned, which made his eyes sparkle even more. For some inexplicable reason, I wanted to hit him. Hard.

I glanced at the clock in the corner of the computer screen again. It was after eleven. How long did it take to schmooze information out of one ditzy, gullible woman? I blew a breath out my nose and contemplated my emotions. *I don't care who he's with or what he's doing.* But my twisted insides disagreed.

Until he'd left for the military, we'd been friends. He was practically like a second older brother to me. This unrest, and maybe something more, swirling around my gut was new. I didn't like it.

I refocused on my screen. It only took me two hours to hold up my end of this partnership. Caleb had a new name and background that would pass anything but the deepest of dives, due to the fact I'd borrowed the name and information from a real former Army soldier. A shiny revamped version of Caleb's ID sat on the table, thanks to my computer program and a few items from the corner store. Now, Caleb just needed to get the interview.

I tapped the keys to enter my new search into the engine. A search with Will's name didn't bring up anything current. His superiors must have reported him as missing by now. And any search combining Nansic and the military bought up the company's charitable donations to military families from last Christmas.

Maybe I needed to cast a wider net. Rookie mistake. The problem was my vivid imagination. Specifically, the graphic images my brain kept throwing in my face of Caleb in the backseat all over *Michelle.* I gritted my teeth and hit Enter.

The list popped up on the screen. I scrolled through the stories and stopped at a breaking news title. *Crazed soldiers described as Rabid Beasts.* I clicked the title and the news story popped up. My breathing increased as the air in the room seemed to be sucked out by a vacuum.

My eyes devoured the words. I scrolled down and whispered to myself. "How have I not seen this before?"

The only way this wasn't a national headline news story was if someone kept it from the press until now.

The sound of the bolt on the motel door sliding open tore my focus. I gripped the table, muscles tense. Caleb appeared through the doorway. His eyes and mouth, both relaxed at the corners, told of more than a few drinks.

I turned back to the screen, my fingernail between my teeth.

"Hey," he said and locked the door behind him. "You still up?"

"Just doing a little research. What did you find out?"

"She's not working in Dr. Nelson's lab. From what she said, all his projects are hush-hush. Not any help there so I started working her for security info." He walked by me and eased himself onto the bed.

The smell of perfume trailed him in a rank cloud. I chewed a chunk of nail off until blood seeped out of the nailbed.

"You need to read this article," I said.

He lay back on the bed. "Read it to me. I think I had one too many shots. Took a little more than I thought to get her to open up about security around the place."

"Okay, I'll paraphrase so I don't use any words that are too big for you."

He grunted.

I waved a hand to clear some of the perfume stink and skimmed the paragraphs to pick out the pertinent points. "Over the last three weeks, four soldiers stationed at your base have lost their minds and started shooting civilians and their fellow soldiers, seemingly without reason or provocation."

He bolted up on the bed. "What the hell?"

"The first two didn't kill anyone, but they brutally beat several civilians. The third shot and killed a civilian. But the worst happened yesterday when a soldier took out six civilians and two of his own squad before another member of his squad shot him. He's in critical condition."

Caleb got up and paced the room, all signs of alcohol gone. "That can't be right. No one would take out their own team."

"Witnesses described the men as acting like rabid beasts. The military is blaming possible PTSD and is investigating but won't comment further," I read from the last paragraph.

"Did they give the names?" he asked.

"No, they haven't released any names. But that isn't all of it," I said.

"What?"

I pointed to the screen. "Officials did say a missing soldier, reported by his squad two days ago, is being investigated for any connection to this string of violence."

"Two days ago. They have to be talking about Will." Caleb paused behind me and read the lines.

A large, calloused hand gripped my shoulder and squeezed gently. The urge to turn around and be enclosed, safe, swept over me. I stood up and took a step toward him.

"It's going to be okay," he said and pulled me close.

I nodded, my throat sealed to the point of choking, and leaned my head against the muscles of his chest. Warmth enveloped me in the circle of his arms.

He put one hand on my upper arm and tilted my head to meet my eyes. "We won't let them get away with any of this. I swear."

Our gazes locked and something deep inside me sparked. My gaze darted to his lips. Heat swirled low in my belly.

Caleb's head moved a fraction of an inch closer to mine. My

hand gripped the fabric of his shirt. A few inches closer and our lips would meet.

He jerked and stepped back as if burned, setting me at arm's length from him.

I grabbed the chair to catch my balance, the heat in my belly doused by his sudden change.

He reached his arm back to rub his neck. "I can't do this."

"Do what?" I asked. My brain struggled to keep up. My desire, his reaction, I couldn't compute it all, couldn't process.

His gaze rested on me. "Nothing. Never mind. I'm going to hit the shower."

He walked past me, the overwhelming floral scent trailing behind.

I sat and turned back to the computer. *God, I almost fell for those stupid blue eyes.* Slapped back to reality, anger fueled my muscles and my words. "Good idea."

He paused while I pounded on the computer keys with more force than absolutely necessary. "Harper, I"

"I have work to do."

He held up his hands and walked to the bathroom without another word.

Pulling out Ren's necklace, I put it under my nose and breathed in the soothing lavender to cleanse my senses of the perfume, and hopefully the turmoil jumbling up my insides. My reactions to Caleb confused me. I needed him as a friend, wanted him as a friend. But some important parts of my body had failed to get the memo.

Trying to sleep was pointless. I stayed at the table, laptop open, searching for any further information on the soldier story. Any articles I found, all from small independent media outlets, spouted the same information as the first. None mentioned the missing soldier, and none mentioned my brother.

Caleb didn't say a word after his shower, didn't even look

my way, but went straight to bed. His soft snoring added background noise to my late-night investigations.

I couldn't see how Will fit into any of this. My overtaxed brain spun like a Spirograph, weaving an intricate design of tangents and possibilities that eventually spiraled into a jumbled mess.

My back ached from sitting in the same position for over eight hours. I blew out a breath. *Start at the center.* I went back to the initial article. The eyewitness reports described the soldiers as *rabid beasts*. I stared at the blinking search bar, my vision blurring like a stuttering video. I typed in rabid animals and hit enter, then groaned at myself. Maybe it really was time to stop.

I reached for the screen to close the laptop when the top story caught my attention, *Local Birds Gone Rabid?* I paused. I'd heard of rabid dogs, squirrels, hell, even cows, but never birds. *Some birds are pretty mean anyway, how can they even tell the difference?* The link took me to a small-town paper in northeast Indiana. Not exactly in Nansic's backyard, but in the grand scheme of things, suspiciously close.

The reporter warned townspeople to be wary of the migrating population of Canada geese stopping in at local lakes and ponds on their way north for the spring. Several reports of serious attacks were coming into the sheriff's office. The violence of the attacks caused local farmers to speculate the geese contracted a new form of rabies, which to this point was only found in mammals. Wildlife officials said a mutation in the rabies virus that allowed it to grow in nonmammal species was highly unlikely, but they were bringing in a professor and her graduate students from Indiana State University to investigate the strange behavior.

I thought of the chemical vats in the factory. Could Nansic be dumping chemicals into local waterways? I started a search on watersheds but only lasted a few nonproductive minutes before the lined maps looked like random shapes.

I collapsed into the fluffy hotel pillow and didn't remember closing my eyes.

The chime of a cell phone and the tapping key sounds in response dragged me from my dreamless sleep. I cracked an eyelid and stared at the naked skin of Caleb's back. Fresh gauze covered his lower spine and the tape roll sat next to him on the already-made bed. Blinking, I looked away and ignored the warm feeling spreading over my skin.

"Why make the bed if the maid is going to come in and change the sheets?" I croaked out the first thought to enter my mind.

He didn't turn but I could hear the smile in his voice. "Habit."

"The best thing about hotels is not having to make your own bed. Leave it to the military to ruin even that."

He dropped the phone and swung a leg up on the bed to turn and face me. "It's not a habit from the military. Ever since I was a kid, my bed better be made or there was trouble. Nothing wrong with that."

"Let me guess," I said and rubbed sleep from my eyes. "Your dad. Right?"

He nodded.

"Who was in the Special Forces your entire childhood." I waited for him to nod again. "So, a habit from the military. See, ruins even the pleasure of being messy."

His lips pressed together, but he didn't argue.

"Who texted you?" I motioned to the phone.

His attention shifted to his back and applying the tape. "Michelle."

"Michelle?"

"The lab tech. The one I was pumping for information."

I threw back the covers and launched myself out of bed, suddenly needing a long shower. "You're such a pig."

"What? No, I didn't mean it like that," he called after me. "I didn't sleep with her."

"I don't want to know." I slammed the door to the bathroom and turned the shower on to drown out the rest of his disclaimers. My hair stood off my head in a three-inch-high rat's nest of red curls. Will always called me Bozo when I let my hair get out of control like this, owing to the fact that I looked like a crazed clown escaped from the circus.

I shouldn't care who Caleb talked to or flirted with. He'd made it obvious last night he wanted nothing to do with me. And I didn't want anything to do with him. Guess he was more into tall, married blondes, like Michelle.

I paused and met my own glare in the mirror. *Thinking about kissing him was just a response to stress.* A tight stomach and burning deep in my chest cropped up every time his face flashed in my mind. *Just acid reflux. He's an ass.* My reflection didn't agree.

The shower tamed my locks to a more respectable height. With one last glance in the mirror to school my expression into one of disinterest, I gathered the nerve to face Caleb again.

I opened the bathroom door to an empty room. A note lay on the desk next to my laptop. *She came through with the interview. Took the IDs.* I paced around the room like a caged tiger. The fake ID would hold up to their scrutiny, but that wouldn't stop someone from recognizing him. Real acid crept up my throat.

Two torturous hours later, and an entire motel notepad filled with drawings of Luna from every angle, the lock clicked and the door swung open. Caleb walked in carrying a bag. "I got breakfast."

I waited for more, then held out my arms. "Well?"

He pulled a slim plastic card out of his pocket and tossed it on the table. "I got the job."

I blew out a breath, with plans of sneaking in and hacking the internal servers already spinning through my head.

"The bad news is I don't start until next week, pending the background check and me completing sixteen hours of online courses," he continued.

"Shit. Five days from now. We don't have five days. Will doesn't have five days."

"I know. Sit down and eat and we'll think of something." He pointed to the chair with no mention or sign of the awkward situation last night, all business.

I sat down and picked at the scrambled eggs. Excitement over the possibility of having Caleb on the inside warred with worry over him being inside the very company trying to kill us.

The chime of a text on Caleb's phone interrupted the silence.

He glanced at the display and typed a quick reply. "Michelle again."

"What did she want?" I asked and pushed the container away.

He wrinkled his nose before he spoke. "You want the piggish answer?"

I glared.

"She wanted to thank me for being such a gentleman. And she said they loved me at the job interview, and she'd be seeing me around work," he said.

Unexpected heat flared across my cheeks. Busying myself with throwing away my food, I kept my face away from Caleb until the emotions passed. I cleared my throat. "We need a plan for the next couple days." I paused. "I have some other ideas that might be worth looking into."

I explained the rabid geese and my theories about dumping contamination into the watershed.

"So, this contaminated water is flowing all the way to an Army base around the world?" He battled a grin. "Or are the geese migrations taking a detour to the Middle East? Vacation, maybe?"

I let my head rest on my arms. "I know. It makes no sense."

"Well, unless there's an underground river going all the way to the Middle East, I'm not sure what this could have to do with Will." He sighed and patted my hand in a brotherly fashion.

Okay, I guess we're going with denial as the way of handling last night. "I just don't know where to go from here. Without getting ahold of the files or memos the scientist mentioned in the video, we're done."

Caleb climbed to his feet, his face taut from the pain in his back. "Okay, so let's get our hands on those memos."

"Do you have a magic wand you've failed to share? They have an *internal* server. I can only hack it from *inside* the building."

He flashed a devious grin. "I didn't say anything about hacking, just good old-fashioned spy work."

CHAPTER FIFTEEN

We sat outside the unlisted address I'd liberated from the DMV records for Dr. Nelson. The neighborhood sported custom family homes set on large lots. I scrunched down in the front seat as a Lexus sedan pulled into the garage, not moving until the garage door lowered behind it.

Caleb smirked with one eyebrow raised.

"What?" I asked.

"I parked where he can't see us, you know," he said.

I straightened in the seat and refused to look his way again. "I was worried he might recognize my hair from the tour."

"He couldn't see even those flames in this light," he chuckled.

I ran my tongue over the front of my teeth but kept my reply to myself. We spent the next two hours in silence watching through the front window as the doctor, his wife, and teenage sons ate dinner and then settled in for the night. Caleb reclined his seat to the furthest setting and shifted to one side, a grimace on his lips.

When only the bedroom lights were on, Caleb popped the door open. "Let's take a stroll."

I scrambled to make my numb legs move without falling on my face and eating the curb. Caleb straightened slowly then limped to the sidewalk.

"Are you sure you can walk?" I asked.

"Walking is good for your back. It's the sitting that's killing me. We need to have a look around." He reached for my hand.

"I'm good, thanks," I said, thinking of the incident last night and put my hands in the pockets of my jeans.

He kept his arm out and faked a smile. "It looks more normal for a couple to be out strolling together, darling."

I considered his reasoning, then slipped my hand in his. "Okay, *honey bear*."

The warmth of his fingers seeped into my frozen skin. We turned together and walked up the street away from the doctor's house. The callouses on his fingers reminded me of the way my hands felt in my sharp shooting days. My fingertip brushed along the ridge of his thumb.

He squeezed my hand in response, which sent tingles up the nerves of my arm. The cool evening air did little to chill the heat flooding my body at the small touch. *I'm just cold and he's warm.* The tug of his arm guided me to one side of the sidewalk to allow a woman out walking a yellow lab to pass. She smiled and nodded.

At the corner, we turned and crossed the street like any couple out for an evening walk.

"Neighbor has a dog, poopsie pie," he said with a metric ton of sugar in his voice.

I had to bite my lip to hold back a smile. He sounded like the guy I'd known. The goofy clown. He could always get to me. "How can you tell, shnookums?"

"Well, my sweet-with-a ton-of-spice-cute-little-ginger, look at the glass on the front door."

He called me his little ginger. The screen door had a glass insert for colder months. The bottom half was smeared with streaks and prints.

This time I couldn't hold back the laugh. "My large-and-way-too-smart-for-his-own-good sweetheart, maybe they have kids," I challenged.

He chuckled, and that silly grin I'd missed so much eased the tension in his face. Before Caleb could answer, the deep *woof* of a dog echoed, and the wooden pickets of the fence shook with scratching.

"Or both," I amended and cocked my hip sideways to give him a bump. As soon as my hip connected with his upper thigh, I remembered his surgery. "Oh God, are you okay? I completely forgot you're hurt."

"I'm fine." He nudged me with his elbow. "It would take a lot more than a little knock to hurt me."

But the breezy mood was broken.

In front of the doctor's house, Caleb paused and pulled me to face him. I stumbled and clutched his arm to steady myself.

"What are you doing?" I whispered, forgetting our fun tête-à-tête, and pulling my arm away.

His eyes twinkled with the reflected glow of the streetlight. "Pretend I'm charming and you actually like me."

"I used to like you," I said, still confused. "I thought we were friends."

His arm wrapped around my waist and pulled me in closer. My heart rate skyrocketed in response to his clean, spicy scent. Warm fuzzies erupted and multiplied in my stomach like a computer virus.

"I've always been your friend, Harper," he said even as he pulled me into a much more than friend's hug.

I mentally smacked myself for my response and stiffened in his embrace. This was Caleb. My friend. Will's friend. Not some guy I get all swoony over. Not that I ever got all twitterpated over guys, but especially not Caleb. When I glanced up, his eyes were scanning the doctor's house directly behind me.

"I don't see any security cameras or sensors, but I can't be sure until I get a closer look," he said and bent his head. Warm lips brushed my cheek in a chaste peck, then he released me.

Electricity shot through my body. Tensing, I turned and rushed ahead like the sidewalk was on fire. His much longer legs caught up in two strides. I kept my head turned to the side to hide my burning face and focused on the bare branches of the tree, starting to bud, on the opposite side of the street. This was a mission. He'd do anything to get the intel he needed.

Back in the car, Caleb started the engine, took a roundabout route, and parked one block over. I took the time to collect myself and forced my muscles to relax. By the time he parked, I could face him without staring at his lips. Mostly.

The doctor's upstairs windows were visible in the space between the houses. I gripped the door handle, my nerves afire with my first foray into the art of breaking and entering.

This was entirely different from cyber breaking and entering from the comfort of my room. You couldn't come face-to-face with your victim, plus I'd never hacked individuals. I wasn't that kind of hacker.

"You stay here." Caleb opened his door.

"I'm not a kid. You don't need to protect me," I protested.

He paused and shook his head, jaw clenched. His voice held reined-in irritation. "We're a team. This is a mission. And you're my eyes. Quit looking for insults and start acting like part of the team. Each member does their part."

My mouth open to deny his words, but nothing came out. He was right.

He held up his burner phone.

My hand fell from the handle and reached into my pocket

for my burner. I swallowed then nodded. "Sorry. I'll text if any lights come on upstairs or if I see anyone coming."

With a jerk of his head, he climbed out and limped across the street. His back had to be hurting. I didn't even know how he was moving, much less doing everything else he'd done in the last week. My eyes tracked his progress until I lost sight of him on the left side of the house. He'd chosen that side to avoid the neighbor's large dog that lived on the opposite side of the doctor.

My hands shook. Visions of Caleb in handcuffs and police lights danced across my mind. I twisted to scan the neighborhood. A car drove by, then another. Each time, I forced myself to sit naturally, not hunch like the criminal I was.

Normal evening sounds blared in my overdriven senses. Crickets, wind, every dog barking sent a jolt of tension through my body. A door slammed somewhere. I craned my neck to find the source then forced in a breath and refocused on the upper level of the doctor's house. No lights. But a dim glow emanated from one window. Had that been there before?

I blinked to clear my vision and stared. A nightlight maybe? Blood throbbed through the veins in my head. I grabbed the burner and opened it then glanced back at the glowing window. A shadow moved from inside the house. The throbbing turned to pounding.

Someone awake upstairs, I typed and hit send.

I blew out the stale breath and scanned the street. At the end of the block, a police sedan with no flashing lights or sirens crossed the intersection, heading toward the doctor's house. In the two seconds it was in my view, my blood pressure spiked to an aneurism level.

Shaking hands pressed the buttons on the burner phone. *Police car. No lights.*

I slid over into the driver's seat and white-knuckled the wheel. My neck muscles tightened with each passing second.

The passenger door popped open. Tense muscles jolted and I nearly flew through the roof.

Caleb slid in and closed the door, a metal briefcase in hand. He threw an arm over the seat, completely relaxed, and gestured at the keys hanging in the ignition. "Are we going?"

I nodded, my stomach still in my mouth, turned the engine over, and pulled away from the curb. At the corner, two more black and white police sedans drove by.

"They must have a silent alarm," Caleb said, a grin creasing his cheeks that reminded me of his expressions when he pulled off an especially funny prank in high school. "That was fun."

CHAPTER SIXTEEN

Nelson family home
 Indianapolis, Indiana

Dr. Nelson closed the door behind the last police officer. He'd sent the boys and his wife back upstairs to try to get some sleep and walked down the hall and into the kitchen. The company's head of Internal Security—a made up position to cover his actual job—sat at the marble breakfast bar, a glass of orange juice in hand. Dunham's buzz cut and self-assurance easily identified him as ex-military, one of Marling's mercenaries on loan from his government connections.

"I got rid of the police, but they're parking a cruiser outside the house for the rest of the night just to be on the safe side," Nelson said and kept to the opposite side of the island. The special security team had always made him uneasy, even before he knew how far they were willing to go for money.

"I'll have a couple guys hang around. But I doubt they'll come back," Dunham said and downed the last of the juice. "You're sure there was nothing incriminating in the briefcase?"

"Nothing. I never bring home anything with labels," he said with surety in his voice, but his mind raced over the collection of papers. Thank God he'd taken the cell phones out and brought them upstairs when he went to bed.

Dunham stood, towering over the doctor by a good six inches. "Good." He took out a phone and punched a contact. "He wanted to talk to you after the police left."

"Marling?" the doctor said into the phone.

"You're sure it was the two of them?" Marling demanded.

"Positive. A neighbor remembered seeing a petite redhead on a walk with her boyfriend right before. No one else would take just the briefcase when there was a three thousand dollar watch next to it."

"You need to get this under control," Marling yelled. "I paid a lot of powerful people to sign off on this safety study. Politicians don't like getting caught with their pants down. Understand?"

"Aren't you on your way back? This is more your ballpark," Nelson hissed. "And I have more important things to take care of."

"I've had a setback with the brother. It'll be a couple more days. By the time I get to the States, the sister better be dead."

Nelson pinched the bridge of his nose and looked toward the ceiling. "I'll figure something out."

"I've had investigators looking into her past." Marling said. "She was treated for anxiety and nervous breakdowns multiple times. Get something prepared to discredit her if any information gets out." The line went dead, and he handed the phone back to Dunham who stood with his arms crossed.

"We know they're close by. What can we do to locate them?" Nelson asked.

"One of the tech guys got an idea since you helped us locate the hacker who has been snooping around. He set a trap. The moment they try to contact him again we'll have their location. I'll keep a team on standby."

Dr. Nelson flipped off the kitchen light, not bothering to show Dunham to the door. "Do what you need. This is getting too close to home."

CHAPTER SEVENTEEN

The tremors in my hands didn't stop until we got back to the hotel room and the deadbolt slid home.

"What did you find?" I asked.

He gestured to the briefcase. "I didn't have a lot of time. But he came home with this and it's locked. Worth a chance."

I leaned over and checked out the zero thru nine, six-digit locking mechanism. "That has a million possible solutions. It'll take forever to open."

"How much you want to bet I can open it in five seconds or less?" he asked.

I crossed my arms. I knew better than to get into this game. "You probably saw the code somewhere in his office or something."

"What was it you called me back on the street? Too smart for my own good?" He picked up the case and held it over his head. His biceps flexed and in one swift motion he slammed the case into the floor on one front corner. Papers spilled out onto the hotel carpet.

Caleb cocked his head to the side.

His expression made me want to hit him, but also to plaster myself against him at the same time. I chose a third option and bent to pick up the papers. "I'd call that brute strength more than smarts."

Manilla files held what looked like three different sets of documents. I opened the first, marked simply *State,* and shuffled through multiple pages of columns of numbers. No headings and no labels made it impossible to tell what the numbers represented. The second file, marked *GOV,* held similar number readouts to the first. The last, marked *Home,* was filled with more papers and longer lists of numbers but the data, whatever it was, had an extra column the others were missing.

"This doesn't look promising," Caleb said, flipping through the second file, his brows together. "Do they make any sense to you?"

I shook my head. "I can send them to Ren and see if he knows anyone who has an analytics program. Otherwise, it could take weeks to figure out what they are talking about, and we can't even be sure this has anything to do with Will."

His nose scrunched at the mention of Ren. He set the papers down and shrugged. "Whatever you think would help. I start the security job in four days, but we may not have that much time."

I typed out a quick message to Ren, asking about an analytics program. He was still on probation for hacking the dean's private emails and releasing them to the campus.

Part of me always knew he wanted more than friendship, but I could never quite picture him that way. My thoughts flashed to Caleb, our near-kiss, and the peck on the cheek. I'd certainly never experienced reactions like those with Ren.

I sat waiting after I sent the email. Five minutes later, Caleb came out of the bathroom, ready for bed. I chewed a fingernail to the quick. No response from Ren. My foot tapped the floor with a manic rhythm.

"You need to get some sleep. We'll hit it early in the morning and see what we can find," he said.

"I'll leave the sound on so if he answers I'll hear it." I pushed aside the prickly feeling in my stomach and went to brush my teeth. *He's probably taking a shower or something.* The computer chimed as I turned the corner to the bathroom. I spun and hurried to open the message, Caleb on my heels.

There is something you would like to see. Follow the link. My finger hovered over the mousepad. Ren wouldn't send anything virulent, but the syntax was off. It didn't sound like him.

"What's wrong?" he asked.

"Nothing, it's just a bad feeling."

"Should we not open it?"

"My firewalls would warn me if there's a problem with the link. Nothing's showing."

I bit my lip and clicked the button. A news story popped up on the screen, a local story from Chicago. *Local college student shot in apparent robbery gone wrong.* The title scrolled across the lower portion of the screen. The film showed an apartment building and flashing police lights illuminating the night in red and blue. Onlookers stood behind yellow police tape, watching while a covered body rolled out on a stretcher.

"Police are saying Jacob Jordan apparently surprised an intruder. The intruder shot Mr. Jordan, a senior at a local college. He died on the scene. Electronics were the only obvious thing taken. Police are asking anyone with information to contact the precinct immediately," the female voice said over the video.

I stared at the screen, my mouth open, as the story started over again on a loop. My brain refused to absorb the information. As it finally sank in, the room spun around me like a tornado with me in the eye. Buckling legs forced me into the chair with a thud. I gripped the table to stay upright.

Caleb gripped my shoulder. "Jacob Jordan. Is that…"

"They killed him," I answered in a strangled gasp. "They killed Ren."

CHAPTER EIGHTEEN

My forehead pressed into the palms of my hands while I forced air into and out of my lungs until the black spots faded from my vision. *They killed him. It's my fault.* I knew he wouldn't leave it alone, but I'd still asked for his help. Ren's face, his smile, his laugh, played through my mind on repeat. The urge to hit something, scream, pound my head into a wall, overwhelmed me.

Instead, I clutched the locket he'd given me like a lifeline over the abyss of my grief and held it to my nose to breathe in the lavender scent.

Caleb paced back and forth in the small space of the motel room. "Shit," he said for the third time.

I cried out and ripped the papers off the desk in a floating cascade. "They killed him over what? This? We don't even have any idea what's going on."

The computer chimed again. A new message appeared. I wiped moisture from my cheeks and stared at the screen but couldn't bring myself to touch the keyboard.

Caleb leaned over the desk. "Could they track us if we open it?"

"Like I said, any malware would set off my alarms. But they're going to track my IP address, now that they know my old handle. We have to get out of here."

He hit the mouse pad and opened the message. This time an image filled the screen.

A choked animalistic cry escaped my lips. Will lay curled in a ball on a dirt floor, with bloody dark red patches on his Army fatigues. His eyes were closed and his body limp.

"Is he dead?" I sobbed, my hand over my mouth.

Caleb didn't answer but scrolled to the bottom of the message.

Turn yourselves over to us or your brother will end up the same way as your friend.

"He's still alive." I closed my eyes against the image of Will, but it was burned into my brain. "What are we going to do?"

"I told Will I'd protect you. There's no way I'm letting you anywhere near these people," he said and slapped the laptop shut. "The only way he has a chance is if we figure out what's going on and expose them."

He was right. They'd kill us all. I forced my head up and fisted my icy hands. Last time, it only took them a few hours to track my location.

"We need to get out of here," I said again but couldn't make myself move.

Caleb bent to pick up the papers from the doctor's briefcase. As he stuffed them into a stack, an ink smeared portion on the bottom of the back of one sheet caught his attention.

"How do you feel about going to prison?" he said and held out the paper.

I stood, my legs as shaky as brittle sticks, and read the print. *Indiana State Penitentiary*, along with the date and fax number, was printed in gritty, smeared ink in the lower corner. Thoughts struggled to make it past the fog of grief in my brain. "It's worth a try. Maybe we can use your new ID card to convince them we're from the company."

I forced myself into action, instead of curling up in a ball like I wanted to do. We packed, checked out, and drove out of the parking lot ten minutes later. I'd pulled the battery on my computer so they couldn't track us—from now on it would be internet cafés and libraries for our tech needs. A quick google search on my burner cell showed the state penitentiary was in Michigan City—right across Lake Michigan from Chicago.

Half a block away from the motel, three large black SUVs passed us going north. I usually wouldn't have paid any attention to oncoming traffic but the three large vehicles in a row drew my attention. My eyes settled on the last vehicle in the line.

The driver was a hefty man with a crew cut. Recognition set in, along with a desert-dry mouth. "That's the mercenary from Chicago. The one from the park."

"Yeah, I saw him." Caleb kept his head straight, his focus on the road. "That was damn fast."

"They were waiting for me to contact Ren. They must have set up a trap to track my IP." I peeked back over my seat to be sure the SUVs weren't turning around to follow us. "The break-in tipped them off we're in Indiana."

He nodded.

"Did the motel ask for the license plate or anything about the car?" I asked, peering out the window for any signs of traffic cams. "I didn't see any surveillance when we checked in."

"No," he said. "And they didn't have any cameras besides the one aimed on the desk."

The SUVs turned into the parking lot of the motel we'd vacated minutes before. Their tech guys were scary good. They'd have to be to have found Ren. My heart spasmed as tight as a noose. He'd died because of me.

"I'm sorry about Jake, or Ren." Caleb broke into my thoughts. "He seemed like a stand-up guy."

I opened my mouth to answer, but no words formed. Having Ren referred to in the past tense sucked all the oxygen from my lungs. Caleb reached over and covered my hand with his. I held on for dear life. I sank into my seat and my misery. Guilt dragged me down while I clutched the plastic bottle containing my lone emergency pill.

We drove the three hours north to the state prison in silence and arrived in Michigan City in the early hours of the morning. Caleb checked us into another seedy motel that wouldn't ask too many questions.

I stood in the doorway and stared at the single king-size bed in the room.

"It was the only room that was clean and ready to go," Caleb said from behind me. "Don't worry. I'll sleep on the floor." He headed straight into the bathroom.

Dazed, I walked in and sat on the edge of the bed, too drained to even change into pajamas. I contemplated the floor. Worn and faded floral carpet covered the cement but offered little to no padding. Sleeping on that with his incisions would be torture.

I sighed and gathered the energy to at least change out of my jeans and into pajama pants. When Caleb finished in the bathroom we switched. Moving like a zombie, I washed out my lone pair of underwear and bra and hung them on the shower rod before I brushed my teeth.

When I finished, Caleb was already curled up on the floor under his jacket looking extremely uncomfortable. I gestured to the other side of the large bed. "Just sleep on that side. You can't sleep on that nasty carpet."

"I've slept in worse places."

"With your back? That's stupid." I crawled under the covers.

He considered the bed, then climbed to his feet. Planting one of the extra pillows in the center of the bed between us, he plumped it and arranged it like he was constructing the Great Wall of China. Still in his T-shirt and jeans, he lay on top of the bedspread and threw his jacket over his shoulders as a blanket.

"What exactly are you afraid is going to happen if you sleep under the covers?" I asked, my tongue loosened by grief.

He reached out to shut off the light and settled in with his arms crossed. "Nothing. You're Will's little sister."

"What's that supposed to mean?" I demanded.

"Just what I said. Now go to sleep." The bed shifted as he rolled away from me.

I stared at his back then flipped to my side and closed my eyes and listened to his already steady breaths. Exhaustion claimed me quickly and took away thoughts about the warm body in the bed.

Warmth surrounded me. My brain slowly came to awareness in a comfortable silence instead of the jolt that usually started my days. I blinked and sighed, feeling rested for once instead of exhausted from nightmares.

A warm weight shifted and readjusted around my body—a toned, firm weight that wrapped around my waist and spooned my back.

I jerked to full awareness, laying stock still. My eyes raced over the motel room trying to place where I was. The previous night flooded back. So much for the pillow barrier between us.

Behind me Caleb stirred. His hand stroked my arm and tightened.

"It's okay. I got you. I'm here," he muttered in sleep-slurred words.

I blinked. He thought I was having a nightmare. I scooched sideways and rolled onto my back. The moment I moved he bolted awake, his arm still across my torso.

"What's wrong?" he asked, his eyes wide.

"Nothing, what are you doing?" I gestured to his arm.

His face relaxed and he rested his head on his pillow, his eyelids heavy. "You were having nightmares. It was the only way I could calm you down."

"I didn't have any nightmares," I started then paused. It was the first time in years I hadn't seen the gruesome images in my dreams. Since Will joined the service, I hadn't slept more than a few hours a night. I blew out a sigh and met his tired eyes. He'd stopped the dreams before they got to the bad parts. "Oh..."

He pulled his arm from my waist. I grabbed his wrist and stopped him from rolling over. "You didn't have to. I'm sorry if I kept you awake."

"I slept good." His gaze met mine. And held.

My nerves became hyperaware of the firm chest pressing against my arm, even through the bedspread. My breath froze in my chest. My eyes darted to his lips and back to his eyes. I couldn't breathe, couldn't move, couldn't think about anything but how his mouth would taste.

I reached up and gripped the back of his neck.

He hesitated for a split second then bent his head and his lips brushed mine. That was the only spark the tinder box inside me needed. Blood seared along my veins and I pulled him closer to get more of his peppery pine smell and salty sweet taste. My lips parted and he deepened the kiss while my arms wrapped around his neck. His lips moved lower to my neck and traced a path to my collarbone, sending shivers over my skin.

Sensation flooded my brain—his sculpted muscles, hot against my skin, the stubble on his chin scratchy against my collarbone. I dove into exploring the wide expanse of his chest and back.

Something about the way he held me made me feel safe. And the way he touched me—not too hard, not too soft—turned me into modeling clay in his hands.

All the racing thoughts in my brain stopped in their tracks. Only feeling was left. Emotions pushed to the surface like seedlings sending out tender shoots of life.

"Harper," he groaned into my neck.

My explorations roamed lower, my fingers slipping to the hem of his shirt.

He jerked back. His hand shot to my wrist, pulling it away before I even registered his movement.

Hungry to feel his touch, I reached for him again. "What are you doing?"

"Wait," he said and rolled away from me. "We can't do this. I can't do this."

Cold air touched my skin where his heat had just been. My clouded thoughts struggled to restart along their neural paths. "What do you mean?"

He got up, his breathing heavy. "I'm sorry. I was taking advantage of you. Your vulnerability."

He might as well have thrown cold water on me. Fury heated the pleasurable warmth in my blood to boiling over. I leaped out of the bed. "My vulnerability?"

"You just lost a friend, and everything with Will. Plus, your issues," he waved a hand.

"You mean my anxiety?" I planted my hands on my hips. "You can say the word. It won't set off an attack."

"I don't want to make your anxiety any worse."

I crossed my arms, daring him to tell me the truth. "If you don't want to be with me, then man up and say it. Just don't treat me like I'm unstable."

"You're not unstable. It's just that when I left, you were a kid." He paused and rubbed his eyes. "And now you're..." He paused again. "Not."

I blinked. "Yeah, I'm twenty-two, that kind of happens in seven years. You've changed a bit too, but you don't see me freaking out about it."

"It's different. This just isn't right." He sighed and turned to make an escape into the bathroom, pausing at the door.

Frustration and bewilderment fought for dominance inside my head.

He glanced at the floor, not meeting my gaze. "Did you want to get your...clothes, before I take a shower?"

My God he's still freaking out over my bra. "What? Can't you say bra?"

His face hardened. "Oh, I can say fucking bra just fine."

"What's the problem then?" I demanded.

"Nothing." He crossed his arms, then mumbled, "It's your bra I'm not used to."

Frustration won the battle. I strode into the bathroom to grab my clothes.

The door shut behind him. I got dressed and dropped onto the bed, deflated. I'd known him for so long. He was Will's best friend. My friend. My brain didn't have a place to put this new attraction, or rejection.

The years of therapy forced on me weren't completely wasted. I knew on some level he was absolutely right. With Will's disappearance, and now Ren's death, the last thing I should be doing was jumping into bed with someone, especially Caleb. I closed my eyes and calmed the battle between the overly rational side of my brain and the side that was still imagining in vivid detail the things I'd rather be doing right now with Caleb.

I put a pillow over my face and groaned into the fluffiness. The bitter sting of rejection still on my tongue, I focused my brain on what was important. Will.

Glaring light peeked around the blackout curtains. It was well into the day.

When Caleb walked out of the bathroom, he was the calm, collected soldier again. He met my gaze, his face stone—all business. "Are we good?"

"Peachy," I said, my voice strong and sure. "We have bigger things to worry about."

CHAPTER NINETEEN

Caleb stuffed the ID badge from Nansic into his jeans pocket. "Let's get over to the prison and see if this badge can get us any information."

We drove the few miles to the prison in complete silence. The chain-link fence topped with razor wire slowly opened in front of our car after a sloth-like check-in process at the prison gate, something about not having filled out the visitor request paperwork ahead of time. After flashing the Nansic badge and some explaining, Caleb pulled into a parking space. I grabbed my laptop, still disconnected and more of a prop now, and put on my best professional impersonation. Hopefully, one company badge would do the trick. It was midafternoon but only a couple cars were in the parking lot. We walked through the empty rows to the visitor's entrance.

Caleb put his hand on the handle. "Ready?"

I swallowed and nodded.

The smell hit me like a blast of noxious air as we walked through the door—unwashed male bodies with a hint of not-very-enthusiastically-applied cleaning products. I swallowed my gag reflex and forced my feet forward.

Fluorescent light glared down from the ceiling, making the monochromatic palette even more noticeable. Some color would go a long way to brighten up the place. A few chairs lined the hallway to a desk shielded by thick glass—bulletproof, I presumed. A uniformed guard stood behind the bar-level counter. He didn't smile or greet us when we approached, but stared, his mouth a thin line.

"Hi there. We are just coming to check on some data." Caleb pulled out his Nansic badge plus the paperwork from the prison for good measure.

It could have been my imagination, but the guard looked even more unfriendly at the sight of the badge. "We aren't allowing any civilians in except legal counsel."

I thought of the empty parking lot. "Is there a better time we could come back?"

He shifted his glare to me. "No, visitation has been shut down indefinitely."

My intestines balled into a hard lump in my abdomen. We needed to see if this was related to Will. I didn't have any other ideas. I slouched against the counter like this was a minor irritation to my workday instead of life or death.

"We aren't here to see any particular prisoner. Is there any way we could just verify some data?" Caleb asked, trying to keep his inquiry as general as possible, and held out the fax we'd liberated from the doctor's bag.

The guard glanced at the fax sheet then picked up the phone. "Yes, sir, I have two employees from Nansic at the visitor's entrance wanting to *verify numbers*." He paused and listened. "Right away." He replaced the phone in its cradle. "It's your lucky day." He pushed a sign-in sheet through the opening in the glass.

Caleb signed the fake name matching the ID I'd made him.

The guard reached down to hit a button below the counter and the door buzzed then slid open.

I shot Caleb wide eyes while the guard wasn't looking.

He leaned in to whisper. "Stay calm."

I nodded but spotted his white-knuckled grip on the handle of his bag.

Walking through the security door sent shivers along my nerves. The bolt slid home behind us with an ominous metallic thud, and panic crept over me like poison ivy. We waited, locked in a tiny cell between the two metal doors, for the door in front of us to open. Utter panic stopped all logic and coherent thought in my brain. I gripped the prescription bottle in my pocket so tight it cracked.

Then, I remembered my name printed on the bottle. A different name than I'd just signed on the visitor log. If they made us empty our pockets and looked at the name—thoughts spun out in my brain.

When the heavy metal door swung open, I stopped myself from rushing out of the confined space. I held onto my laptop and concentrated on one step at a time, still strangling the prescription bottle, until the sensation eased to a bearable level.

Another guard met us at the end of the hall.

"Follow me," he said and led us down a hallway lined with office doors, away from a second set of double barred doors marked *Visitation*.

My anxiety lessened with every step away from the metal bars. We climbed a set of stairs to the second floor and walked down another hallway. The guard, no more pleasant than the first, knocked on a wooden door. A plaque, inscribed with *Warden Teller*, hung from the door.

"Come in," a voice commanded.

The guard opened the door and stepped aside. A memory

flashed in my mind of walking into the principal's office when I got caught hacking.

We stepped into an ordinary office. Cream paint and decent, if common, landscapes decorated the walls. Behind the desk a heavyset man with salt-and-pepper hair rose from his seat. A deep scowl creased his tired face.

"I've been calling for days, and they send two techs to see about the problem? I asked for Nelson to come himself," he grumbled, not offering a hand or introduction.

"I'm sorry, sir, but Dr. Nelson is tied up with other projects," I said without thinking, my voice steady.

"Other projects? We have a crisis here and he sends two kids, barely out of school?" He paused and eyed me. "Are you even out of school?"

"I'm an intern, sir." I straightened as tall as my five-foot-one frame allowed.

He rolled his eyes and sat back down in his leather chair.

Caleb and I followed suit, sitting down, and waiting for him to volunteer more information.

"So, what exactly is the plan?" he asked with a sigh.

"The doctor sent us to gather more firsthand information from you, sir, so we can formulate a plan," Caleb said.

"I sent him everything he asked for," he exclaimed and threw his hands in the air. "You want firsthand information? How about I throw you out in gen-pop for a few minutes and you can see for yourself." His face reddened. "Get the hell out of my office." He reached for the phone on his desk. "I'll call and give the good doctor a piece of my mind right now."

I leaned forward. "Sir, please. I understand it would have been better for Dr. Nelson to come himself but unfortunately that wasn't possible. If you could go over the problems, we will convey the urgency and get you answers."

He eyed me for several beats, the phone suspended halfway to his head, while my organs constricted into a black hole.

"Fine," he said finally and replaced the receiver. "But something better happen fast."

Caleb scanned the sheet of random numbers. "When did you first notice the problems starting?"

"Last month. Like I told the doctor. At first, I didn't think too much of it, being a high-security prison and all, we get fights. But things have gotten worse, much worse."

"In what way?" I asked and took out a pen and paper to jot down notes.

"I've got half my population in the infirmary and my isolation tanks are full so inmates can cool off. Problem is they aren't cooling off. Now, forty of my guards have been attacked. The prison is on complete lockdown. Does that sound serious enough for you?"

"And you think these outbursts by the inmates are because of our project here?" Caleb asked.

The warden leaned halfway across the desk and jutted his finger at Caleb's face. "Don't you try to tell me it's not your fault. I've worked in the detention system for over thirty years. Your DX-200 is doing this."

My memory sparked at the mention of DX, sending blazing bolts through my nervous system. Dr. Nelson talked about it before he was cut off in the video from Will. I shot a glance sideways at Caleb.

"We aren't questioning your judgement, sir," I said, my palms up. "We're only here to gather facts."

"Like hell you are." His face went from red to purple. He opened his mouth again, but the intercom beeped on his phone. He punched the button. "What?"

"Sir, we have another altercation in Block C," the voice said.

"Dammit," the warden exclaimed and hefted himself out of

the chair. He reached in a desk drawer and pulled out a flash drive. "You give this to the doctor and tell him if he doesn't get his ass down here with some answers, I'll release it to the media. No amount of money is worth this."

He tossed the flash drive at Caleb and stalked to the door, not waiting for us to follow. I scrambled out of my chair. The guard who had escorted us waited outside.

"Get these two out of here," the warden snarled as he passed and rushed down the hallway.

"Yes, sir," the guard said and motioned for us to follow him.

We took the same path to the visitor's entrance and waited at the security door until it buzzed and unlocked. The door swung open, and I restrained myself from running down the hallway and out the exterior door. Instead, we walked out and didn't speak until we were in the car with the doors closed.

"We make a great team." Caleb flashed a grin. "You did really good in there."

"I thought I was going to pass out," I confessed.

"You did good, Harper. Looks like we're definitely on the right track," Caleb said and started the car. "You want to play it now?" He motioned to my computer.

"I'm not going to underestimate their computer techs again. Better to be safe and use a public computer."

"You're the geek, what you say goes."

The small internet café boasted secluded corners, homemade pastries, and—with a generous tip and a well-placed, blue-eyed wink from Caleb—a borrowed laptop from the barista. I'd chosen a corner table to give us some privacy. The shop was busy for a weekday afternoon, with only a few tables free.

Caleb set down an oversized mug of coffee and a plate with

two golden pastries next to the computer. The flash drive was open and ready to view. He pulled a chair next to me. I glanced around the shop for the tenth time.

My stomach growled at the scent of the filled croissant and mocha. I'd never actually liked the taste of coffee, but with my sleep habits I couldn't get through the day without a liberal dose of caffeine. The chocolate at least made it palatable.

"Let's do this," Caleb said and took a big bite of his croissant.

I hit play. The camera trained from an angle high on a wall over the cafeteria of the prison. Inmates sat in groups at tables with benches bolted to the floor, trays in front of them, talking and eating. The buzz of the conversation on the video was unintelligible. I turned the computer volume up to the highest setting.

One inmate at a table off to the left stopped eating, gripped his spoon, and stood over his benchmate. With no warning or apparent provocation, the man stabbed the plastic utensil into the other inmates back then ripped it out and repeated.

I gasped, unable to comprehend a sliver of plastic causing so much damage to human flesh.

The entire cafeteria erupted.

Expletives exploded from the computer speakers. "Motherfucker" blared over the quiet hum of the café. I jumped in my seat, bumping the coffee cup in my rush to stop the continued rush of obscenities.

Heads turned in our direction.

"Sorry." Caleb waved and flashed a sheepish grin.

One woman at the table across from us waved. "No worries." Then shot her own smile Caleb's way while she thrust her shoulders back and did her best to put her assets in a good light.

I mopped up the mocha I'd spilled and made a point to meet

her gaze. She held mine and flipped her perfectly straight, highlighted blonde hair over her shoulder. No apologies there. My teeth ground together.

"Ready to try again?" Caleb asked, oblivious to the stare down or the woman.

I shifted my attention to the screen and hit play one more time. The instigating inmate stood over his bloody victim, beating him until the man stopped moving. The crowd around the two formed a circle. Fights broke out amongst the spectators.

"Doesn't look too significant," Caleb said. "A prison fight."

The inmate, covered in the blood of his victim, reached down and grabbed the bench they'd been sitting on, grunting and straining. The bench shifted as the anchors gave way.

Caleb shook his head. "No way, man. It's bolted into concrete."

The inmate lifted the bench over his head, veins bulging in his neck, and swung the bench at the onlookers who, locked in their own battles, didn't see the metal bench coming. The blow crushed one man's skull, sending blood, bone, and brain across a section of floor.

No longer hungry, I set the croissant on the plate. I forced myself to watch, to see what this video could show us about the mess Will was involved in.

"Look at his face," I said pointing to the instigator. "He looks crazed, out of his mind."

"He may look like that all the time."

I nodded. The fight escalated, the first man bashing in skulls until his opponents, some begging for their lives, were nothing but bloody puddles.

"Where are the guards?" I asked.

Caleb pointed to the upper edge of the screen where a line of riot shields unsuccessfully pushed into the crowd. "They don't seem to be making much progress."

I focused on the main fight, one gruesome beating after another, but not on the actions themselves. Instead, I took in the scene as a whole. The wide eyes, bulging veins, straining muscles—all of them similar to the utter rage of the instigator.

"Oh, damn," Caleb said and reached out to hit the stop button.

"What?"

"That guy just bit off part of the other one's face." He shook his head. "Trust me, you don't want to see it."

I stared at the frozen image on the screen. "Rabid beasts."

"What?"

"From the description in the articles about the soldiers. They were described as rabid beasts," I said.

Caleb contemplated the image. "You're right. Whatever this DX-200 is, it's causing rage or psychotic breaks. And they were testing it on the inmates." He leaned back and put a hand to his chin. "Overproduction of testosterone, maybe? That and adrenaline could explain the increased strength and rage but..." He leaned in to examine the frozen battle. "With increased catecholamines, hmm."

I stared at this science-spouting Caleb like he was an alien.

"Why wouldn't the prefrontal cortex be controlling the outburst though?"

My wide eyes met his. "Don't ask me. You lost me at catechola-whatevers. Have you learned all this in your classes?"

He dropped his hand from his chin and shrugged. "Just finished endocrinology."

I'd always known Caleb was smart, much as he'd tried to hide it in high school and play the goofball. "Okay, Doc, so what are you thinking?"

His gaze dropped to the floor. "Ah, I have to finish my time before I can apply to med school." His gaze moved back to the screen. "One thing's for sure. This is no normal prison riot. It has to be related to the DX-200."

"Would they use soldiers for testing as well?" I asked, incredulous the military would be okay with their soldiers being used as lab rats.

"Wouldn't be the first time. Guys from 'Nam are still dying from Agent Orange in their tissues fifty years after the war. And that was supposedly safe."

I shook my head, anger pouring through me like red-hot lava. "That's messed up. People risk their lives to protect this country and the government tests something on them without their permission?"

"They don't need permission. Your life belongs to the government until your commitment is up." Caleb shrugged. "Plus, with all the needles they jab us with it would be easy to slip something in." He considered the last bite of his croissant. "Or they could have put it in the food. The higher ranks never ate with us."

I chewed on my lip to keep my fear and anger from pouring out, then looked up from the computer. The flirty blonde was still watching our table. But this time her expression was anything but inviting.

She glanced down at her computer, then leaned over to her friend and pointed to the screen, whispering behind her hand. Her eyes darted to Caleb. Tingles crept up my back like hundreds of scattering spiders.

I snatched the flash drive, not bothering to hit eject, and grabbed Caleb's hand. "We should go now."

He scanned the room and took in the blonde and her friend, who were now both staring, wide eyed and whispering. The friend held her cell phone to her ear.

"What now?" he grumbled.

We hurried out to the car. While Caleb put some distance

between us and the café, I searched the internet on my burner for a clue as to what spooked the women.

"Holy shit," I said.

"What is it?" he asked.

"News story has you as a wanted man. Special Forces deserter wanted for suspected murder. They're saying you're armed and extremely dangerous and to report any sightings to the police."

"Deserter?" His grip on the steering wheel tightened and our speed increased. "They're calling me a deserter?"

"And murderer," I pointed out. "You might not want to get pulled over for speeding."

"I served with honor for the last seven years," he fumed but slowed to the speed limit. "I've been protecting this country from our enemies, risking my life, getting blown up." His jaw worked like he was chewing something bitter. "My dad is going to see this story."

"He'll know it's bullshit," I said. "Are you okay?"

"I'm just wondering who exactly the enemy is." He paused. "And if I've been fighting the wrong war all these years."

I laid a hand on his arm. "We knew when they ambushed us in the park there was a connection up the chain of command. The question is how high it goes."

"If those chicks at the café called the police, Nansic is going to know for sure we've been to the prison."

"Where should we go?"

"All that matters right now is putting some distance between us and here. We can figure out the details later," he said.

"Wouldn't they expect us to run away? Maybe if we go south, toward Indianapolis, we can stay off their radar."

"Moving around is going to be a lot harder now."

"That's the entire point." I stared out the window. "To box us in."

CHAPTER TWENTY

Dr. Nelson's research lab
 Nansic Headquarters
 Indianapolis, Indiana

A stack of messages waited on his desk when Dr. Nelson came back from his dinner break. The top four were from the warden at the state prison and the last was just a number. With gritted teeth, Nelson picked up the phone and dialed the direct line to the warden's office.

The warden answered on the second ring.

"Warden Teller, this is Dr. Nelson returning your messages."

"Where the hell do you get off sending two green kids down here to gather information?" the warden shouted.

Nelson sat up straighter in his chair. "What kids?"

He listened to the description of the petite redhead and muscular man with her, his heart sinking with each word. "What did you tell them? I need to know everything you said."

"I couldn't tell them much, seeing as I had another riot on

my hands. Get your ass up here and fix whatever it is you did to these men."

"I'm working on an injection that should decrease the aggression."

"Work faster," the warden shouted. "I gave them the video for you."

"What video?" Nelson demanded.

"The fight in the cafeteria. I swear I'll release it to the press if you don't figure out what's going on and do something," the warden ranted.

Burning acid crept up Dr. Nelson's chest. "Send me that video, immediately."

Nelson hung up the phone over Teller's continued shouts. He blindly reached in his drawer for the almost empty bottle of antacids and popped four into his mouth.

Wishing for a few fingers of scotch, he grabbed one of the two burner cells from the drawer—the one that never rang—to make the call he dreaded. This could be his death sentence. As he hit the keys for the one number on the phone, he heard a sound behind him.

"I've got those slides prepared for you, Doctor," his lab assistant, Jim, said from the doorway.

Relieved for an excuse to put off the call, Nelson dropped the phone back in the drawer and turned his gaze from the wall to the cleaned cages on the lab bench. No more blood and fighting, only vegetative rats wandering aimlessly around the cages.

CHAPTER TWENTY-ONE

We didn't stop for the night to sleep, but took turns driving south, abiding by all the traffic laws. We passed Indianapolis, and Nansic headquarters, and kept south toward Kentucky. In the early morning hours, Caleb snored in the front seat. He'd fallen asleep within seconds. How he could crash with the entire country looking for him was beyond me.

I'd found news articles from every major city in the midwest about Caleb and the numerous crimes he was supposedly involved in. They showed his military picture from when he enlisted—younger, in uniform, and his hair close-cropped. His longish hair and scruffy appearance, typical in Delta, hid his features a bit. At least we had that going for us.

Two hours into my driving shift and Caleb's nap, we approached the outskirts of Louisville, still on the Indiana side of the border. The tank was down to less than a quarter. I pulled off the highway and into a gas station. Stopped at the pump, I contemplated the still-sleeping Caleb.

His arms were crossed over his chest with his hands tucked into his elbows. He looked younger, vulnerable. Sleep softened his chiseled features down to smooth marble. A shadow of the boy I'd known was there, under all the bravado and muscle.

It was like my whole world was shifting, like gravity was reversed. Plus, the tingling heat he sent to my core with a simple look didn't help matters. This attraction to Caleb messed with my head.

He grumbled in his sleep. The thought of him waking up with me creeping out over him pulled me back.

"Caleb." I reached out a hand and squeezed his shoulder.

He sprang awake like a Jack-in-the-box on steroids. "What? Where are we?"

I flinched. "We're outside Louisville. I didn't know if you wanted to grab some snacks and drinks."

His wide eyes settled back to normal. "Sure. Any requests?"

"Caffeine."

I rubbed my arms against the spring chill and leaned against the side of the car. In the blackness of early morning, the illuminated inside of the gas station was easily visible through the windows. I watched Caleb, his head down, walk around the aisles grabbing snacks and drinks as well as a baseball cap.

Tires crunched into the deserted gas station. A police cruiser pulled to a stop in the bay between me and the door to the convenience store.

I strained to stay in my relaxed pose against the car while two officers climbed out of the vehicle. One opened the gas cap and started fueling while the other stretched and looked around.

The pump handle clicked. I bolted at the sound and grabbed the gas pump with shaking hands. Caleb finished paying at the counter and headed to the door. The second cop observed him with interest, a frown on his face.

If he placed Caleb... I wanted to scream, shout for Caleb to notice the danger in his path. Instead, I scooted around the pumps and the back of the police car to the second policeman. "Excuse me," I said in my most innocent voice.

The officer turned his attention from Caleb to me, the frown scrunching his face like a bulldog. Behind him, Caleb walked out the door and froze, eyes wide.

"Yes?" the officer asked.

"I just wanted to check I'm headed the right way," I said and smiled, spouting the first thought that came to mind. "I'm trying to get to Wabash?" The town from the article about rabid geese was the first to pop in my head and out my mouth. "I'm supposed to meet my professor there to study some geese. My cell phone died and I'm afraid I got turned around in Louisville. Am I on the right highway?"

Caleb, recovered, slapped the cap on his head and strolled around the front of the police car to our driver's side. I heard the door open and close.

The officer nodded. "Yeah, you just keep heading north on 65 until you hit Indianapolis then get on 69."

"Highway 65 to Highway 69. Okay, thanks a bunch," I said and waved to the first officer.

I walked at a normal pace to the passenger door and slid inside.

"Shit, that was close," Caleb said and turned over the engine.

"You have no idea. He was eyeballing you."

He tugged the cap lower on his head and drove to the exit of the gas station. "You're a natural, you know. You didn't miss a beat."

"I'll sign right up for counterintelligence," I joked.

Ready to continue south, Caleb drove toward the highway. The police car pulled out of the station behind us.

"Get on the northbound ramp," I said.

He paused. "Why?"

"I told him we were going to Wabash."

Caleb turned onto the northbound ramp—back the way we'd come. I kept my eye on the patrol car in our rearview mirror while Caleb obeyed every traffic law. I was grateful the cops couldn't see my guitar-string muscles.

"Try to relax," Caleb said. "We're just driving to Wabash."

I rolled my shoulders but didn't take a full breath until the patrol car finally took an exit ten miles down the highway. Caleb's grip on the wheel loosened, too.

An idea niggled in the back of my mind. "What if we actually did go to Wabash?"

"What's in Wabash?"

"Rabid geese. Both the instances overseas and the ones at the prison have to do with extremely violent behavior. The same with these geese. What if it's connected?"

"I doubt they'd be looking for us in a small town so it wouldn't hurt to lay low there. But I was thinking they were putting something in a vaccine or drug and dosing the inmates and soldiers with it. How would geese get DX-200 in their system?" he asked.

"I know, I was thinking the same thing. But if the geese are involved, obviously it's not a vaccine or drug. I doubt they're stuffing pills down geese's throats, so ruling those out would give us more information."

He adjusted in the seat to take pressure off his back. "We've got about two hours to figure it out before we get there."

Fields of dirt flew by outside the window. We were still on the highway. The sun loomed high over the horizon. Heavy machinery moved along rows, planting the earliest summer crops. Desperate to keep my mind occupied and less likely to spin out, I googled inane queries on my burner phone like *crops planted in March in Indiana*. Likely, seed potatoes were going into the ground, my search revealed. I watched the farms pass by. Thoughts of Ren, Will, and DX-200 ricocheted around my head like rubber balls shot out of a cannon.

Ren was always trying to get me to eat more fresh vegetables. Emotions bubbled to the surface. I breathed and focused on the tractors, the tiny green plants. The vibrant color of the leaves promised all the vitamins and health benefits of superfoods.

The fields outside Nansic headquarters flashed in my mind, a new bouncy ball to add to the chaos of my brain. But this one grew bigger as I watched sprayers move over the fields of plants beside the highway.

"Holy shit." I jerked forward in my seat.

Caleb's warm, strong hand gripped mine. "What is it?"

"What about the test fields?"

"The ones at Nansic?"

"What if they're spraying a chemical on the test fields?"

He nodded as understanding dawned. "And the geese flew through the chemicals. It would fit. The geese would be flying north. Indianapolis then Wabash could be on their migration route for spring."

"The tour guide said they were testing new pesticides to control the superbugs." I leaned forward. "What if DX-200 is a pesticide?"

"That would explain how the geese got exposed. Then they sprayed it on food that they fed to the prisoners and the troops at the base. It's all conjecture unless we can prove it's the chemical they're testing," he said.

"Make a detour. We need a sample from those test fields."

I reclined the seat as far back as it would go and adjusted for the hundredth time. Nine hours of sitting in a car pulled off of the road after a day of driving circles around Indiana—with all our stops—was getting to me. With Caleb's face on the news, staying in public places was a no-go. I'd made a run into a convenience store to grab food and drinks, then we parked in the trees a mile outside Nansic Headquarters to wait for dark.

Caleb lay in the seat, pretending to sleep. His taut muscles gave him away. My attempts at casual conversation were met with grunts and one-word answers until he claimed fatigue and closed his eyes.

My gaze fell to his lips. The memory of their moist heat on my skin ran tingles over my body. The thought of his hands and the sensation of his touch pooled molten lava low in my belly. I wanted to reach out and feel his biceps again, so different from anyone I'd dated.

I licked my lips. The unspoken questions had hung between us like fog since the incident in the motel. I couldn't stand it anymore. "I know you aren't sleeping."

"Okay," he said and kept his eyes closed. "Maybe I'm trying."

"We need to talk." I shifted in my seat to face him.

He cracked an eye. "About?"

I bit back the sarcastic reply that jumped to my tongue out of habit. "Don't play dumb. We need to clear the air."

"Why do girls always want to talk?" he muttered but inched his seat up and waited.

"There seems to be some chemistry between us." I paused. Shit. How do you say you're attracted to someone without sounding completely desperate? "I'm"

"Listen, I was thinking with the wrong head." He motioned to his pants.

I blinked and stared, waiting for him to continue. Several

beats passed. Nothing. Men. "Okay, so where does that leave us?"

"You've changed." His gaze darted to my chest then back to my face. He cleared his throat. "You were a kid when I left. You're not now."

I swallowed and waited.

He shook his head. "Nothing can happen. You're Will's little sister."

The disappointment and pain his words caused surprised me. "What is that? Some kind of bullshit guy code?"

"I guess you could call it that." He held my gaze. "But also, you need a guy who you don't have to worry about, someone whose job doesn't give you nightmares."

Anger fused with attraction in a fire meets explosives scenario. My fists tightened. "Don't tell me what I need." I pointed a finger in his face. "You regret kissing me? Aren't interested? Just say so. Quit hiding behind excuses."

"Harper—" he started.

"You know," I interrupted him. "You've changed too. And I don't just mean that you can lift more now. You used to be honest with me. You treated me like a person. Not just Will's little sister." I glared across the short distance. "We laughed together. We had something special, and you threw it away when you left." I jerked the door handle open and climbed out of the car, then leaned against the cool metal. I wasn't sure what bothered me more—the rejection or the fact Caleb might be onto something.

I'd always dated shy, subdued guysthe exact opposite of military adrenaline junkies I'd grown up surrounded by. *Damn it*. I hated it when he was right. It was likely a self-defense mechanism to avoid guys who would put themselves in danger. I chewed on a fingernail. There was also a reason none of those relationships lasted longer than a few months.

Dusk settled and the sun sank behind the trees, about to disappear over the horizon. The chill of the evening air cooled my overheated skin. The driver's side door opened and closed behind me. Boots crunched in the dead grass and twigs on the ground.

Caleb rounded the front of the car. "Harper. You've always been special to me. That's why I can't... Why we can't..."

"I think it's dark enough." Not able to bear any more excuses, I stopped him. I wiped my hands over my face, then turned. "Ready to go steal some vegetables?"

A frown creased his forehead. He opened his mouth, closed it, then nodded.

CHAPTER TWENTY-TWO

The fields surrounding Nansic spread around the south side of the main research building unprotected by any fence or barrier. We trekked through the trees to the test fields from the hidden car.

"I can't believe they can just spray chemicals into the environment without knowing they're safe," I ranted to myself and stepped over a branch. Another caught my face and I swatted it away. Though I loved to paint nature, I didn't enjoy stumbling around in it, especially not in the dark.

"I'm sure there're regulations," Caleb spoke for the first time since the car. His voice was quiet. "And ways to get around them if you know the right people."

"The government is supposed to protect us. Not let companies poison us."

Night settled in. Caleb took the lead, pushing through the underbrush. With a sliver of a moon overhead, darkness enveloped us like a blanket. My foot caught on something. I tripped and hurtled forward. A squeak escaped my lips and my arms shot out to break my impact with the ground.

Instead of the cold ground I hit warm muscle, just as solid

but gentle. Caleb's arms wrapped around me. My face pressed into the lower portion of his chest, giving me a deep breath of his spicy scent. My hands grasped for purchase on his hips, while I regained my balance.

"Sorry, can't take me anywhere," I grumbled and let go.

His arms stayed wrapped around me. "Are you okay?"

I wanted to sink into him and pound my fists into his chest at the same time. *Okay? No, I'm not okay!* Emotion hit me like a tsunami. I hadn't realized how much I'd missed Caleb until I had him back. Now with a whole new spin on our relationship, my brain couldn't catch up with the way my body reacted to him. Throw in his rejection, and he might as well have put my heart in a blender. The only thing holding me together was the few scraps of pride still left to my name.

I firmly pushed on his chest. He didn't get to comfort me. "I'm fine."

He let me go. I paused, waiting for him to say something else but he just nodded and turned away.

We stumbled the rest of the way through the dark to the fields, not daring to use flashlights. Caleb held up a hand and crouched at the edge of the trees, scanning the area. I squatted next to him, nerves on high alert. It didn't seem smart to be so close to people who wanted us dead.

"I don't see any guards," he whispered. "There could be cameras, though."

"I doubt they have a problem with people stealing kale."

"You get a variety of plant samples and I'll get the water." His voice was calm, all mission-mode.

I nodded and he set off to the collection pond I'd seen on the tour. I scrambled forward toward the edge of the vegetable field. Halfway in, my legs shook like brittle twigs holding up my body. My head darted back and forth, certain armed men would come storming out. I fell to the dirt at the end of a row of kale and snapped off a leaf. The plastic bag slipped from my hand and blew a few feet in the breeze.

Scrambling after it, I must have looked like a deranged monkey. I gripped the bag and stuffed the leaf inside along with several more from other varieties of taller plants nearby.

The blaring cacophony of sirens practically sent me out of my skin. Lights flashed and somewhere far off a door slammed. The beat of guards' footsteps pounded toward the fields. Fueled by fear, I darted back to the tree line faster than a gazelle chased by a cheetah. Once in the darkness of the brush, I crouched and scanned the area. Voices grew closer. Men dressed in uniforms checked the fields.

My head swiveled, looking for Caleb, while I made myself as small as possible in the bushes. A few feet from where I hid, a guard paused and listened—so close I saw the five o'clock shadow on his face and smelled his cologne.

"Another deer?" he called to his companion.

The second guard shrugged. "Could be, but we need to be sure. I'll check the monitor in the holding pond."

My hacker senses went on alert at the mention of the monitor, wondering if it was wi-fi enabled. I filed it away for future consideration. *More pressing issues at the moment.* The guard by me moved a breathable distance away, doing a grid-search on the field where I'd stolen the plants.

My hands tingled and my sharpened senses buzzed. Around the field several more guards in blue cargo pants and polos appeared, weapons at the ready. Nansic took their vegetables seriously. I crouched, ready to run. A hand gripped my shoulder. I spun, one leg cocked, ready to use every dirty move I knew.

"Easy, it's me," Caleb hissed from the darkness.

I let my hands fall to my sides.

He motioned to stay low and follow him. We made our way

back into the trees quickly and silently, away from the guards and guns.

Once we were a safe distance I spoke. "Did you get the water?"

"Yeah, I saw the surveillance cameras but one of us must have tripped a motion sensor."

"A bit too close for comfort."

CHAPTER TWENTY-THREE

Dr. Nelson's research lab
Nansic Headquarters
Indianapolis, Indiana

Dr. Nelson clipped the slide onto the stage of the microscope and adjusted the focus. His breath caught in his lungs, praying the slide would show promising results. The pink tissue came into focus with freckles of blue throughout the nuclei of the nerve cells.

He swallowed and changed to the next slide. Same result. More blue freckles. With an increasingly acidic stomach, he filed through the remaining slides. All the same. The brain tissue in each rat showed cell death.

"You okay Dr. Nelson?" Jim asked from the other lab bench where he'd finished cleaning up the cages and disposing of the carcasses of the test rats.

The doctor straightened from his slumped position. "I'm fine, Jim. Why don't you head home? We'll need to start over again tomorrow with the next set."

"Are you sure? I can stay and help."

"No. Go home," Nelson said. "See you in the morning."

"Goodnight, Doctor," Jim said and closed the door behind him.

Alone and unobserved, he dialed Marling's number. It took several seconds for the call to connect. Marling picked up on the third ring.

"Have you stopped the absorption yet?" Marling asked without greeting.

Nelson sighed, his eyes still on the blue freckled slides. "It's not that simple. I made progress with the affected adrenals so the more immediate endocrine problem is solved, but I can't stop absorption."

"Great! So, that's fixed the immediate anger issues," Marling said.

"Yes."

"Good job, Doctor. We can move ahead with production."

"No, we can't move forward. I'm telling you I can't fix the long-term problems," Nelson insisted. "If we continue—"

"I read your memo." Marling cut him off. "I also read the side effects won't show up for twenty to thirty years. It'll be impossible to link them to our product."

"You can't move into production yet. I won't let you do it." Nelson stammered.

"As if you have a say," Marling laughed.

"This isn't part of the plan," Nelson whispered. "You'll ruin everything."

"Ruin everything? What are you taking about? We aren't turning away from billions of dollars in profit because of a few hiccups. Do you have any idea what a pesticide that kills all the resistant insects is worth? We'll completely control the market. Not just in the States but the entire world."

Nelson pinched the bridge of his nose and spoke under his

breath. "Small minded idiots getting in the way of the bigger picture."

"What?" Marling asked.

"Nothing," Nelson said, recovering his composure. "The girl. We have no way of locating her."

"I'm on my way back to the States now. I have some ideas on how to lure her out."

CHAPTER TWENTY-FOUR

With our two samples in bags, we drove the few hours north. We pulled into town a little before eleven p.m. The sign on the side of the road read *Wabash, Indiana, population 10,666.* We drove down an old-fashioned looking main street with brick buildings and a retro movie theater. A stop at the one roadside motel in town proved futile as it was full of curious visitors wanting to see rabid geese.

The possibility of a night sleeping in the car, with Caleb, was enough for me to suggest the historic bed-and-breakfast we drove past. It would use up more of our dwindling cash than I'd like, but I needed some space. And a shower. At this point, we'd both pass for grungy homeless people more than college students.

Caleb's few days' worth of scruff and longer hair would hopefully be enough of a difference from the clean-cut military ID photo so he wouldn't be identified. He pulled into a space outside the Victorian-style-mansion-turned-B&B.

"You sure?" he asked.

"No," I said but opened the door. This was a risk, but we needed to clean up somewhere before we went to meet with the scientists. Caleb climbed out after me and pulled his baseball cap down over his head.

The sign on the door said the last check-in was eleven o'clock, which was in three minutes. Caleb pushed the small brass antique ringer and stepped back. It took a few minutes before the door opened and a gentleman with white hair, who was only a few inches taller than me, stood before us.

"Do you have a reservation?" he asked with a quizzical smile.

"I'm so sorry to bother you. We don't have a reservation, but we've been driving for two days and the motel on the highway is booked up. We were hoping you might have a room open?" I said.

He contemplated Caleb and me for a moment. "Let me guess, college students here about the geese?"

"Is it that obvious?" I grinned. "Yes, we're hoping to join in on the research. Have you seen them?"

"It's the darnedest thing. Geese can be mighty mean birds, but I've never seen them act that way," he answered then opened the door wider. "Let's get you out of the dark and into a room."

"Thank you," Caleb said and carried the bags over the threshold. The caretaker locked the door behind us, and I followed him to a desk. Beside it sat a table with a large glass beverage dispenser. I marveled that the water had plenty of ice, fresh looking strawberries, and mint leaves, even at night.

"Just sign in here." He pushed a large leather-bound book and pen across the desk.

I signed my name and Caleb's fake name. Caleb pulled out his wallet and handed his forged ID across. The caretaker barely glanced at it and handed it back.

"The room is one-sixty a night, breakfast is included, and

you'll want to come down a bit early before all my wife's famous coffee cake muffins are gone," he said with a grin.

Caleb handed the cash over. "Do you need a credit card?"

"Good ol' American dollars always work here. Besides, I hate paying those fees." He waved for us to follow him up the curved staircase.

I breathed a sigh of relief and ran my hand over the ornately carved wood of the banister while I took in the floral wallpaper and crystal chandelier. We climbed two flights of stairs.

"The third floor is the bridal suite. Our best room," he said, then unlocked the door and waved us in.

My mouth hung open at the words *bridal suite* and I snapped it shut. Just what I didn't need. I forced myself not to look at Caleb's face.

I walked into an enormous suite filled with ornate wood furniture. It took up the entire third floor of the house and the varying pitch of the walls told me this was once an attic. Off to one side stood a wide doorway leading to a spa-like bathroom and in the center of the room sat an enormous, canopied king size bed. The only other place to sleep was a chaise lounge. I had no intention of repeating what happened the last time Caleb and I slept in a bed together. The lounge it would be.

"If you need anything, ring the desk, but there are some nice soaps and shampoos in the bathroom made by hand right here in Wabash," he said and backed out the door.

"Thank you so much." I grimaced and touched my hair which could have passed for dreadlocks at this point.

Caleb turned the bolt then walked over to set the bags on the lounge and faced me.

His gaze tightened my chest. I grabbed my travel bag out of the backpack and headed for the bathroom.

A claw-foot tub sat in one corner and a large shower in another. Fifteen minutes later, I emerged, pink from scrubbing, and smelling faintly of roses. Caleb sat on the lounge, his shirt off, towel in hand.

"I'll sleep on the couch," he said and headed to the bathroom.

"I can sleep on it. It'll hurt your back."

"I'll be fine. You take the bed." His tone didn't leave any room for arguing.

The nightmares woke me every few hours. By dawn, I was more than ready to get out of the down-stuffed fluffiness of the bed. I glanced around the room. Every time I looked at Caleb, flashes of kissing him flooded my brain. No matter how deep I buried the memory, and the oh-so-heated feelings it brought up, it resurfaced like a weed. I dressed in the bathroom then headed straight out of the bridal suite.

"Where are you going?" Caleb asked from the lounge. His feet and legs hung off the end from mid-calf down.

"To get some breakfast," I said and closed the door behind me. Just looking at him set off a storm of confusion and upset. I needed to get my head on straight.

The smell of fresh, cinnamony heaven led me to the dining room. A thin woman with an apron was setting out covered trays on a sideboard.

"You're just in time. I set out a fresh batch of muffins and coffee. Egg casserole will be out in a few minutes."

"Thank you, they smell delicious."

She went through the swinging door to the kitchen, and I grabbed a plate, oversized muffin, and coffee.

I stood at the window with my plate and contemplated the curved path and arches outside. It reminded me of my mom's garden. Will and I had chased each other around playing make believe games when we were kids, often with Caleb in tow. Almost always, Will played the hero and I the damsel in distress with Caleb the villain, of course. The memory tightened my stomach into a hard ball around the muffin I'd just enjoyed.

A thought I'd been ignoring forced itself to the surface. Even if we proved Nansic was poisoning people with a pesticide, it wouldn't get Will back. I had no idea *how* we could get Will back.

I pushed away the weakness washing over me and focused on what was in front of me. *Geese. First, I have to figure out if the geese are part of this.*

Half an hour later, Caleb came downstairs with some other guests, chatting about the weather.

"I need to go get ready," I excused myself without looking his way.

He came back upstairs as I finished putting my hair in a ponytail.

"Are you going to be running away from me all day?" he asked.

"I don't know what you're talking about," I said, still looking in the mirror.

"I knew talking wouldn't help anything," he said under his breath.

I grabbed my jacket off the sink and spun to face him. I *wanted* to hate him. It would be so much easier than this. Whatever *this* was. I'd gotten better at compartmentalizing over the years. Time to shove these feelings about Caleb in a box and bury them deep. "You're right. For once. So, let's stop talking and go see if we can save my brother."

He eyed me then stepped out of my path. "Lead the way."

We got directions from the innkeeper's wife and set out across town to a small pond. The researchers from the college set up tents away from the water and the geese. Ropes ran between trees with signs attached, warning against the dangerous animals. Spectators, researchers, and a few camera crews covered the once empty fields.

With the pond on one side, we had no choice but to weave our way through the news crews. I gripped the pill bottle in my pocket and listened for the plastic *tap* of the lone pill.

Caleb donned his ball cap. Only his blazing blue eyes were recognizable from the military picture.

A deputy, hardly older than me by the looks of his baby face, held up a hand when we approached the roped off area. "Sorry, this area is closed to the public."

"We're with the university, sir," Caleb said.

I flashed him my university ID.

The deputy's chest puffed up at Caleb's use of sir. "Professor March is over there in that tent." He pointed to the last tent in the row of four. "You'll need to check in with her."

We nodded and ducked under the rope. The professor's tent hummed with activity. Students and research assistants scurried in and out like bees around a hive. In the center sat the queen. Only this queen wore faded jeans and knee-high galoshes.

"Professor March?" I asked and approached her chair.

She glanced up from the computer, took in the two of us, and puckered her lips like she'd eaten something sour. "If you're here hoping to get thesis material, you'll have to wait. We don't need any help and I don't have the time."

"We have a theory we'd like to discuss with you," I said, glancing at Caleb.

She returned her gaze to her computer screen. "We have several working theories. Thank you anyway."

Caleb reached out and pushed the laptop screen closed.

"Don't touch my computer," the professor growled, her face scrunched up like an angry pit bull.

Caleb leaned over the table and held out the water samples. "We know where the chemical causing the aggression came from."

"How do you know it's a chemical?" she demanded. "We never released that to the media."

"Call it a lucky guess," I said and pulled the bags of leaves out of my pocket. "Our samples should be a match for what you found in the geese."

She eyed the baggies then returned her gaze to our faces. "And where did these samples come from?"

"If they're a match, we'll tell you what we know," Caleb said.

"This better not be a prank to waste my time. I've got a serious problem on my hands. We're documenting detrimental behavior patterns never seen in these animals." She rose from the table and waved for us to follow her to another tent. Lab equipment spread around the various tables. She closed the flap behind us and latched it shut.

"Professor," called a guy in his early twenties. "They sent the NMR results from the lab."

We followed her over to the table and waited while she looked over the printout. "Are you sure this is right, John?" she asked him. "This doesn't match any registered chemical."

John studied Caleb and me a little too closely for my comfort. I hoped he'd been too busy to watch much news. I resisted the urge to shift and forced myself to meet his gaze without blinking.

"Sorry, I don't think I've seen you around. I'm John, Professor March's graduate student," he said and held out a hand.

Caleb shook his hand. "Nice to meet you, John. We're a bit late to the party. Just dropping off some samples to be tested."

I nodded and smiled.

The professor sighed and chewed her lip. "Okay, let's see what you've got. We don't know where this is coming from so if what you two have is a match then I have some questions."

John's eyes rounded. "They have a sample of the chemical?"

"Possibly," I said and handed over the baggies.

He darted over to a table with the excitement of a kid with a new toy.

"How long will it take to know if it's a match for what you found?" Caleb asked.

"A couple hours to do preliminary tests. To be certain, we'll have to send samples back to the university for further evaluation. Which could take a few days."

My throat cinched tight. We didn't have a few days.

Instead of standing over John's shoulder, we ducked outside.

"Remember to stay back from the animals," Professor March called behind us.

The lakefront spread to one side, peaceful and calm, the opposite of the hubbub of activity on the other side of the ropes. We walked toward the water, away from the cameras, which were more of a threat in our eyes than the geese. A flock of geese milled around the water's edge, while what I assumed to be two graduate students crept up on one side of the flock.

"They don't look aggressive," I said. The flock moved away from the not-so-sneaky-students. "I guess I was expecting foaming at the mouth or something."

One student made a grab for a smaller goose, lunging and hugging the animal to prevent damaging its wings. The bird honked a distress call. A commotion erupted out of the reeds at the water's edge.

"Oh shit, look out. Here comes one," yelled the second

student, pointing to the moving reeds where not one, but two large geese exploded from the vegetation. They beat their wings as they ran, their necks extended and beaks open, honking.

The first student dropped the goose he was holding and scurried back, tripping over a root and falling flat on his back. Two geese lunged at the downed student, scratching with their clawed feet and biting at his head. The claws inflicted a surprising amount of damage. He screamed and covered his face with his hands. Within seconds, blood gushed down his neck from the multiple wounds.

"Stay here," Caleb said and raced across the grass toward the attack.

"Caleb, don't," I said, glancing at the reporters behind the ropes. He didn't even pause. Always the hero. Always had to save the world, just like Dad and Will.

The second student yelled and ran to help his friend. Instead of retreating, the geese continued the attack on the ground, ripping chunks of hair and skin off the boy's head. Grabbing his friend's hand, the student dragged him several feet. The geese followed, thrashing their wings against the legs of the standing student.

Caleb reached the fight, taking the downed student's other hand and yanking him to his feet while the birds turned their attention to the new threat.

Shouting behind the lines drew my attention away from the attack. The camera crews, attracted by the chaos, turned their lenses on the scene. My blood turned to sludge at the sight of the lenses trained on Caleb. I chewed on a fingernail but stayed away, hoping Caleb's beard was enough to mask his identity.

One goose bit Caleb's extended hand, whipping its head back and forth until a chunk of flesh ripped out in its mouth. Caleb let go of the stumbling student, fisted his free hand, and swung. He connected with the tiny head of the goose with a solid *thwack*. The bird dropped to the ground and didn't move.

On their feet, the two students rushed to the tents while Caleb fended off the remaining bird. Both of its wings hung at awkward angles, the bones broken. But still, it didn't stop its attack. Caleb half-crouched, ready to leap to the side, and backed up, never taking his eyes off the violent bird.

Under other circumstances, the sight might have been humorous. But these geese were nothing to mess with. Caleb lunged to avoid a bite, his hat falling to the ground.

I held a hand over my mouth. My stomach twisted.

"Back up," a voice commanded from behind me.

I turned to see the professor, a rifle in hand. She took aim and fired a white dart into the chest of the goose. It squawked then dropped to the ground at Caleb's feet. His head jerked around and focused on the gun in the professor's hands.

She marched to the unconscious birds and crouched by their sides. Gently, she lifted a damaged wing. "Damn. That will make three this week we've lost."

I caught Caleb's eye and looked to the still-rolling cameras. He grabbed his hat from the ground and pulled it on as he angled his back to the lenses.

"What will happen to them?" I asked the professor.

She lifted one bird in her arms. "This one will have to be put down. We'll see if we can learn anything new from the tissues. We'll release the other one if he doesn't have serious injuries."

We followed her back to the tent, out of view of the cameras, Caleb holding the second goose.

"Smart move, punching him," she said to Caleb. "I'll have John bandage up the bite for you."

Blood ran down his fingers from the two-inch wound on his hand. "I never knew geese could break the skin."

"These certainly can," she answered. "The theory is an overproduction of adrenaline is giving them vastly increased strength."

The two students Caleb rescued sat to one side of the tent, John already cleaning the various gashes and bites.

She laid the bird on the table and smoothed the feathers over the creature's head. Opening a bin, she pulled out a vial and syringe, then measured out the clear liquid. With quick hands, she injected the medicine into the goose then reached for a stethoscope and listened to the chest until the heart stopped beating.

"It's a shame, but with the broken wings this is most humane," she said and covered the bird with a towel.

"It isn't normal for an animal to hurt themselves, is it?" I asked, my eyes still on the towel.

"Absolutely not. Under no usual circumstances would an animal damage itself this way. It's suicide."

"Can I help you with that bite?" John asked, having finished up with the traumatized students. "It was pretty brave of you to step in."

Caleb raised his eyebrow and held out his hand. "They looked like they could use some help."

"You might even make the news. Some reporters wanted to talk to you," John said, his attention on cleaning the wound.

Heroics catch camera lenses. The students needed help, but in our situation, Caleb shouldn't have stepped in.

He shot me a glance as if reading my mind. "I'm assuming I don't need to worry about rabies?"

John let out a bark of a laugh. "It's not rabies, no matter what the news says. You'd be more likely to have an infection with a cat bite. Their mouths are filthy in comparison."

"Good to know."

The professor studied Caleb, her brow scrunched. "You

don't seem like a student. Where did you say you're going to school?"

"In Chicago," I said and turned to the professor. "How much longer before we have the test results back?"

Before she could answer, another student rushed into the tent, papers in hand. "Professor March, you're going to want to see this right away. We found a new behavior pattern."

She took the papers and scanned the contents. "When did you first notice the behavior?"

"Yesterday, we thought it changed, but we weren't sure. But, as you can see, it's gotten much worse today," the girl answered.

"Damn. What the hell is this?" the professor said to herself then turned to glare my way. "I don't have any more time to mess around. Tell me what you know or get out."

Caleb spoke before I could. "Like we told you, we don't want to waste any of your time until we're sure we are dealing with the same problem."

"Then let's rush those tests." She slammed the papers onto the table "Not only do I have violent geese, now I have geese forgetting how to swim."

CHAPTER TWENTY-FIVE

We waited two hours, out of sight of the press cameras and out of the way of the beehive of activity our samples created. Caleb's burner phone blew up with texts.

"Who's texting?" I asked after the third time.

"Michelle. She's reminding me I have to get those online classes done before I start in three days."

"We don't know if they've figured out who you are," I said.

He nodded. "But it would be a good option to keep open if they haven't."

I swallowed. Caleb could walk right into a trap. My fingers itched to hold Luna. Stroking her fur would have calmed my anxiety. I rubbed my hands over my arms. Not the same effect.

"We don't have a lot of choice. But I have to log sixteen hours for the classes, so I need to get started," he said.

"The classes aren't a problem. I don't want you getting caught," I said with more emotion than I'd intended.

He raised his eyebrows.

"Oh, don't go getting full of yourself," I snapped. "I just don't want to be up against these people alone."

"That's what I figured."

"Give me half an hour with a computer and you'll look like you've been a good boy and done all your homework."

He grinned. "Where were you when I needed you in high school?"

"You never asked for my help." I turned and approached John where he was working at a lab table. "Is there a library around here?"

We followed John's directions to the local library and settled in at the last two computers in the row, which offered a little privacy. My hands paused over the keys. I flexed my fingers to shake away the nerves. My chest squeezed until my ribs crushed my heart. I pushed images of Ren's sheet-covered body from my mind. Grief was a funny thing. I'd forget for a bit and feel normal but then the smallest thing would bring it all rushing back.

"You good?" Caleb asked from over my shoulder.

I blew out a breath and began tapping keys. "Yep, I'm going to reroute through some dummy servers, just to be safe, but this shouldn't take long."

He nodded and sat in the chair next to me and scrolled through news stories on his computer. The basic setup of the website the company used for the classes was easy to navigate. I broke past the firewalls in minutes and hacked Caleb's account. I adjusted the time for the classes to look like he'd completed the sixteen hours. Contemplating the test scores, I entered an eighty-five. Respectable but not outstanding.

"Really?" Caleb said. "If we're going to cheat, at least give me an A."

I smirked. "We don't want them to suspect anything."

"I could ace that stupid test."

I tapped the keys and entered a ninety. "There, happy now?"

He turned back to his own computer.

I hesitated for a moment, then logged into my anonymous account. I hadn't checked it since Ren died. There were tons of messages from my former hacker colleagues, most with the subject line of Ren. I scanned the emails and froze. Ren's email address glared from the list.

Shaking fingers clicked on the message, sent the day before he died. It contained two lines of text and an attachment.

Did some more digging. Be careful, they have friends in high places.

I opened the attachment. A picture popped up. *Oh, Ren, this is probably what got you killed.*

I leaned closer to the screen. The vice president of Nansic stood next to another suit-clad man. The camera angle and time stamp made me think Ren got the image off a security feed. An added caption read *Marling with a congressman. Time stamp puts it during a closed special funding meeting.*

"Harper, you need to look at this," Caleb said from beside me.

I tore my eyes away from the photo to glance at his computer. He turned up the volume a notch so I could hear. A news story played on the screen, showing the tear-stained face of my mom. She stood in front of our house, pleading for information leading to the location of her lost daughter. Me.

Moisture sprang to my eyes at the obvious desperation in her voice. I swallowed the thickening in my throat. It was one thing to know she was probably worried about me. It was another to see the evidence on her face and hear it in her voice. If only I could call her.

The camera backed out a bit. My mom's arms cradled the half-orange, half-black striped face of Luna. Mom's hands moved over her fur. At least my sweet girl could give one of us comfort.

The news anchor came back on, talking about how Will had

been MIA for the past week and was possibly killed in action overseas serving his country. My face flashed across the screen. I'd supposedly run away after suffering a severe nervous breakdown due to my mental health history. On top of that insult, the picture they showed was from the time period of my mistaken venture into short hair. The Bozo Effect was in full force.

"I guess it was inevitable," I said. "I'm surprised a missing person would be on national news though."

"They must be pushing the story to get your face out," he said. "And letting you know they can get to your mom."

My mom's voice continued. Her words penetrated my brain. "Harper, if you can hear me, remember the poodles. Please honey, remember."

"Poodle. That's one of our code words." My brow pulled together. As a safety measure, and because I thought it was fun as a kid, my family came up with code words to communicate with each other in times of emergency. Kind of like the codes my dad used with his Special Forces squad. Even if our aunt picked us up from school, I wouldn't leave with her until she gave the all-clear code word.

"Yeah, what's that one mean?"

"She's telling me to stay away, not to contact her."

Caleb nodded in agreement. "She knows something isn't right."

"They wouldn't hurt her. Would they?"

He shook his head and put a hand over mine. "There isn't anything to be gained by hurting her. She doesn't know anything."

I tore my eyes away from Luna and my mom. Gesturing to my screen, I said, "Look at this."

"What was Marling doing in D.C.?" he asked, leaning over. "Isn't that Congressman Briarwood?"

I remembered the congressman's face from the news program I'd watched in the hotel a few days before. "I think you're right. Isn't he the one pushing a stronger military?"

Caleb's brow pulled low over his eyes. "Yeah, he's the one who is all about supporting our troops and military funding. But what the hell is he doing with that snake?"

"Ren said this was during a closed special funding meeting. How much you want to bet the project had something to do with DX-200 and the Army base?"

"If they have someone in the government on their side, it could explain how they found out about the meeting when I reached out to my CO," Caleb said, his shoulders tense and his hands fisted as if he wanted to hit something. "They caught wind of it when it ran up the chain of command stateside."

"Until we're sure what DX-200 is, it's impossible to gather much more information about what they're doing together."

He stood. "Let's go see if the preliminary results are in on those tests. And hope the professor is too busy to catch your story on the news."

We headed back to the goose pond, ducking our way through even more film crews behind the ropes. The sight of the reporters and cameras made me twitchy after seeing myself on the news. I resisted the urge to pull my shirt over my face to hide. The professor was in her tent, pacing, when John let us in.

"There you are. I've been waiting an hour for you two to get back," she exclaimed.

My chest tightened, and my muscles tensed to bolt. If she'd seen the news and figured out who we were we needed to get away fast.

"They finished testing the water and plants you brought in," she continued.

I let out a stale breath. "Is it a match for what you found in the geese?"

"Everything looks the same," she said. "I can't be one hundred percent certain until we send it off to run the NMR, but I'm ninety-five percent sure your chemical is the same unidentified chemical we found in these geese." She put her hands on her hips. "You need to tell me where you got those samples."

DX-200 is a pesticide. I licked my lips and met Caleb's gaze. He glanced back at John, who was watching from the doorway of the tent.

"We need to talk in private," he said.

Professor March waved at John to leave the tent. He let out a sigh for our benefit but closed the flap behind him.

Caleb stepped closer to the Professor and spoke in a low voice. "We may put you in danger by sharing this information."

Professor March's brows shot up to her hairline, but she nodded. "I have to know what's causing this."

Caleb laid out our suspicions about Nansic and DX-200 being their new pesticide, as well as our run-ins with the mercenaries. Her jaw dropped open when Caleb got to the shoot-out in the middle of Chicago, but she stayed silent until he finished.

I watched her, afraid she wouldn't believe the outrageous-sounding scenario.

"I don't doubt a company would put profits over public safety." She waved a hand through the air. "These companies have turned science on its head to have it say what benefits their profit margin. Massaging data is practically the norm." She shook her head. "But I have a hard time swallowing government officials would not only turn a blind eye but would actually be involved."

Caleb pressed forward. "We don't know how much the government knows or how many are involved. But we know about Nansic. If their chemical is causing this problem with the geese, that in itself would be something they would cover up."

"As much as I don't want to think it's possible, I don't see any other explanation for what we're seeing," she said finally. "I guess it was just a matter of time before they resorted to silencing people permanently."

"Do you have any idea how the chemical is causing the violent behaviors?" I asked and sat in a chair, my legs weak with relief.

She pulled out images of brain scans and handed them to Caleb and me. I looked at six different pictures of brains, different sets showing small regions lit up with varying colors. The colors highlighted different areas, but that was as far as my limited knowledge got me.

"So, it is the amygdala and, I'm guessing, the hypothalamus? These are a little different from what I studied in A and P," Caleb asked.

She nodded and pointed to the first set of pictures. "This is a normal *Branta Canadensis,* or Canada Goose, brain. The amygdala in the affected goose is lighting up, showing a concentration of the chemical. It's one area controlling fear." Her finger moved to the middle set. "Here you can see the concentration in the bird equivalent of the hypothalamus and pituitary gland, which controls hormone function, including adrenaline." She pointed to the last set of scans. "And here you can see the difference in size of the frontal cortex. In the affected geese it's shrunk considerably, we think because of cell death. This would reduce higher thinking and impulse control."

"So basically, they are becoming easily angered with no impulse control," I said.

"To put it simply, yes, but it's much more complex." She ran a hand through her hair and sat behind her makeshift desk.

"The inability to feed and swim is a new symptom, and I can only guess what those scans will look like."

"It took months for the prisoners to show symptoms, but the geese are showing symptoms almost immediately." Caleb handed back the scans.

She shook her head. "Likely because the geese had direct exposure when the crops were sprayed while the prison subjects would have ingested the chemical in much smaller doses. It went through the digestive tract and took longer to build up in the tissues."

"Direct exposure also explains why a higher percentage of geese were affected than in the prison population," Caleb added.

I looked back and forth between the two of them trying to keep up on their science-speak.

She nodded. "It could also have to do with differing brain chemistry between species and a hundred other possibilities." She switched on her computer and pulled up a satellite image of the area around Nansic headquarters. "We haven't seen any other animal species exhibiting this rabid behavior but maybe this flock flew directly through the spray and inhaled it or landed in the water collection pond."

"Or we may not have found the other affected animals yet," I mumbled.

"When will the NMR confirm this is the same chemical?" Caleb asked.

"A couple days," Professor March answered. "From what you've told me, it sounds like the best thing for the two of you to do is to stay in town out of sight."

Frustration boiled up. Sitting around and waiting for confirmation was not on my agenda. Figuring out a way to take Nansic down and get Will back was. "Is there any other information you have that might be helpful in proving what they've done?"

"I can't connect what's happening here to the base overseas and the prison unless you get me samples. Even then, with politicians behind them, it's going to take an enormous amount of irrefutable evidence to prove they're responsible. I've seen companies wriggle out of responsibility when there was ironclad proof."

I bit my lips. Going back to the prison to ask for samples would be suicide.

"Take my blood, or tissue, whatever you need for the tests," Caleb said quietly from beside me.

My brow furrowed. "We don't know if you've been exposed," I said, then snapped my mouth shut. They'd been testing DX-200 in the prison for almost a year. Caleb was on the base until he was injured three weeks ago. My organs churned and cinched tight, unable to think about the possible consequences. "You can't have been exposed."

He grimaced. "There's one way to find out and right now I'm the only potential source of proof they're using soldiers as guinea pigs."

I gripped the plastic sides of my chair until my hands went numb.

"I can pull some blood and tissue samples and send them to a college that's been helping with the goose samples," Professor March said gently.

"Thank you," Caleb said.

I didn't want to watch the professor take samples from Caleb, but I couldn't tear my eyes away. I stared, hands fisted, while she pulled several vials of blood then jabbed a large bore needle into several places of Caleb's muscle to collect tissue. First Nansic threatened to take away my brother forever, now they might take Caleb as well.

"A brain scan wouldn't be a bad idea, but that would raise questions," the professor said as she bagged the samples, labeled them and put them in a cooler marked *Biohazard*. "We'll see what the tests show and go from there."

"How long will these take?" My voice broke and I cleared my throat in hopes of covering up the emotion.

"Two or three days."

Caleb rolled his sleeve down over the band-aids and threw me a weak smirk. "If I turn into a major asshole in the meantime, do me a favor and knock me out with that dart gun."

CHAPTER TWENTY-SIX

We got back to the bed-and-breakfast in the early evening. We'd stopped at a diner, but I couldn't even contemplate eating. Caleb being exposed to the DX-200 had never occurred to me. But obviously it had to him.

I climbed the stairs from the foyer, Caleb close on my heels. A woman clutching a white bathrobe to her chest, her hair in a towel, rushed down the stairs. I hugged the wall to let her pass.

"There's no hot water," she complained.

The voice of the owner carried up the stairs. "The water heater must be actin' up. Just replaced the darn thing. I'll get up to the attic to check it right away."

I continued to the third floor and unlocked the door to our suite. The walls of the large room pressed in on me, the silence deafening. I paced the hardwood floor, avoiding Caleb's gaze. We'd barely said two words since we'd left the professor's tent.

"Do you want to tell me what's on your mind?" he asked.

I didn't pause in my pacing. "I can't believe I didn't realize you might have been exposed."

"It's pointless to talk about," he answered. "We need to be

thinking about how we're going to prove Nansic is spreading poison, and we need to get Will back."

"It's not pointless to talk about. You could get sick. You need to see a doctor before it hurts you." I kept my voice level—barely.

"Right, I'll see a doctor as soon as I get out of prison for desertion." He held out his hands to stop me, but I turned and paced the opposite way, knotting and unknotting the flannel shirt around my waist.

"What if we went to the media? If it's out in the open, it would be harder for them to come after us or the professor," he said, sitting on the lounge as he watched me.

I stopped, ran my hands through my hair and suppressed the urge to scream. The room swam before my eyes. "I need some fresh air," I said and grabbed my hoodie. "I'm going to sit in the garden and clear my head."

"Harper, it's freezing out there."

I walked out the door before he could protest further and ran down the stairs then out to the side yard garden I'd seen that morning.

The chilly air took some of the heat from my blazing cheeks. I pulled my sweatshirt tight around my torso and followed the path to a bench. The flower gardens lay dormant, only the early spring plants daring to send up shoots and tiny flowers. I blew out a foggy breath then allowed the cold air to fill my lungs. It smelled of damp earth.

I leaned back against the rough wood of the bench and forced images of a hulked-out Caleb, insane with anger, from my head. The DX-200 made those prisoners into mindless beasts. The thought of Caleb affected tightened my chest like a vise.

Several minutes passed. My fingers chilled to ice along with my toes. I couldn't stay outside all night, though it was tempting.

With a sigh, I rose from the bench and turned up the path to go back inside.

All I remembered after getting up and taking a few steps on my chilled legs was blinding light and a wave of heat a million times worse than the puff of opening a hot oven. The sun expanded and blasted out of the third floor of the house. I felt weightless for a moment, sailing like a bird through the air, then the pain of impact and nothingness.

When my eyes cracked open, they focused in on the third floor of the bed-and-breakfast. The entire top of the building was gone. Flames engulfed what little remained of the third floor and most of the second. My heart cramped and twisted. My mind screamed. *Caleb.*

I scrambled to my feet with my hearing muffled like I was underwater, and lurched toward the door. Though no one could survive the inferno that had just been our room, I couldn't stop myself from rushing to the wide wooden steps leading to the porch.

The front door flew open before I reached it, people spilling out like water from a hose. Thick, black smoke billowed from the opening and I covered my nose and mouth with a hand. The woman in the bathrobe stumbled in front of me and I grabbed her arm to keep her from falling. She clutched my torso as I led her to a grassy area away from the flames and eased her down.

"Thank you," she gasped, coughing.

My ash-stung eyes searched the survivors for Caleb, hoping. A few stragglers, smeared with soot, stumbled out the door. No sign of Caleb.

The innkeeper's wife collapsed on the grass staring at the house. She grabbed my arm. "Frank. Frank is still in there. He was going up to check on the water heater."

I turned to face the inferno. Heat pushed against my skin from the blaze. I didn't think, didn't consider, but ran up the steps and through the front door. The blistering temperature and smoke stopped my progress a few feet inside. I threw my arm over my face, ripped my flannel from around my waist, and plunged it into the water dispenser by the desk, then covered my nose and mouth.

"Frank," I yelled over the crack and sizzle of the fire. "Caleb." I crept to the stairs and ran up the half-flight to where the stairs turned. The house groaned like the fire was hurting it. I glanced to the ceiling and the bubbling plaster. I yelled again, turning to the next half-flight.

"Help," a choked voice called from up the stairs.

"I'm coming," I yelled and rushed up the last few steps.

On the second-floor landing, Caleb pulled an unmoving form across the carpet. He fell backward, the other man landing on top of him. At the sight of Caleb, alive and moving, a sob of relief escaped my lips.

He struggled to breathe the soot-filled air. The thick smoke stung my eyes and burned my lungs even through the wet cloth.

"Harper," Caleb choked out, coughing. "The ceiling is going to go."

I ran to his side, took a deep breath then pressed the cloth to his face. I grabbed the unconscious man's arm, seeing it was Frank, and pulled with every ounce of strength in me to get him off Caleb's legs. He grabbed the other arm with his free hand, the flannel pressed to his face. Together, we pulled Frank across the hallway to the stairs and down to the first landing.

Pressure built in my lungs from holding my breath and I gasped out the old air and, out of reflex, sucked in the ash-filled air. With a painful spasm, my lungs rejected the smoke and I hunched over in a coughing fit.

A loud crack echoed from the floor above. Caleb pressed the

flannel to my face and grabbed Frank with both hands. Straining, he lifted the smaller man across his shoulder, and we rushed down the last few steps and out the open front door.

We made it to the grass, collapsing in a black-smeared, coughing heap, before the ceiling gave way and the second floor fell into the first with a *whoosh* of heat that singed my eyebrows. The firetrucks had arrived after I went inside. Firemen surrounded us, pressing oxygen masks to our faces and assessing Frank.

We backed away to make room for the paramedics to work on him. I gobbled down the sweet-tasting, clean air then hunched over, gagging and hacking. Caleb fell to his knees on the grass, then buckled and toppled over.

"Help," I screamed, dropping next to him. I lay my hand against his chest to feel for movement, my stomach folding in on itself until I felt his chest rise. Blood oozed from a gash across his forehead.

Two paramedics rushed to Caleb, one checking for a pulse at his neck. He nodded at his partner. They rolled Caleb onto his side and secured the oxygen mask over his nose and mouth. "We need a board over here."

They secured Caleb, still on his side, onto a hard board and lifted him to the ambulance. I stood outside the door, shifting from foot to foot and pressing my mask into my face. One paramedic lifted the oxygen mask from Caleb's pale face and opened his mouth then put a scope inside. "Burns along his throat and likely burns to the bronchi. He needs a CT."

The second paramedic nodded and handed over a different mask, which they slipped over his face.

"Is he going to be okay?" I choked out.

"Does he have any breathing problems? Asthma, lung disease?"

"No, I don't think so," I said, my mind racing.

"His pulse is stable, and the EKG looks good. He should be okay, but we need to take him to the hospital to treat him for smoke inhalation. Plus, check out the gash on his head."

"No," Caleb said from the gurney, his eyes wide open, trying to pull the nebulizer from his face. "No hospital."

"Sir, the effects of smoke inhalation can be delayed and, if not treated, cause permanent damage to your lungs." The paramedic put a hand on Caleb's shoulder to ease him back against the gurney.

He relaxed into the pillow. His bloodshot eyes met mine. I nodded. His fake ID should hold up under scrutiny at the hospital. As long as no one recognized him.

To my left, paramedics lifted Frank into another ambulance, his wife close behind. She rushed over and clutched my hands. "Thank you. Thank you so much for getting him out."

"I hope he's okay," I said around my mask and squeezed her hands.

"Miss, we need to check you out as well," the paramedic said.

I waved him off. "I'm okay. I was outside when the explosion happened."

"At least let me take a look at you," he said, hopping from the back of the ambulance and approaching me.

I let him peer down my throat with a light, check my blood oxygen saturation and other vitals. "I don't see any burns in your airways and your vitals look good. Just keep that oxygen on for the ride to the hospital and let us know if you start to feel dizzy or nauseous."

I nodded and climbed into the back of the ambulance, taking the seat next to Caleb. We rode in silence during the short trip to the county hospital. Talking hurt too much and was a pain around the masks. They unloaded the gurney at the ER entrance and handed us off to the doctors and nurses. I waited outside the curtain while they removed Caleb's smoke-filled clothes and examined him. A nurse brought me a plastic bag with his wallet, pocketknife, and watch.

The doctor stepped outside the curtain. "Are you family?"

"Yes," I said without hesitation. "How is he?"

"He has a mild concussion and he's lucky the bronchi aren't more severely burned. He inhaled a considerable amount of smoke. I don't know how he didn't lose consciousness under those conditions. We need to monitor him and run some blood gasses." He paused and flipped through the chart. "I also restitched the incisions in his back from his surgery. He needs to follow up with his surgeon though."

"Thank you," I said. "Can I see him now?"

He pulled back the curtain. Caleb lay on his side looking ghostly with a green tinge, a pink, plastic basin clutched in one hand. A nebulizer hummed on the table, the mist flowing up to his face.

"How are you feeling?"

"Better than I would have if you hadn't been stupid enough to run into a burning house," he groaned through the mask. "Seriously, isn't it pretty well-known not to run into a fire?"

I sat in the chair next to the bed. "I had to get Frank out," I paused and added softly, "and you."

He met my eyes over the rim of the puke basin. "I'd just gone down to the second floor when the explosion happened. If I'd been in the room, they'd be identifying me with dental records."

I swallowed and slid my mask from my face. My hand found his and I held on, not able to talk. An edge of the curtain being yanked back sent me jumping halfway out of my chair.

A policeman stuck his head through the gap. "Okay if I ask you two a few questions?"

I glanced at Caleb. Looking half dead and with the mask on,

there was no way the officer would recognize him from the news, but I was a different story. I slipped my mask over my face and nodded. Hopefully, the soot dulled the easily identifiable red of my hair.

We answered his questions but didn't offer any additional details, giving him just enough information to not appear suspicious.

"I can't say it was smart not to wait for the fire department, but from what the doctor says, you saved both their lives with your quick thinking. It was a good idea to soak the shirt in water." The officer smiled. "Your room was on the third floor?"

"That's right," I said.

"When you went upstairs, did you smell any sulfur odor?"

I shook my head and glanced at Caleb. He answered, "No."

The officer pursed his lips but nodded.

"Do you know what caused the explosion?" I asked.

"One witness mentioned the hot water wasn't working shortly before the explosion, which could indicate a pilot light out or a gas leak." He put his pen back in his pocket. "We'll have to wait for the official report."

We nodded but didn't comment.

"We'll keep the reporters outside and away from you all so you can rest." He moved to the curtain. "We'll release the basics—continued investigation, possible gas leak, no casualties. So, they may try for an interview."

I waited until the curtain fell closed behind him, then turned to Caleb. "What do you think?"

"That was no gas leak." He tried to push himself off the bed and failed. "I've been around enough tactical explosives to recognize a controlled blast. The initial damage from the explosion was limited to the third floor." His gaze met mine. "It was meant for us."

"How did they find us?"

"The reporters filming the geese attack? Someone recognized us? We need to get out of here."

"As soon as the police release their statement that there were no casualties, they'll know for sure we survived," I said and bit my lip. "It's not safe to go back and get the car. They may be watching."

"They would have had someone at the scene after the bomb to be sure they killed us, so they already know."

The moment Caleb said the words, all the faces of the EMTs, first responders and onlookers flashed in my mind. He was absolutely right. *Mission success 101: confirm you take out the target.* One of those people had set the bomb. *I should have realized.*

Caleb broke me from my thoughts. "Do you still have the rest of our cash?"

I shook my head. "It was upstairs. All I have is about thirty bucks in my pocket and the flash drive the warden gave us."

"One thing at a time. First, we need to get out of here. They could try again any time," he said and pushed himself to a sitting position.

"Don't the doctors need to get the test results back first?" I put a hand on his shoulder. "They were pretty worried about your blood gasses."

"I have to get you out of here." The hospital gown fell open, revealing a large swath of skin. "Let's go"

I averted my eyes. "You don't have any clothes."

His body swayed as he searched the room. "Where did they take them? Where's my knife?"

"The clothes were ruined. I'll have to buy you some. But I have your knife." I grabbed his arm to keep him steady, my brows together. His eyes were on me, but they weren't seeing me. He stared past me.

"Why don't you sit down?" I said.

"No, we have to leave. Hand me my knife," he said and tugged out of my grasp, pulling the tubes from the nebulizer. He ripped the mask off his face and yanked off the lines for his pulse ox and heart monitor. The machines beeped their disapproval. He took two steps toward the curtain before his knees buckled.

"Caleb," I gasped and lunged to break his fall. The teacher's voice from my first aid class filled my mind: *Don't try to catch them but protect the head if you can.* My hands slid under his skull and we crumpled to the linoleum in a heap.

The curtain pulled aside before I could call out for help. The doctor stood over us, lab printouts in hand.

"He seemed confused and wanted to leave, then he just collapsed," I said from under Caleb's weighty torso.

"Nurse," called the doctor as he squatted and put two fingers on Caleb's wrist. "His lab results just came in. The carboxyhemoglobin levels are high, which indicates carbon monoxide poisoning."

Two nurses rushed in and together the three rolled Caleb off me and onto a lifting device, then moved him to the gurney. Slipping the nebulizer back over his face, the doctor shook his head.

With fists clasped to steady my shaking hands, I climbed to my feet. "Is he going to be okay?"

"Confusion is common with levels as high as his." He turned to the nurse at his side. "He needs to be on the first helicopter."

The nurse rushed out.

The beeping from the machines subsided when they reconnected the various leads. Caleb's heartbeat and oxygen levels displayed on the screen.

The familiar tide of choking terror rose through my torso, forcing logic out in front of it. I clung to the prescription bottle in my pocket and hung on to what little shred of sanity I had left. "What's happening to him?"

"He needs a hyperbaric chamber. The closest one is in Indianapolis," the doctor said. "We'll transport him by helicopter and get him in the chamber as soon as possible."

My leaden legs would no longer support me. I landed with a thud in the chair, my breathing strained. The oxygen mask hung loosely around my neck. "I need to stay with him."

"We only have enough room for the patients we're transporting to Indianapolis. I'm sorry."

My eyes followed the peaks and dips on the monitors, as if I could will the lines to stay in normal ranges. I let their rhythm soothe the whirlpool of anxiety threatening to pull me under.

I couldn't bear to think of Caleb, alone and vulnerable, flying right into Nansic's backyard. He looked smaller and weaker in the hospital bed, not like the muscle-bound soldier who'd showed up at my door only a few days before, but more like the lanky guy I'd known most of my life.

"When will they move him?" I croaked out.

The doctor paused at the edge of the curtain. "They're preparing the chopper now, so in the next fifteen minutes."

I held Caleb's limp hand, pulling myself together one stitch at a time, until the nurses came to take him out to the helipad. Though his breathing was ragged, it remained steady. I stood in the empty alcove, a thin sheet of fabric separating me from the busy emergency room. Tears dripped down my face in sooty rivulets.

After a minute, I blinked, wiped the moisture from my cheeks, and clenched my jaw. Caleb couldn't be left alone and vulnerable. With a deep breath, I dropped the oxygen mask into the chair and strode from the emergency room.

CHAPTER TWENTY-SEVEN

The tent flaps rustled in the wind. The brisk walk from the hospital to the pond at least kept the chill in the spring air from seeping into my limbs. But in the few miles I walked, it seemed like every part of my body hurt. I hadn't noticed the plethora of bruises and pain until after they had taken Caleb to the helicopter.

As I'd hoped, there was still light inside the main tent beside the water. I'd banked on Professor March being a workaholic. I lifted the shiny plastic flap and stepped into the circle of light cast by two portable lanterns. The professor sat behind her computer, typing away at the keys. She glanced up. "Did you forget something?" she asked, then paused as she took in my soot-smeared, bedraggled appearance. "What happened to you?"

I smoothed my palms over my dirty clothes and shook my head then rounded the table to stand beside her. "I need your help. I'm sorry to ask, but I don't have anyone else I can go to."

She stood from her chair as her brow pulled together. "Were you in a fire?"

"Nansic found us." I reached over the computer and pulled

up the live news story outside the bed-and-breakfast. The Victorian building was now a smoldering ruin with firefighters still spraying down hotspots. A reporter stood in the foreground talking about how it was a miracle no one died in the apparent gas leak.

"They started a fire?" she asked.

"No, they set a bomb. Caleb barely made it out. He's on a helicopter—" I choked on the thickening in my throat. Saying it out loud made it more real. "Flying to Indianapolis."

Her eyes widened. "You're sure it was a bomb?"

"Caleb's sure. I need to borrow a car. They could be watching." My muddled thoughts refused to form coherent sentences. I took a breath and tried again. "If they find out where Caleb is, they'll kill him."

"Slow down. Why don't you sit down for a minute?" She glanced at my dirty clothes. "We can get you some clean clothes."

"No," I insisted. I had bigger things to worry about than smelling good. "I need to leave now."

"I can take you," a voice said from behind me.

I spun on my heel. John stood in the doorway, his hand holding the tent open.

I shook my head. "I don't think that's a good idea."

"I told him everything," Professor March said. "You can trust him. He hates these companies just as much as I do."

"It isn't safe to be around me." I shook my head. "If I could just borrow a car..."

John moved closer to the table, lowering his voice in a conspiratorial whisper. "Don't worry about me. I spent all last summer on the *Marine Guard*." He smiled as if his statement explained it all.

I blinked and tried to focus. I didn't have the time or the inclination to ask what he meant.

"It's an antiwhaling vessel. It—never mind, he knows about the dangers," the professor explained.

"Being on a boat is a bit different from people shooting at you and trying to blow you up," I said to John.

He straightened his stick figure frame, his chest puffed out like a rooster. "I'll do anything to stop corporate greed from destroying our planet."

I thought of Caleb in the hospital mere miles from Nansic headquarters. I didn't have time to argue. "Fine. Thank you. We need to leave now."

John threw a bag of clothes and his laptop in the back of his car and we hit the road. The drive took an hour and forty-five minutes with not much traffic at midnight. John filled the time by telling me all about his adventures on the ocean, saving whales from whaling ships. After five minutes, I stopped listening to his tirade.

I glanced over as he waved his bony hand to emphasize his point. His thin forearms disappeared into the pushed-up sleeve of his shirt. The contrast between his skeletal frame and Caleb's substantial one struck me. Transfixed on John's waving hands, I longed for the firm grip of Caleb's fingers on my own.

"Don't you think?" John asked.

I shifted my gaze, my mind trying to catch up. "Well," I stammered.

"I know you probably already researched it, but I doubt they've looked at the gut bacteria and nitrogen-fixing bacteria in the soil and how they're affected." John saved me from having to answer.

That was the second time I'd heard someone talk about nitrogen-fixing bacteria in relation to the pesticides. I made a mental note to do some research after Caleb was out of the hospital and safe. "Do you think that could affect the geese as well?"

"The effects on gut bacteria definitely should be checked out. I'll ask Professor March if we can run some more tests on the deceased geese. It would be good for looking at longer-term side effects. I mean, we know the current pesticides affect them." He seemed to take my attention as a green light to continue his rant. "There could be even more long-term effects of these types of chemicals that we don't know—lower intelligence, fertility issues, higher cancer rates. Not that those bastards care."

I nodded like I understood what he was talking about. We reached the outer limits of the city and I used google to help navigate to the hospital. It was near the city center, close enough to Nansic headquarters for mercenaries to get there in a matter of minutes. I scanned the parking lot for any familiar faces or out-of-place men.

We drove past the emergency entrance and passed the landing pad. A green helicopter sat on the cement. Caleb was already inside the hospital. I opened the door before the car came to a complete stop and hopped out.

"Thanks for the ride, get back to Wabash," I said to John over my shoulder.

"I'll stay and help you," he protested.

I leaned over to meet his eyes. "I'm good. It's not safe to be around me." I closed the door on his objections.

The information desk sat opposite the hospital entrance. "I need to find a patient that was flown in for the hyperbaric chamber."

"Are you family?" the receptionist asked, her eyes scanning my smoke-stained, sooty clothes and face.

"Yes." I answered without expanding. "Please, I almost lost him in the fire."

"I'll have an aid take you to the hyperbaric room," she said and lifted the phone from its cradle.

My eyes darted around the lobby, scanning the faces for any familiar unfriendlies. "Has anyone else come to see him?"

"Not that I'm aware of."

I let out a stale breath.

The aid led me three flights up to an observation area with a large window into a white room. An oblong chamber sat on the far wall. It looked like an enormous blue vitamin capsule. With Caleb inside.

His eyes were closed. Machines monitored his vital signs. I wrapped my arms across my chest, reassured by the steady beeps. The door opened, making my heart jump past my throat and well into my sinus cavity.

A doctor approached with an electronic tablet.

"How is he doing?" I asked.

The doctor tapped his screen a couple of times. "He's been in the chamber for over thirty minutes now. He should wake up soon. We'll be monitoring his blood gasses, but he'll need to stay inside for several more hours and possibly come back for further treatments."

"How does this help smoke inhalation?" I waved at the enormous contraption. My hoarse voice hurt my throat.

"The chamber is airtight. We pump a higher concentration of oxygen in at three times the pressure of normal air. This helps to increase the oxygenation of the blood. The carbon monoxide he inhaled from the fire is tying up too much of his hemoglobin, which caused his confusion," the doctor answered.

I took in the blue tubes running from the oxygen tanks into the chamber, the pressure gauge on the side reading forty psi, and the oxygen reading one hundred percent.

"It's at its maximum pressure right now. After another hour we'll reduce the pressure slowly."

I nodded. "But he's going to be okay?"

"We'll know more after he wakes up." His eyes drifted over my dirty clothes. "I'll see if a nurse can round up some clothes for you to change into."

The air turned to cement in my lungs, and I couldn't bring myself to ask the question on my tongue. *What if he doesn't wake up?* I turned back to Caleb's immobile form as the doctor left.

Helplessness had me pressing my forehead against the observation glass. Over the short time we'd been together, Caleb had somehow squeezed his way out of the friend-zone and firmly into my closed-off heart. If I never saw his dorky smile again, never heard his deep voice challenging me, never felt those strong arms around me...losing him would be my undoing.

Tightness built in my chest, encasing my ribcage in a vise. I struggled to push the panic down. Reaching into my pocket, I gripped the small prescription bottle with its one pill left and fought the urge to take it. Instead, I lifted the necklace Ren gave me to my nose but instead of lavender, the stone smelled of fire and smoke.

The room fell into a rhythm. The beep of the machines and the soft whoosh of the air from the chamber lulled me into a daze. Forty minutes ticked by on the clock. Nurses checked on Caleb every fifteen minutes, adjusting the pressure gauges and tapping notes in his chart on their tablets. The pressure on the chamber was down to one and a half times normal air. Still, he didn't wake up.

"Harper." A voice from behind me jolted me from my trance. I spun, my hands in fight position, on my toes and legs bent.

John held up his palms in surrender.

"What are you doing here? I told you to go back to Wabash," I exclaimed and dropped my hands.

He approached me and put an arm around my shoulder. "I told you I'm not afraid of corporate thugs."

"I appreciate your help, but what about the tests on the gut bacteria?" Ren's lifeless body on the gurney flashed in my mind. I couldn't stand more blood on my hands.

"I already texted the professor. She's going to order the tests first thing in the morning. I'm staying to help you," he answered. "I wouldn't miss this adventure."

I resisted the urge to smash his face up against the glass and demand if Caleb in the chamber looked like an adventure.

A nurse came in the room, a gray sweatshirt and pants folded in her arms. She held them out. "Why don't you go change into these."

I glanced through the glass to where Caleb lay, still unconscious. A hand lightly gripped my shoulder. "I'll watch him," John said. "You go change."

I nodded and accepted the clean clothes from the nurse.

She showed me to a bathroom off the hallway. With the door closed and locked behind me, I stared at my reflection in the mirror. Soot smeared my skin and ash dulled my red hair to nearly brown. I washed my face with wet paper towels, but the soot smeared more. Finally, I dunked my head under the running water in the sink. Gray water ran down the drain. The smell of smoke hit my nostrils, and memories from the fire flooded my mind. I swallowed the bile rising in my throat and continued scrubbing until all I could smell was hospital soap.

Pink-skinned and still dripping, I took off my filthy shirt and pants, replacing them with the clean sweats. I patted my hair with more paper towels and threw the ruined clothes in the trash. Feeling slightly more human, I opened the door and walked down the hallway to the observation room.

John turned when I walked in and smiled. "You look better."

I glanced past him to the adjoining room where a nurse was adjusting the gauges on the chamber. The material of his scrubs strained across the expanse of his shoulders. Without making notes in the electronic chart, he turned and walked out of the room.

"They're lowering the pressure again. Must be a good sign." John motioned to the hyperbaric chamber.

I stared at the door the nurse walked through, nerves prickling my skin. "That's a different nurse than was in before."

"Shift change?" John shrugged. "I hit the vending machine and got you something to eat." He held out a package.

Ignoring his outstretched hand, I stepped to the glass, my gaze on Caleb. He seemed to be sleeping peacefully. My attention shifted to the pressure gauge. The pressure read twenty psi. I looked at the oxygen gauge. My heart stopped in my chest, momentarily paralyzed.

The oxygen gauge read zero.

The monitors on Caleb's vitals had changed. His pulse rate and blood pressure were climbing steadily.

"Get the doctor," I yelled and bolted through the door into the hyperbaric room. Through curved glass Caleb lay motionless, his chest not moving. I grabbed the hose leading from the oxygen monitor and followed it to the knob on the wall. Gripping the knob with sweaty palms, I twisted. It refused to move. My spindly muscles didn't compare to the grip strength of the brutish nurse.

With a snarl, I squeezed as hard as I could. The grips of the knob ripped into my skin, but I twisted harder. Finally, it gave way. I cranked it all the way open. The hiss of air moving signaled the reintroduction of oxygen to the chamber.

I rushed to the window and pressed my hands against the

glass. He lay still, not breathing. The oxygen level climbed to one hundred percent. The monitors blared alarms as his heart rate climbed out of the normal range. Then the erratic line on the screen dropped to a straight, flat line. His heart had stopped.

"No, no. Breathe, damn you." I pounded on the glass. I needed him out. He needed CPR.

I scanned the control panel. Too many buttons. Too many knobs. My gaze focused on a red button marked emergency. Without hesitation, I slammed the button down. A soft *hiss* signaled the escaping pressure from the hyperbaric chamber. The reading on the pressure gauge fell.

Too slowly.

Behind me, the door flew open and two nurses ran in, obviously alerted by the alarms. Neither was the large man I'd seen in the room minutes before.

"No one is allowed in here," the younger of the pair exclaimed.

"He's not breathing," I cried. "We need to get him out of there."

The older nurse assessed the readouts on the chamber and Caleb's nonexistent vitals. "Call a code."

The younger nurse hit a button on the wall that read code blue, then picked up the phone and punched in some numbers. After a moment she said, "Adult code blue hyperbaric chamber."

Within seconds, an announcement erupted from intercom. "Adult code blue. Hyperbaric chamber. Adult code…"

The older nurse put a hand on my shoulder to focus my scattered attention. "How long since he stopped breathing?"

"I don't know, maybe a minute?" I answered and stepped out of her way as an entire army of medical personnel poured into the room. "We have to get him out."

"The chamber is decompressing. We can't open it until the emergency protocol has run or he could seize."

"How long?" I demanded.

She glanced at the gauge. "Thirty seconds, the pressure is almost at room air."

I crossed my arms over my chest and bit my fingernail, my feet moving across the floor. I couldn't stand still. I waited, doing nothing, while Caleb lay dead. Thirty seconds lasted years while I stared at his waxen face.

The doctor rushed into the room and spoke with the nurse. The younger nurse rushed in with a cart and readied the defibrillation pads. Everyone stood at the top of the chamber, ready to pull him out.

At last, the chamber clicked, and the end popped open. They leapt into action, one sliding the gurney out while another started compressions, and yet another put a mask over his mouth to force air into his lungs.

The doctor stood back, assessing the situation. "Get the pads on him."

One nurse placed the defibrillation pads on Caleb's bare chest. "Clear."

Everyone stepped back and for one second the frenzy stopped.

The room spun around me and I leaned against the wall to stay upright. I covered my face with my hands, unable to watch. I heard the buzz of electricity and the impact of Caleb's body slamming back into the gurney.

The medical staff leapt back into action.

"No pulse. Charging."

My legs gave way and I slid down the wall into a puddle on the floor, my hands still pressed over my face. The image of Caleb's still features loomed behind my closed lids.

CHAPTER TWENTY-EIGHT

The buzz and thump sounded again. This time followed by a beep. Then another.

"We've got a pulse," the doctor said.

A sob escaped my lips, but I couldn't take my hands away from my face. I pressed my palms against my closed eyes until the tears receded. Huge gulps of air calmed the spasms in my chest. I listened to the steady beep of Caleb's heartbeat until the doctor's voice penetrated my awareness. "I need you to return to the observation room."

I pushed away from the wall supporting me. They ushered me back through the door and locked it behind me. I was alone in the observation room with John, who was smart enough to stay quiet. Caleb lay motionless, hooked up to a myriad of monitors and machines but out of the hyperbaric chamber.

I took Caleb's knife from the bag and slid it into my pocket. If I saw that *nurse* again, he'd have a nice surprise coming. Scenarios ran on the hamster wheel that was my brain. Nansic knew where we were. And they'd be back.

Without Caleb awake, I couldn't do anything except press my forehead against the glass. John gave up trying to talk and left to get some real food. I had two choices—risk another attempt while waiting for Caleb to wake up or leave him. Not really a choice. Instead of my pill bottle my hand closed around the knife in my pocket. Let them come try to take away another person I loved.

My mind froze around the word. *Loved.*

I closed my eyes, not even bothering to fool myself that I meant it in some kind of platonic sense. *I love Caleb.*

My heart shifted to choke my throat shut. *When the hell did that happen?* Somewhere between the flying bullets and cheap motel rooms, I'd fallen for him—not just a little, all the way. Or maybe the feelings had been there for years.

And now he might die.

An hour later the doctor came into the observation room, creases marring his tan face. "We have to look into a few things, but the good news is his blood gasses are back in the normal range."

I couldn't care less about his cover-the-hospital's-ass-from-a-lawsuit spiel. "When will he wake up?"

"We're going to move him to the ICU."

My guts liquefied, but I nodded. It was only a matter of time before Nansic tried again.

I sat and held Caleb's hand after they moved him, the knife in my other hand and one eye on the door.

John returned with takeout, but my Styrofoam container sat untouched on the tray.

With each passing second, my hope that Caleb would wake up diminished. My brain spun with what little I knew about oxygen deprivation and brain cells playing out in my head. I couldn't give up on him. Not to save my own skin. Not for anything.

"Harper?" Caleb's throaty voice jerked my head from the bed where I'd rested it.

"Oh my God, you're awake," I gasped and gripped his hand in both of mine. Relief washed over me like fresh air.

"What happened?" he asked.

"You have carbon monoxide poisoning."

"Where are we?"

"Indianapolis."

He struggled to sit up. "What? They could find us. Go. Leave me."

"We have you under an assumed name." John stepped forward. "They won't be able to find you again."

Caleb's eyes widened. "Again?"

I resisted the urge to kick John. Barely. "There was a problem in the hyperbaric chamber."

"They'll figure out they failed and come back." He paused to breathe and coughed. "You're not safe here."

"I'm not leaving without you, so I guess I'll take my chances," I said and held his gaze.

A knock at the door stopped his response. The doctor entered the room, a tablet in hand. "It's good to see you awake, Mr. Walker," he said, using Caleb's fake name. "How are you feeling?"

"Not bad, considering. When can I get out of here?" Caleb answered with what I was sure was false bravado.

"Your labs look good. The blood gasses are back to normal ranges. But your body's been through a lot, especially so soon after major surgery." He motioned to Caleb's bandaged back. "Let's check you out before I make any estimate of how long you'll need to stay."

John and I stepped out of the room while the doctor examined Caleb. Five minutes of pacing and watching for mercs later, the doctor called us back inside.

"What's the verdict?" I asked.

He tapped entries into the tablet. "I've explained to Mr.

Walker that he needs to stay for observation for a few days. The rest is up to him to tell you himself."

He finished typing on the pad and set it on the counter to wash his hands. "It's best to keep you on liquids, no solid foods. I'll have the nurse bring you a tray." He dried his hands on a paper towel and walked out the doorway.

I turned to Caleb. "So, what did he tell you?"

"I'm fine." He threw the covers off his bare legs. "We can leave now."

"Yeah, right." I held out a hand to keep him from climbing out of bed. "You don't want to tell me? I'll find out myself."

"They can't tell you anything without my permission," he said.

"He's right Harper," John chimed in. "HIPAA protects privacy."

I rolled my eyes for both their benefit and walked over to the tablet on the counter. It took thirty seconds to bypass the security on the device.

"I told you to leave it alone, Harper," Caleb said and swung his legs over the side of the bed.

I scrolled down the various test results. The numbers meaning nothing to me, I stopped at the doctor's comments. "The patient is exhibiting signs of severe smoke inhalation as well as abnormal response to neuro exam. Ordering CT scan to rule out CVA. Recommend observation pending results of testing."

"What's a CVA?" I demanded.

Caleb sat with his arms crossed over his chest, glaring. "A stroke, basically. Are you done invading my privacy now?"

"Why would you have a stroke? From the oxygen deprivation?" I gasped, setting the tablet on the counter and sitting in the chair next to the bed.

"It could be a lot of things. One being the exposure to the

pesticide. We saw similar damage in the geese brains," John said.

I opened my mouth, but no words formed. My brain froze at the thought of Caleb suffering the same effects as the prisoners in the state penitentiary. I snapped my desert-dry lips shut.

Caleb yanked the hospital gown tighter and gripped the handrail to stand. "It doesn't matter. We don't have time for more tests."

"The doctors might be able to do something if you've been exposed to the DX-200. Maybe we should at least see if they can help," I said.

"We both know chances are slim. How do we even explain what they need to look for? I'm not going to sit around a hospital and wait to see what kills me first, the chemical or the mercs." His bloodshot eyes met mine. He forced himself to stand on weak legs.

I jumped to put a hand under his elbow. I couldn't support his weight, but I'd try. Careful to avoid his surgical incisions, I put my other hand around his waist. Vibrations came up through his torso from his shaking legs. "You're sure about this?"

"They can't force me to stay and undergo tests. We're leaving." He released the rail and swayed like a tree in the wind.

"Okay. You need some clothes." I gestured to the hospital gown.

"I'll see if I can get some clothes from the nurse," John volunteered and headed out of the room.

"You should have left me." Caleb glanced down.

I shook my head then pulled his knife from my pocket and snapped it open with ease. The muscle memory of playing with my dad's knife returned quickly. "Not a chance."

"What? No frying pans handy?" A ghost of a smile tweaked his lips. "You always were stubborn."

"It comes with the red hair."

John returned a few minutes later with a set of gray sweats and a nurse close behind.

She approached where Caleb perched on the edge of the bed. "What is this about you leaving?"

"I'm signing myself out." He stood and reached for the clothes, his arm shaking with the effort.

Struggling to keep us both upright, I steadied him, his torso pressed into my side. He regained his balance and leaned against the rail with the sweatpants in hand. With jerky movements, he got his legs into the pants and pulled them up underneath the hospital gown.

The nurse watched his progress then sighed. "I'll find the doctor."

He refused my help to put on the shirt, obviously trying to prove he was well enough to leave. It would take a lot more to convince me.

The doctor returned with the nurse and did his best to persuade Caleb to stay, listing the myriad of life-threatening complications, but, in the end, gave up and got the forms to leave against medical advice. By the time he signed the paperwork, Caleb could at least stand without help. The nurse insisted on wheeling him out in a wheelchair, which he agreed to under protest.

I glanced at the clock for the tenth time in as many minutes. We needed to get out of the hospital before Nansic figured out a new plan to kill us. They could arrive any moment.

We rolled past a security guard, and he followed us to the elevator, likely to cover the hospital from a potential lawsuit.

John offered to run ahead and pull the car around to the side entrance. Hopefully avoiding the main entrance would throw off anyone looking for us. That, plus Caleb checking out early, would be our only chance at slipping away if they were still watching the hospital.

We rode down the elevator in silence, the adrenaline in my bloodstream increasing with each floor we passed. By the time we reached the ground level my heart jackhammered around, bouncing off my ribs. The doors slid open, and the security officer walked out first. I peered out into the empty hallway like I was doing a bad spy impersonation.

I turned to the nurse's raised eyebrows and waved her forward. Outside the glass door, John parked his car illegally in a fire zone then jumped out and ran around to open the passenger door. The glass doors slid open, and the nurse pushed Caleb out to the waiting car.

"I'll help Caleb. Why don't you drive, Harper?" John threw me the keys.

I let out the breath I'd been holding and walked around to the driver's side. *Almost home free.* My muscles froze as a police cruiser pulled toward us. I barely resisted the urge to leap into the car, like a guilty person would do. We're the victims here, I told myself.

The police car pulled to a stop in front of John's car, blocking it from pulling forward. Two police officers got out and approached.

"Excuse me, Mr. Walker? The ICU said you'd checked out. We had a few questions for you," the officer said to Caleb.

"About the fire?" Caleb asked and gripped John's arm to help pull himself to a standing position.

The officer held up a hand. "That and a few other things."

They knew who he was. I tried to breathe but failed.

John and Caleb took one step toward the car when the first shot rang out.

The nurse looked around, startled, as if she didn't quite understand what was happening. Bullets pelted the open car door, which shielded John and Caleb. The passenger window shattered, glass spilling onto the ground. I dove into the car for cover and jammed the key into the ignition.

The officers ducked behind their own vehicle, and one returned fire while the other called for backup. Their car offered us some additional protection.

The security guard pulled the nurse down to the ground but not fast enough. She clutched her chest where multiple bullet holes ripped her shirt. The guard applied pressure to the wounds while he pulled his revolver. The return fire stopped the rain of bullets on us momentarily.

"Get in," I screamed to John and Caleb.

Caleb lurched into the passenger seat with John's help. As bullets started flying again, a gasp escaped John's lips. He stood outside the car door and stared down at his torso with wide eyes. Blood soaked the shirt over his chest and abdomen too quickly. He stumbled back then fell to his knees on the concrete a few feet from the car, his mouth gaping.

CHAPTER TWENTY-NINE

"Go," Caleb gasped as John dropped to the asphalt.

I froze, my gaze on the gruesome scene—John, the spreading blood, the nurse slumped against the security guard, her shirt stained crimson. A bullet whizzed past my window, its hum unmistakable.

"Go!" Caleb ordered.

I broke into action and slammed the car in reverse, flooring the gas so we peeled out of the loading area. Careening around a corner, we clipped a curb. I swung the car around in the opposite direction from where the bullets came from and slammed it into drive. Caleb bounced sideways in the seat, struggling to close the passenger door. It slammed shut and I focused on maneuvering out of the parking lot without hitting anything or anyone.

A bullet hit the trunk with a metallic *thunk*. A black SUV raced after us. Shots fired in our direction from the passenger side. A man's head and torso leaned out the window, an automatic weapon in his hand.

"Oh shit. Get down!" I yelled.

The police cruiser screeched around a corner alongside the SUV, gaining on the larger vehicle.

Bouncing over another curb, I swerved left out of the hospital parking lot, bullets peppering the back end of our car. We rounded the corner fifty feet ahead of the SUV just as the cruiser angled in front of the larger vehicle in the entrance of the parking lot. It careened to a stop in front of the SUV, blocking it from following us.

City traffic swallowed our car, and I slowed to avoid drawing attention. We passed more police vehicles, lights and sirens blaring, headed for the hospital. Caleb turned to watch out the back window for pursuit. "Take the next left then a couple more turns to throw off anyone tracking us."

"Do you see anyone?" I asked.

"No, but that doesn't mean they aren't watching." He motioned to the traffic cameras. "Get farther away from the major streets and we can fly under the radar."

I took the next several turns until we entered a much less busy part of Indianapolis that didn't have traffic cameras on the streetlights. Caleb faced forward. "I don't see anyone. For once, the police had perfect timing."

I shook my head, numb. "I can't believe I left him there."

"Harper, you had to leave him. The hospital is the best chance he has," Caleb said softly.

The cold chill of the still fresh grief for Ren and fear for John stole over me. "He wouldn't listen. I told him it wasn't safe to stay. Now he might be dead."

"It's not your fault."

I forced myself to focus on the road and steered around another turn. Large buildings gave way to apartment buildings and small businesses. "Where are we going? What are we going to do? We don't have any money."

"I don't know yet. Get farther out of the city and we'll find a place to hole up." He slumped into the seat, his face and lips pale.

CHAPTER THIRTY

Nelson family home
Indianapolis, Indiana

The smell of garlic and chicken greeted Dr. Nelson as he closed the front door. He breathed in the heavenly aroma, his mouth already watering. Setting his new briefcase and keys on the hall table, he walked into the kitchen and wrapped his arms around his wife's waist.

"Dinner smells fabulous." He nuzzled her neck.

She laughed. "You've been so stressed out over work I thought you could use a treat."

Dr. Nelson closed his eyes and rested his head on her shoulder while she browned the chicken in the cast iron pan. Tense muscles in his neck relaxed for the first time in what felt like weeks.

"You spoil me." He allowed himself to lean against her, warmth seeping into his tired body. "I'm sorry if I've been distracted. I'll make it up to you, somehow."

"Just as long as you promise me you won't miss Matthew's

trip to MIT." She squeezed his hand with her own. "Let me get this in the oven."

The doctor leaned against the kitchen island. On the counter to his left, a radio played a classical piece. The music spilled out of the speaker and flowed over him in a soothing wave. He turned up the volume and grabbed a sparkling water from the refrigerator while enjoying the symphony.

"Traffic through the city was terrible tonight," he said.

"Must have been because of the shooting at IU Health Hospital. They closed the area down for over an hour from what they said on the news."

Dr. Nelson swallowed the bubbly water, his relaxed muscles tightening. "Shooting?" The cell phone in his pocket buzzed.

"A drive-by, I guess, but not gang related," Isabel answered. "They have two men in custody."

Dr. Nelson clicked his screen and read the text from Marling. *Need you back at the office.* His stomach churned with what felt like razorblades.

"Honey? Did you hear me?" his wife asked. "Jeremy?"

Dr. Nelson set the bottle on the counter. "I'm sorry, dear, what did you say?"

Her brow pulled together and she reached out a hand to grip his arm. "Are you all right?"

He waved away her hand and straightened, forcing a smile. "I have to go back to the office."

"Right now?"

He strode to the doorway. "Don't hold dinner."

"But—"

Dr. Nelson drove the twenty minutes to Nansic headquarters in less than fifteen while he scanned the highlights of the shooting on his phone. The mug shots of the shooters sent his reflux into overdrive. He recognized the former military men working on Marling's special security team.

He rushed through the entryway, waving off the night guard's greeting and swiped his security card with shaking hands. Swearing at the slow elevator, he pushed past the opening doors, and strode down the hall and barged into Marling's large corner office without knocking.

Marling sat in his leather chair, scotch in hand, contemplating the view of the fields out his window.

"What the hell have you done?"

"Thank you for coming in," Marling said calmly. He swung the chair to face Nelson.

"The story is all over the news," Nelson pushed.

"We have bigger things to worry about. The idiots holding the brother screwed up. I'm trying to keep that story under wraps so we can use him to lure these two out." He slammed his crystal tumbler on the desk. Amber liquid splashed over the lip. "We need to find the sister and the fucking Delta Force asshole before they cause any more trouble."

"What about the mercenaries in police custody?" Nelson demanded. "What if they implicate us?"

"They know they'll be compensated for keeping quiet," Marling answered.

Nelson leaned across the desk. "A drive-by shooting in the middle of Indianapolis?"

Marling waved a dismissive hand. "Only because they somehow survived the explosion in Wabash."

The blood pressure in Nelson's head throbbed to the point of having an aneurism. "Explosion?" he shouted. "First you push human testing, then you insist on moving forward with production, now you're letting your thugs set explosives and kill people?"

Marling rose from his chair and pointed a finger in Nelson's face. "I'll do whatever it takes to protect everything we've built. A little redhead and a random soldier aren't going to jeopardize this company."

"This company or your share of the profits?"

Throwing back the scotch in his tumbler, Marling assumed a disdainful expression. "Get back in your lab, Doctor. Our timeline has moved up. You better have the DX-200 safety reports on my desk first thing in the morning."

CHAPTER THIRTY-ONE

I did my best to drive and keep an eye on Caleb at the same time. After a few blocks, his eyes drifted closed. I fought panic until the steady rise and fall of his chest reassured me.

Several miles later when the suburbs loomed on the horizon, I pulled into yet another motel. Caleb needed to rest in an actual bed, and I needed to think. I checked in and paid with cash I'd found in John's wallet in the center console of the sedan, then moved the car to the far corner of the parking lot in front of our room.

"Caleb, wake up." I gently shook his shoulder.

He jerked awake, eyes round, then relaxed when he took in our surroundings.

"I already got us a room." I held up the keys.

"Sorry, I didn't realize I passed out."

My worry over his condition increased when he accepted my help getting out of the car and into the room without protest. The moment his head hit the pillow, he was out again. I spent the night pacing, peeking out from behind the blinds, and checking Caleb's breathing, until the sun rose over the rooftops.

Thoughts of the possible complications of his injuries,

mercenaries breaking down the door, and how to get Will back, kept sleep a far distant dream. The reality of the situation hit me. We were barely keeping ourselves alive. We couldn't possibly find Will and save him unless something drastic changed.

I scrolled my phone for any news on John's condition. Our shootout was the lead story. My heart screeched to a halt when the story mentioned two fatalities. I scrolled down and saw a picture of the nurse who'd wheeled Caleb out. My breath came out a choked sob. A picture of the nurse and her family, a husband and two young children, showed under the ID photo.

The rustling of sheets and coughing alerted me that Caleb was awake. He looked over my shoulder, gripping it.

"She's dead because of us," I sobbed. "Her kids lost their mother"

"You didn't kill her. Nansic killed her," Caleb said.

The police hadn't released the identity of the other victim, an unidentified male. It was John.

"We left him there," I whispered. "He left his wallet in the car. They don't even know who he is."

Caleb turned me into his arms. "It was the only thing we could do. His only chance."

"We need to call Professor March. She would know how to get ahold of his family," I whispered.

"Let me take care of it," Caleb said.

I left the room under the pretext of getting him food, but really, I just couldn't listen to the conversation. With the hood of the sweatshirt covering my hair, I walked on autopilot a block over to a diner to get breakfast, my mind occupied with how to stop Nansic.

I waited for the takeout in the diner, keeping my hood up and head down to avoid anyone recognizing me. The television at the end of the counter was on but the volume was too low to hear. The hostess walked out of the kitchen with our food in a bag. I stood to accept it when Will's face on the television screen froze my hands in mid-reach.

His military photo filled the screen.

"Can you turn that up? Please?" I gasped.

The hostess's brow drew together but the sheer desperation in my voice stopped any questions. She grabbed the remote.

"...missing for the last week has been found. The remains, identified by the dog tags, were discovered in a burned-out building early this morning."

Rushing blood filled my ears, drowning out the rest of the news anchor's words. The world spun around me like an amusement park ride and I lurched sideways, collapsing into a chair. The hostess's concerned face floated in front of my eyes, her lips moving, but no sound penetrated my brain.

Blackness crept in on the corners of my vision and I leaned against the wall. Hands gripped my shoulders. Another face appeared before mine, a man this time. Fingers pressed against my wrist. More hands guided my torso horizontal across the row of chairs. I stared up at the ceiling, gasping for air.

The roaring in my ears receded, and questions penetrated my haze. The words *ambulance* and *police* drove away enough of the shock to at least respond.

"No." I pushed myself up onto my elbows and waved away any help. "I'm okay."

"Take it slow. Your heart rate is close to two hundred," the man who'd been taking my pulse said.

I sat up and gripped the side of the chair. "I'm fine now."

They backed up. "Is there someone we can call for you?"

"No. Thank you," I said, the strain still evident in my voice. I rubbed my hand over my eyes and looked back at the television. The screen showed the weather forecast. I lurched to my feet.

"Whoa, take it slow. Why don't you wait for the paramedics to check you out?" the man asked.

I shook my head and stepped toward the door. I'd already drawn too much attention to myself.

"Wait," the hostess, who was still on the phone with emergency dispatch, called after me. "Your food."

Numb hands grabbed the to-go bag and I hurried out the door. I didn't remember the walk back to the hotel. Suddenly, I was standing in front of the door fumbling with the key, unable to unlock the bolt. The door flew open, and Caleb stood in front of me.

Our eyes met and I saw my own torturous pain reflected. He'd seen.

I threw myself against his chest, pent-up sobs breaking free.

CHAPTER THIRTY-TWO

Caleb sat on the bed, his back to me while he watched the television screen, the volume low. I blinked sleep from my eyes and rolled over. Throbbing erupted in my head. My brain reoriented and the memories flooding back—Will's picture on the news, Caleb holding me through violent sobs, laying down to rest.

My movement caused Caleb to turn and face me. "You're awake. How are you feeling?"

"How long was I asleep?" The pounding in my head made me squint my eyes at the light coming through the curtains.

"About six hours," he responded, coughing. The color was returning slowly to his pale cheeks.

I sat up. "You should've woken me."

"Why? You needed to sleep."

"I need to...I mean, we should..." I paused. With Will dead there was no time constraint, no rush to save him. The reality hit me. Will was dead. I waited for the fear and anxiety that had ruled my life for the last ten years to paralyze me. But my worst fear had already come true. Will was gone.

Instead, pure fury flooded my brain.

"I'm sure they already notified your mom, or they wouldn't have released his name to the media, but do you want to call her?" he asked.

I threw the covers back and set my feet on the floor. "No. She warned me not to contact her. Nansic would definitely have her phones tapped to trace if we call. I mean, I want to talk to her, to see her, but we'd just be putting her in danger."

"Okay." He eyed me for a moment, watching.

"I'm going to take a shower," I said, suddenly aware of my own grime, never completely washed off from the fire.

"Do you need any help?" he asked. At my raised eyebrows, he continued. "No, I just mean I didn't know if you were feeling up to it."

His calm voice and body language reminded me of a zookeeper in a cage with an unpredictable animal. It dawned on me he was waiting for me to fall apart again. I let out a sigh.

"I'll call you if I need anything." I closed the bathroom door behind me.

The shower washed away the soot as well as the tears flowing down my face. But these tears weren't of fear or despair. Instead, a white-hot rage burned through my brain, along all the neural pathways anxiety once flowed, and spilled out as tears. The rage raced through my muscles, filling them with pent-up energy begging to be violently released on the people responsible for taking my brother and Ren. This must have been how Will felt when our dad was killed.

Nansic had to be stopped.

I dried off and cringed at putting on the same dirty gray sweats. A knock at the door stopped me as I slid one leg into the pants.

"Yeah?" I called though the door.

"I found a bag of clothes in John's car. I thought you might like something clean."

My throat closed at the thought of wearing John's clothes. I blinked and reined in the emotion. He'd have wanted me to use them. I cracked the door wide enough to accept the folded garments. "Thanks."

The flannel fit except for straining across my chest, and I cuffed the jeans, but John wasn't too much bigger than me so they worked. At least they were clean. Too bad there wasn't a clean bra in the bag. I washed my now pathetically stained lace one and hung it on the rod.

The TV screen clicked off when I walked into the room.

Caleb's gaze swept over me, sticking on the fabric pulled tight over my breasts. He yanked his gaze to my face, blinking.

I watched red seep up from his neck and spread over his cheeks and crossed my arms over my unsupported chest.

"Anything more on the news?"

"Nothing important," Caleb answered, covering his mouth as he coughed again. He was acting stronger than he felt. Putting on a façade for me.

"Caleb, I'm not going to break," I said and held out my hand for the remote. He handed it to me and wisely remained silent. I clicked on the news. The tail end of the story played.

"Military officials have not determined the cause of the fire, but arson is suspected. The soldier, William Bradley the Fourth, as well as two other unidentified victims, will be autopsied when the remains have returned to the United States."

Anger compressed my jaw and ground my molars together. I clicked off the television. "We're going to make them pay. Things are going to get messy."

CHAPTER THIRTY-THREE

Nelson family home
   Indianapolis, Indiana

Dr. Nelson set the tumbler of gin on his desk in his home office and fished the ringing phone from his pocket. The number from his lab lit up the screen. He stared at the cell for several seconds while debating on answering it.

"Don't answer that," his wife said from the doorway, her arms crossed over her chest. "You are not going back in to work."

He met her gaze and sighed. "I have to answer. I left Jim to make observations. There might be an emergency."

Her lips puckered while he hit the green button and put the phone to his ear. "Yes?"

"I think you might want to see this, Doctor," Jim said.

"What is it?"

"The rats have reached the last stage of deterioration," Jim answered. "They can't eat, drink or walk."

"Already?" Nelson sat up and reached for his briefcase. "They were fine when I left."

"The effects seem to have been delayed, not stopped. They've gone down faster than the previous tests."

Nelson stood and started for the door, past his wife's glare. "I'll be right there."

CHAPTER THIRTY-FOUR

We sat outside the doctor's house in the beater Caleb had bartered for. His watch and knife were gone, but he'd insisted there was no choice. Being involved in a drive-by put John's sedan on the top of the police watch lists. Not to mention a car riddled with bullet holes tended to draw unwanted attention. Plus, he'd traded for our other requirement. A gun.

A spring poked through the hole in my seat, jabbing into my back. We'd rolled the windows down despite the chill to alleviate some of the cigarette-and-god-knows-what-else smell. At least the engine ran.

Tapping the keys of John's laptop, which Caleb found in the trunk along with the bag of clothes, I checked for any new information on the investigation into Will's death. Nothing.

We'd been camped out across from the doctor's house for hours, waiting for our chance. I closed the laptop and rubbed my eyes. "It doesn't look like we're going to catch him at home without the wife and kids."

Caleb pointed his chin toward the house. "The garage door is opening."

The doctor's Lexus pulled out with a single occupant in the

driver's seat. We hunched down in our seats as the car's headlights lit up the inside of our car and waited until the doctor drove past. I turned the key in the ignition and followed at a respectable distance.

"Where the hell is he going at ten PM?" I wondered aloud.

We followed the Lexus through downtown Indianapolis, my chest growing tighter with every turn. We rounded the corner and drove up the now familiar street to Nansic headquarters.

"Does this guy do anything but work?" Caleb ranted while he scanned the parking lot for security cameras. "Looks like we're going to have to do this here."

I pulled into a space a couple of aisles over from Dr. Nelson's assigned spot and in the shadow cast by a tree in front of the lot lights. We jumped out of the car, easing the doors closed and approached the Lexus from behind. The doctor got out of his car and Caleb pulled his gun from his waistband.

Caleb rushed the doctor, with me close behind, and slammed the man up against the side of the car before he ever saw us coming.

With the gun pressed to the doctor's temple and his hand over the shocked man's mouth, Caleb leaned in. "Hello, Dr. Nelson. You're going to come with us without any trouble or this is going to get ugly. Give me your car keys."

The doctor nodded, understanding, and dropped the keys in Caleb's palm then held his hands up in surrender.

With the back door open, Caleb shoved the doctor in the center of the backseat of the Lexus and tossed me the keys, then climbed in. I scrambled into the driver's seat. The engine purred to life and I drove us out of the lot and into downtown Indianapolis.

Behind me, Caleb kept the gun trained on the doctor. "Pull over on this side street."

I pulled the car to the curb but didn't turn in my seat to face the doctor. Instead, I glared into the rearview mirror. The rage inside me focused on the balding man and I restrained myself from climbing over the seat to choke the life from him with my own hands.

"You killed my brother." My voice came out as a harsh whisper.

"No, I had nothing to do with that," he exclaimed. "Marling was in charge of everything overseas."

"So, you killed Ren," I growled.

"Who? I mean, no," he stammered.

My eyes narrowed and met his in the mirror.

"You mean the hacker? I…" He fell silent.

My hands fisted in my lap.

"We know about the DX-200. And the experiments on the soldiers and prisoners in the state pen. You've poisoned the food in the prison and on base," Caleb said. "You're going to give us what we need to take down Nansic."

"I can't." He held his hands up again.

"Okay. We can start with shooting your knees." I turned to look him in the eye. "That's nothing compared to what they did to Will."

"No, you don't understand. Everything is on an internal server. I can't bring anything out of the building," he clamored. "I can't get you any proof."

Caleb pressed the muzzle of the gun to Nelson's knee. "You brought home paper before."

"That was before you broke into my house. Now, Marling has his men go through everyone's belongings before they leave the building. I can't even take a stapler home."

I closed my eyes and swore under my breath. "Okay. Then you testify to what you know."

"That won't accomplish anything besides getting me and my family killed," Nelson exclaimed.

I leaned halfway into the back seat, crowding the doctor's space. "I don't think you understand the problem you've created with your little science project, Doctor."

He sat back. "I've taken care of the rage problem, but I can't solve the long-term effects. I've delayed the onset of the brain deterioration, but the outcomes are amplified now. That's what I was coming back to check. You have to believe me. I've told them but the company doesn't care. I sent memos with all the research, all the results and problems, to everyone involved and they only care about profits."

"It's not just humans we're talking about. Animals are experiencing the same side effects after exposure." I pulled up the most recent article about the geese in Wabash and handed him the computer.

He deflated like a leaking balloon. "This entire thing has gotten out of hand," Nelson confessed. "I'm a researcher. I never wanted to hurt anyone."

He was either an amazing actor or completely sincere. I still couldn't be sure which was the case.

"If that's true, tell us what we need to know," Caleb pressed.

"It won't matter," Nelson insisted. "This goes all the way to Washington D.C. We're paying off politicians to get the military contracts for testing. These are powerful people. They'll never let it get out."

"If the public knew what was happening, they wouldn't stand for it. Government officials aren't above the law," I said.

He shook his head and I swore I saw a glimmer of something in his eyes before a mask of sadness enveloped his features. "I admire your optimism. Unfortunately, that's not the way it works anymore."

"You tell us what we need to know and let us worry about how to take the company down," Caleb demanded.

Nelson seemed to examine Caleb, really taking him in.

"You're sure you can stop production and take down the company?"

"I'll take them out or die," Caleb responded without blinking.

Nelson leaned back and rested his head against the seat, seeming to have come to some kind of decision. "Fine. I can't be a party to this mess anymore, but you have to leave me out of it. They'll kill my family."

"Unlike you, we aren't murderers." I cocked my head to the side. "We don't want to see anyone else get hurt."

"You're going to have to hurry. They'll find you. And Marling has pushed DX-200 into production," Nelson said. "In a matter of months, it could be sprayed on crops across the world."

We drove Nelson back to the parking lot at Nansic after liberating his cash from his wallet to help our pathetic financial situation. His couple hundred dollars would at least pay for the motel for a week.

Being careful to check for security, we parked the Lexus and picked up our car.

"How can they not care that billions of people and animals will lose their minds over the next thirty or forty years because of their pesticide?" I asked incredulously.

"With the delay in symptom onset, it would be hard to find the source," Caleb said. He released the latch to recline the passenger seat.

I glanced over at his pale face. His usually vibrant blue eyes were dim with exhaustion. "Are you all right?"

He nodded. "Just tired."

His force and presence made it hard to believe he'd been

dead for several minutes, mere days before. Now he was paying the price for the false bravado he'd shown the doctor. Worry over the possibility he'd had a stroke had spurred on an hour of research on what to watch for. So far, I hadn't seen any of the red flags, but I couldn't put the possibility out of my mind.

"You need to rest."

He put a hand over mine on the steering wheel. "I'm fine, Harper. We have more important things to think about."

My gaze focused on his hand over mine for a moment. Except for after we got the news of Will's death, we hadn't touched.

With a last squeeze, he pulled his hand away and closed his eyes. I drove to the motel, a semblance of a plan forming in my mind by the time we arrived.

The next morning, Caleb gasped as he leaned over to make the bed.

"Don't make the bed. Lie down on the bed," I ordered. "I'll go out and get you some food and clean clothes."

He raised his eyebrows.

"If we're going to have a chance at stopping these bastards, you need to be healthy. So, lie down and rest." I didn't mention his trembling hands or shaking legs. No need to bruise his male ego.

With a shake of his head, he acquiesced. His soft snores followed me out the door. I dialed the professor's cell phone after I got into the car.

She answered on the second ring. "Harper? Are you guys okay? What's going on?"

"We're safe for now, Professor," I said. "I'm sorry to ask anything else of you, but..."

"You have nothing to be sorry for. Believe me, I want this company to pay for what they did to John. What do you need?"

"I was hoping you might know someone who can help us," I said and explained what I had in mind.

After hanging up with the professor, I sat and stared at the phone for several minutes. My fingers itched to dial my mom's cell number. She had to be beside herself with losing Will. Guilt over adding to her upset twisted my heart. I snapped the phone shut.

I got back to the motel, food in hand, as well as a bag of new jeans, shirts and underwear. Picking out underwear for Caleb was...interesting...but necessary since John's travel bag didn't have anything to fit Caleb's much larger frame, and the gray sweats were taking on a brownish hue.

I opened the door. Caleb was nowhere in the closet-sized room. I froze until the sound of the shower relaxed my muscles. I set the food on the table and opened John's computer, pulling up the chair.

Ten minutes later, the water shut off. Caleb came out of the bathroom, a towel wrapped around his waist a not-so-large motel towel that left part of one thigh and hip exposed as well as three quarters of his legs. He knotted the scrap of fabric at one side and leaned over my chair, both hands on the table.

I blinked and forced myself to turn and not think what would happen if the towel slipped. Heat thrummed through my veins. Flashes of our kiss played through my mind on repeat. Maybe the towel slipping would be a good thing. I bit my lip to hold in a sigh.

"What are you looking at?" he asked, his attention on the computer screen and oblivious to the discomfort his near nakedness caused me. *Yet he can't handle seeing my bra and panties.*

I swallowed and yanked my gaze from his body before I

answered, "I was just doing some research on, um, stuff." I glanced sideways and my eyes got caught up on the view of his lean waist, abs and the light trail of hair leading lower.

"You good?" he asked, a smile playing at the edges of his lips.

Flustered, I snapped my gaze to his face. He straightened with a grimace and raised one annoying eyebrow.

"I wasn't sure if you like briefs or boxers. So, I went with boxer-briefs." I said the first thing that came to mind and grabbed the bag of clothes, tossing it his way. "Hope everything fits."

"Thanks. Anything would be better than those sweats at this point." He took the bag into the bathroom.

A smirk spread over my lips while I waited for a reaction. Mere seconds later I got it.

"Seriously?" he called.

"There wasn't a lot to choose from."

He walked out of the bathroom in a shirt with a pair of boxer-briefs hugging his thighs and hips. The gray T-shirt sported the saying 'I Don't Need Sex', in bold lettering, then in smaller print, 'The Government Fucks Me Every Week.' The fabric clung to his shoulders and arms like shrink-wrap, straining across his pecs. He held out the other shirt I bought with a glittery pink unicorn on the front. "You're telling me these were the only options?"

"It was that or 'I think I might be pregnant'," I said, holding back a giggle.

He shook his head and returned to the bathroom. "That would have been better than a freaking unicorn."

"I guess fashion trends are different in Indiana," I said with a snort and leaned on the table, pent up tension spilling out of me as gasping laughter.

"Maybe you should shop somewhere besides a thrift store," he shot back.

"Hey, within our budget there wasn't a lot to choose from."

"I should be grateful you didn't get me pink bedazzled jeans." Buttoning the jeans, he walked out and shook his head, his expression softening as he watched me regain control. "As long as you're enjoying yourself."

"There would have been a better selection if you didn't have such wide shoulders."

"I'll keep that in mind." He ripped off the tag and glanced at the clearance sticker. "I can see why they were fifty cents."

I handed him the takeout burger and fries and a bottle of water. The laughter faded into uncomfortable silence, and I busied myself with my food. Just as I chewed the last bite of my burger, the phone buzzed in my pocket.

"It's the professor," I said and answered.

Caleb listened to my end of the conversation until I hung up.

"It's all set up. We need to leave now," I said.

CHAPTER THIRTY-FIVE

I rolled down the window in the car, unable to stand the noxious odor anymore. "I seriously think someone died in this car."

"Nah, it's just puke and cigarettes," Caleb answered from the back seat, rubbing his arms against the cold air. His body was recovering, but the temperature was getting to him. I sighed and rolled the window back up.

He pulled the ball cap lower on his head to hide his features.

"I don't think anyone is going to recognize you with that shaggy face," I teased.

"Better to be safe than sorry," he answered. "Are you sure we can trust this guy?"

"I looked him up. He's the real thing. He's gone to jail to protect his sources in the past. Plus, he's been published in every major news outlet and has a reputation for breaking tough stories."

"Let's hope he's willing to do that again."

A car pulled up behind us. Caleb eased his gun from his waistband. I heard the soft click of the safety being switched off. A single figure exited the sedan and approached our car on the passenger side. I rolled down the window from the driver's side controls.

"Harper?" the man leaned down and asked.

"Yes. Mr. Webber?" I responded even though I recognized his features from his profile picture.

He nodded.

"Get in." I motioned to the empty passenger seat.

He climbed in. His nose wrinkled when the stench hit him.

"You're sure you weren't followed?" Caleb asked from the back seat.

"I took every precaution. Professor March gave me some basics of your situation, so I understand the danger. Tell me what I can do to help you."

I turned in my seat and launched into the events of the last week, which seemed like a year, in retrospect. I explained Will's call and disappearance, the connection with Nansic and the violent behaviors in soldiers. When I got to the prison, I showed him the video the warden gave us. Then I explained the tests with the chemical from the fields and the one affecting the geese, as well as Dr. Nelson and the confirmation he'd given.

"Anyone near us is in danger so you need to be careful who you share details of the story with," I cautioned after I'd finished.

He nodded while he jotted handwritten notes. "If the corruption goes up as high as you think, then yeah, I'd say we need to be extremely cautious. Don't worry, I'd only share the story with my editor, not even she knows my sources. This Dr. Nelson, he's willing to talk?"

"He needs assurance you won't use his name. He's worried about his family's safety." Caleb spoke for the first time in several minutes.

"I'll die before I reveal a source." Webber met his gaze and held it.

"I hope you mean it, because that's exactly what this may come to," Caleb warned.

"We'll need the doctor to corroborate all of this. Internal documents would be irrefutable evidence they knew the effects of this pesticide and continued with production. Without that we're building a circumstantial case," Webber said.

"But you're willing to write the story?" I asked, gripping my phone in my hand while I held my breath.

Webber ran a hand through his salt and pepper hair. "This is a tremendous story. The story of a lifetime. You bet I'll write it."

I released the breath and handed over a copy of the flash drive from the prison. "I'll send you the pictures I took of the printouts we took from the doctor. The originals burned in the explosion. The professor said she would have more results within a day from the examination of the dead geese and Caleb's tissues. That should give you more proof."

He shook his head. "They can still deny knowledge of the delayed dementia. They can say they fixed the anger problem and didn't know there were any further side effects of ingestion. You said yourself the doctor didn't know about the geese."

"What about trying to kill us? Killing John and Ren?" I demanded. "If the mercenaries in custody will talk, they can link the company to murder."

"I doubt they'll cooperate, but I'll try to get an interview with them. See if I can persuade them to link Marling to the orders," he said. He switched off the digital recorder and gathered his notes. "Give me a day. Meet me back here at the same time."

Caleb threw the deadbolt home behind us. I scanned the small motel room and sighed. The tension in my muscles refused to relax. I'd expected some type of relief after our meeting with the journalist. The responsibility was now his to get the story public so Nansic would pay for their crimes. Instead of relief, I was more nervous with nothing to keep me busy.

"So, I guess now we wait?" I sat on the bed then stood and began pacing.

Caleb's rough hand caught my arm. He pulled me to a stop. "This is going to be a long twenty-four hours if you're pacing the entire time."

I glanced down at his fingers, wrapped around my forearm, then back up to meet his gaze. "I can't stand waiting. It bugs me."

"They're going to pay. You should be proud of yourself," he murmured.

"We should be proud," I corrected. "I would've been dead last week without you."

He stepped closer and wrapped his arms around my torso. "You saved my ass, too. I'd say we're even."

My arms returned the hug, seemingly of their own accord. His peppery sage smell hit me, making me want to rub my face in his shirt.

"I can't believe you ran into a burning building to find me," he said, his breath on the top of my head. "I don't remember if I ever thanked you."

The image of Caleb without a pulse on the hospital gurney flashed in my mind, thickening my throat. "When I thought I'd lost you... I—there were so many things I never got to tell you."

"I'm still here. You can tell me now," he whispered.

I love you. The words begged to jump off my tongue. I tilted my head up and found his face inches from my own. We stared at each other, neither speaking, for several long moments. I blinked first, memories fresh from the last time I'd kissed him and been rejected, then slanted my eyes to the floor.

His finger angled my head back up to meet his gaze. The heat I saw there ignited the flames I'd tried so hard to snuff out over the past few days.

His arm constricted and pressed my body against his. "Harper, I'm so sorry. If I'd been over there with him—"

"Shhh." I put a finger over his lips to stop his sentence. "It's not your fault." Nervous tension melted into liquid heat. All that mattered was Caleb being here, with me, now.

"Maybe I could have done something," he choked out.

I glided my hand up over his chest, then higher and ran my fingernails over the skin where his skull met his neck. His eyes half closed and he groaned low in his throat. His tense muscles softened under my touch.

Releasing me, he cradled my face between his hands and slowly guided my lips to his for a gentle kiss.

"What about your guy code?" I asked, then wished I could stuff the words back in my mouth.

"I tried." He hung his head. "I tried not to care about you, to see you as the kid I left behind." He met my gaze again. "But it isn't working so well."

I didn't need any more. I leaned up on my tiptoes to reach his mouth and pressed my lips over his. His hand came up to my neck and cradled my head while our lips danced together. I sank into him and our connection snapped into place. Where it should have been all these years.

He lifted me like a feather, and I wrapped my legs around him. We lay on the bed then he dove back into kissing me. I ran my palms over the muscles of his arms surrounding me. For the first time in forever, a sense of peace, of rightness, filled me.

CHAPTER THIRTY-SIX

I woke from a deep dreamless sleep, encased in male heat. Caleb's arm tightened around me, pressing me into his chest. I rolled over to face him and snuggled my face into his neck. We'd stayed up late talking about stupid stuff, everything from my favorite flowers, daisies, to his secret favorite TV show, Buffy the Vampire Slayer. I was sworn to secrecy never to let his squad find out.

His breath quickened and he tilted my chin up to catch my lips with his.

"Did you sleep well?" he asked after he broke away.

I nodded into his chest. "The best I've slept in a long time. How about you?"

"I slept great. You didn't even kick or hit me this time."

"You never told me I hit you," I exclaimed, looking up to his face.

He grinned. "It's okay. You didn't hit anywhere important."

I shook my head and pushed off him to roll over and sit on the edge of the bed.

"Where are you going?" he asked.

"We can't stay in bed all day. Besides, I need a shower."

After a long shower, I emerged scrubbed pink and smiling. While Caleb got dressed, I opened the computer and found a message from the professor to my new email account, one Nansic wouldn't be watching.

The results from the goose autopsies were in. I skipped the science talk, which might as well have been in French, and stopped at the pictures and notes Professor March attached on the end. Even I could spot the abnormalities with the gaping holes in the tissues. Plus, it matched up with what the doctor told us about continued side effects he'd seen in the rat tests.

The note explained that the nerve cells were dying because of chemicals disrupting the normal activity in the nucleus of the neuron, causing cell death resulting in sections of the brain dying, similar to dementia. That explained why the geese were losing the ability to swim and feed as the symptoms of exposure to the chemical progressed.

I bit my lip and pushed away the thought of Caleb ending up like the geese if he was indeed exposed.

I made a mental note to ask Dr. Nelson if there was any way to know which soldiers on the base ate the DX-200 treated food. *Caleb might not even have been on base when the tests started.*

"You know, I think rainbow might be my new favorite color," Caleb said, walking out of the bathroom and striking a ridiculous pose with one arm up in the air and his hip thrust to the side.

Stopping the *what if* merry-go-round from starting in my brain, I stuffed the worry away and focused on the moment in front of me. I couldn't help but snicker as he strutted around in the sparkly unicorn T-shirt, the only clean one left. He reminded me of the never-serious guy I'd grown up with.

He lifted one eyebrow in my direction. I launched a pillow at his face. My aim was on. He recovered and pulled back his arm as his phone chimed.

Our eyes met, and playfulness morphed to tension on two rings of the cell.

"Is it Webber?" I asked.

The pillow dropped, forgotten, from his hand and he leaned over to check the phone. "Yeah, he wants to meet early."

"Webber will print his article and that will be the end of the company," I said with more conviction than I felt while we drove to the parking garage.

Caleb nodded and glanced at his watch. He checked his rearview mirror for the hundredth time before he turned off the busy street into the garage. We stopped at the machine, got our parking pass, and waited as the wooden bar rose to let us pass. As before, the lot was nearly empty at this time of day. Caleb pulled through one of the many empty spots in the center lane of the second level and we waited.

Webber's car pulled in a few spots over. The journalist rushed from his car to ours. I turned in the passenger seat to face him. A band clamped tight on my chest. He didn't look happy.

"What's wrong?" Caleb asked.

"My editor shut down the story," Webber answered.

My brow pulled together while my intestines tied into a Celtic knot of organs. "What do you mean? Does she want more proof?"

Webber shook his head. "No, it doesn't matter how much proof we give her. She won't touch it."

"So, we take it to a different editor," Caleb said.

"You don't understand. This came down from high up, the owners of the media outlet shut it down. No one will touch a story about Nansic. No journalist, no newspaper, no television channel. I'm sorry, but there's nothing I can do." Webber rested his head on the seat and closed his eyes.

"There must be something. Someone who will publish it," I protested.

His eyes shot open. "No one. Whatever the higher-ups threatened my editor with it was bad. I've never seen her back off from a story."

Caleb straightened. "The owners of the media outlet shut it down? You weren't supposed to tell anyone but your editor about the story."

"I don't know how they found out. All I know is my editor was on board and as excited about the story as I was until she got a call from the higher-ups."

"This feels wrong." Caleb said and checked the mirrors then scanned the near-empty garage. "You're sure you weren't followed?"

Webber leaned forward, peering around the garage. "I took every precaution. Like I always do."

"We should get out of here. I've got a bad feeling about this," Caleb said.

Webber opened his door and stepped out and backed toward his car. "I'm sorry I can't help."

The sound of screeching tires stopped him short. Two black SUVs sped toward where we were parked from opposite directions. Webber turned and ran, his eyes wide.

CHAPTER THIRTY-SEVEN

I wanted to look away, shield myself from the certainty of a scene like my nightmares, but I couldn't. My hands tightened to fists as I bit back a scream.

The SUV barreled down on Webber from behind. The journalist stumbled and pitched forward, catching himself at the last moment before he fell to the ground. He recovered enough to make a desperate leap to the side of a concrete column. The bumper glanced off the concrete, taking out a sizable chunk but missing the reporter.

The first SUV screeched to a stop in front of us. Caleb slammed our car into reverse and floored the gas before the second vehicle could pull in behind to block us in.

Smoke wafted up from the tires as Caleb whipped the car in a ninety-degree turn and pulled ahead of the SUV, driving backward. With one hand on the steering wheel, his torso twisted in the seat to look out the back window and steer down the narrow lane of the parking garage.

Short gasps of breaths burst from my lungs and spots dotted my vision. Blacking out would distract Caleb. Forget the 4-7-8 breathing. The technique was somewhat lacking, in mercenaries-out-to-kill-you scenarios.

The mercenary in the passenger seat held a gun out the window, trained on our car. He had a clear shot into the entire front seat.

"Look out," I yelled, pointing at our pursuers a mere ten feet from the front bumper. There was nowhere to hide. My blood froze in my chest while I waited for the bullets that would kill us.

Caleb gripped the back of my seat, his eyes on the lane we barreled down. "Hold on."

He twisted the wheel as the first bullet left the barrel of the merc's gun. Our car whipped sideways around the one-eighty turn, tires squealing, screaming mere inches from the concrete pillars and parked cars.

The windshield exploded. Square chunks of safety glass peppered us from several fist-sized holes. Fire raced through my shoulder, like a burning blade ripped through my flesh. I gasped, my breath stolen by the pain. I pressed my hand over the wound out of reflex.

Blood seeped out around my fingers and oozed in rivulets down my torso. If the bullet hit any major blood vessels, well, pressure would only put off the inevitable.

Caleb straightened the car and floored it down the ramp. My body slammed into the door sending a fresh jolt of agony through my shoulder. I gripped the handle to steady myself. Caleb gained some ground around the corner, the compact car being more maneuverable than the bulky vehicle. But we were still well within firing range.

The passenger recovered from the turns and lifted his weapon to fire again.

"Caleb," I gasped. "Go faster."

"Hold on," he said again and jerked the wheel sideways.

Darkness crept into my vision and I sank deeper into the seat, unable to withstand the pressure of the turn. We barreled down the ramp.

"We're almost out."

I twisted my head and saw the street racing toward us. Cars drove steadily in both directions. We broke through the wooden gate, not slowing for the stop sign, and into traffic.

I closed my eyes and braced for the impact of oncoming cars. Caleb jerked the handle of the emergency brake and we spun through the intersection. My body pressed into the seat. The sound of horns and screeching tires blared from every direction.

The car jerked to a halt then Caleb accelerated, forward this time. I dared to open my eyes. We sped down the street, weaving through traffic. A glance behind confirmed the mercenaries had made it through the intersection unscathed.

I looked forward and immediately regretted it. The traffic in both lanes slowed at a yellow light. Instead of braking, Caleb sped up.

"Caleb?" My grip tightened on the door handle.

The light turned red, and Caleb swerved into the oncoming lane.

"Caleb?" I said again, my voice a squeak.

His fingers tightened around the wheel. "Hold on."

"You keep saying that," I yelled.

We entered the intersection. Cars closed in on us from both sides. Caleb veered left then right to avoid the oncoming cars and swerved back into our lane out of the intersection. Behind us came the sound of a thunderous crash. The SUV careened sideways, T-boned, and pushed in front of a brown delivery truck.

A gasp exploded from my chest. Caleb took his foot off the gas and we slowed to a less life-threatening speed.

He took two random turns and blended in with traffic as much as the Swiss cheese that was left of our car would allow. We drove in silence, dealing with our own shock. I rested my head against the seat, unable to hold it up any longer.

"That was close," Caleb said, glancing sideways. "Harper? What's wrong?"

I took my hand away from the bullet wound in my shoulder. Blood covered the entire surface. My shirt dripped crimson down to my waist. Lots of blood. Too much blood.

"You're shot," he gasped. "I have to get you to a hospital."

"No," I exclaimed. "They would find us for sure. You'll have to patch me up."

"But—" he started.

I met his gaze. "Caleb, you've had training. We can't risk a hospital."

His lips pressed together, and he returned his attention to the road, steering with new purpose. I tried to keep my eyes open, but blackness crept into the edges of my vision.

Then I was in Caleb's arms being carried through the door to our motel room.

He laid me on the bed like I would break. Even the slight pressure on my shoulder sent fresh waves of agony through my body. I bit my lip to stifle my cry. He rushed to our stash of first aid supplies.

I blinked several times to focus.

Ripping through the supplies and tossing things to the side, Caleb muttered to himself then gathered up the packages in his arms and brought them to the bed. He dropped the lot next to me, still muttering, and began tearing open packages.

"This is going to hurt," Caleb said and gripped my shirt. "We need to make sure the bullet is out."

I nodded, thankful he was a medic on his Special Forces team.

In one fast movement, he ripped the fabric, tearing the shirt in two, exposing my shoulder. Two inches below my collar bone blood oozed from the bullet hole.

"I'm going to roll you to see if there's an exit wound. Ready?"

I clenched my teeth then nodded.

Supporting my arm with one hand, he rolled me onto my side.

I gasped against the pain until he laid me back flat on the bed.

"There's no exit wound."

Even I knew that was bad.

He covered his face with his hands then ran them through his hair. "I'm going to have to get a few more things." With his lips pressed together, he checked his wallet for our pathetic cash supply then returned it to his pocket before leaning over me. There was no way we had enough money. He pressed sterile bandages to the wound and put my hand over it. "Hold this here until I get back."

I pressed on the wound until I wanted to scream.

At the door, he paused and turned back to meet my gaze. "I won't be gone long."

The door closed behind him. Cold crept over my skin that had nothing to do with the temperature in the room. I stared at the ceiling and focused on breathing in and out. My eyelids sagged and I pressed the bandage harder to keep myself alert.

Minutes crept by. My arm sagged, too heavy to hold up any longer. Blood soaked through the sterile pad, the dried patches sticking to my fingers. Weights pulled my eyelids shut. I felt my hand slip but couldn't hold it up any longer. The tickle of the blood running over my skin barely penetrated my brain. Blackness washed over me like motor oil, thick and heavy.

The only thing keeping blood pumping through my veins was the pressure on the wound, but I couldn't bring myself to care anymore. I sank into death and let go.

CHAPTER THIRTY-EIGHT

Searing pain in my shoulder dragged me back. I opened my eyes. Caleb's face hovered over me.

"Hold on, Harper. I've almost got the bullet." His free hand gripped my shoulder, steadying it. Metal forceps dug deeper into my flesh. "Try to hold still."

I couldn't have screamed if I wanted to. Agony stole the oxygen from my lungs. I could only gasp and grip the bedspread with my free hand. I tried to focus on anything but the pain—the scratchy bedspread beneath me, the ugly curtains, the steady sound of traffic from the street. No coping mechanism was a match for the anguish.

Metal scraped metal inside my shoulder.

"Damn it," Caleb swore. He repositioned the forceps, sending fresh hell through my torso.

"There it is." He withdrew the forceps a centimeter at a time until the bloody tips hovered over my skin, bullet squeezed between them. I lifted my head to see the slug. A droplet of my blood slid from the copper tip and spattered on my skin. My head dropped to the bed. I fought to stay conscious.

"Try to hold on a little longer. I'm going to clean this up and put in a couple stitches," Caleb said and dropped the bullet on a gauze pad. "Ready?"

"Go for it," I managed. The cold of the antiseptic washed over the raw wound like icy fire. I tensed but held still while Caleb mopped up the excess liquid in smooth gentle motions. Moments later, the needle pierced my skin. I bit back a scream.

"Almost there," Caleb breathed, not taking his eyes off the sewing job. With practiced hands, he placed four sutures. A gentle tug on the last stitch and a snip with the scissors ended the process.

I melted into the mattress, no energy left. My shoulder still burned like the fires of hell.

Caleb sat back and closed his eyes.

"Thanks," I managed weakly. Without the pain tethering me to reality, I slipped away into oblivion. I gave up the fight and let the blackness take me away again from the steady throb of my shoulder.

When I woke, Caleb was snoring in the chair next to the bed. I stared at the ceiling and blinked the dryness from my eyes then adjusted my position. Fire raced outward from my shoulder at the slight movement. I gasped.

Caleb flew to his feet, his eyes alert and on me. "Harper, are you okay?"

"As good as can be expected after being shot, I guess." My voice came out in a dry rasp. I grimaced.

"Drink some water," Caleb said and grabbed a bottle. "You lost a lot of blood, so we need to push fluids."

His arm wrapped around me like I was a child. He supported my weight and raised my torso, holding my shoulder as steady as possible, so I could take a drink.

I gulped down the water then collapsed in his arms, exhausted. He pushed pillows under me then laid me back down. Usually, I would have protested such nursemaid treatment, but I couldn't support my weight.

"I feel so weak," I said.

"Getting shot takes a lot out of you." He took my hand. "I've seen guys three times your size as weak as a newborn kitten once the adrenaline wears off."

"Glad to know I'm not just a wuss," I said and forced a feeble grin to my lips.

He sat back in the chair. "Do you feel like you can eat anything?"

"I don't think so." My stomach rolled, the water sloshing around.

"It helps to get a little something in there, simple carbs, like crackers or something."

I nodded. "Crackers don't sound too bad."

He sprang to his feet, halfway to the door. "I'll run across the street to get you some." He paused and turned back. "You'll be okay for a few minutes?"

"Take your time. I'm not going anywhere."

He returned in five minutes with various crackers and a couple types of cookies from the convenience store.

I motioned to the discarded medical instruments. "Where did you get the money for the supplies?"

"I stole them," he said, not even blinking at the admission.

I wasn't sure what answer I'd been expecting. "I guess I'm lucky you didn't get caught."

I munched on a chocolate chip cookie. The sugary junk food calmed my nausea, and I sipped the water without fear of throwing up. Caleb ate his own snacks in the chair, staring at the wall as he mechanically chewed and swallowed. His phone chiming broke the silence.

"Who is it?" I asked.

"Michelle."

"The tour guide from Nansic? Why is she calling?"

"I was supposed to start work tomorrow," he responded. "Don't worry. I won't answer it."

"What are you doing?" I demanded weakly. "You have to start the job. It's the only chance we have left."

The phone rang again while we had a staredown.

"I have to get you out of the country," he insisted.

"I can't be moved for days," I said. "Answer the call."

His mouth pressed into a firm line, but he flipped the phone open. "Hello?"

He listened for a minute. "Yeah, I'll plan on being in at seven." He paused. "Great, well, I'll see you tomorrow."

I pulled myself to almost sitting and clamped my mouth against the wave of nausea.

He set the phone on the bedside table and rushed to my side. "Do you have a death wish or something? Lie down."

"We have things to do to get you ready."

"Lie down or I'll call right back and tell them I quit," he threatened.

I relaxed into the pillows and stared at the ceiling, my bravado spent.

"What are you thinking about?" he asked.

"They followed Webber to find us," I said.

Caleb nodded. "They knew he was working on this story."

"You think it was Nansic or their government contacts?"

"Could have been either. I always knew the media was skewed, but I didn't realize a company could kill a story because it made them look bad," he said and shook his head. "I guess I shouldn't be surprised at this point."

"They can't get away with it," I said, anger strengthening my voice.

Caleb rose from the chair and paced the room. "I don't see how we're going to stop them. Our only chance to survive is to run. Maybe South America, some place they wouldn't look." He crouched by the bed and took my hand. "I almost lost you. I need you to be safe."

I raised my eyebrows. "Yeah, I know how you feel. It's kind of like having someone you love in a war zone."

"I get it. I know you've been dealing with this for years, but I'm serious."

Shifting my position, pain shot through my shoulder and chest. I gritted my teeth and got my good arm under me. "I'm not running away. Even if I die trying. I'm taking these bastards down."

"Harper, even if I get inside the company, how is it going to help? We're out of options here," Caleb protested.

"No. If the media won't help us, then we have to do it ourselves."

"What do you mean? Release the story?"

I shook my head. "It's going to take more evidence to take them down without a respected journalist's name. Take the job so we can get inside. We have to get to their hard drives."

Caleb's eyes widened and his mouth opened to protest then closed again. Finally, he nodded. "Tell me what you have in mind."

"I'm going to reach out to some of my hacker friends," I said and held up a hand when I saw the protest on his lips. "Trust me, we're a tight group. And they killed one of our own."

At my insistence I wasn't dying on him anytime soon, Caleb started his job at Nansic the day after the shooting. He was steadily recovering from his near-death experience. Weakness after being on his feet for long periods of time and a residual cough were the only remaining effects. Compared to me, he looked like an Olympic athlete.

He trimmed his shaggy beard down to a well-groomed length but it still hid his facial features enough to ensure no one would recognize him from the news, although the story had died off a bit. He took the bus to work as it was our only option for transportation with the car looking like something out of an action movie.

The moment Caleb walked through the door after his shift, he rushed to the bed. "How are you feeling?"

"Fine, just like the last fifty times you texted me." I waved him off. "Do you think they suspect anything?"

"Hang on," he said and went through his routine of peering out the blinds and watching for signs he was followed.

I chewed on a fingernail and waited.

He turned. With a drawn brow, he pulled my finger from my lips. "Okay."

I rolled my eyes. "Start from the beginning."

"It was pretty boring," he said and sat in the chair. "I was in classes for the entire morning then I followed my trainer around the rest of the day."

"Do you have access to all parts of the building?"

"Right now, my card gives me Zones One and Two clearance. I have to get through my six months of probationary period before I get access to Zone Three. Zone Four, which is the research labs, won't be for another year. They want to protect proprietary information." He shrugged.

"So, what is in Zones One and Two?" I asked, hoping he would say the server room.

"Mostly the areas open to the public, as well as the basic employee areas and the test fields."

"What about the server room?"

He shook his head. "Sorry, the server room is Zone Four."

"We don't have a year to wait for you to get clearance." I pressed my lips together and blew a breath out my nose. "We'll have to get creative."

On day three after the shooting, I got some research done for the plan taking shape in my mind. A bandage across my chest and arm stabilized my damaged shoulder, keeping the pain to a deep throb. Caleb returned at five from work and set a prescription bottle on the table.

"What are those?" I asked.

"Michelle gave them to me," he answered and stripped off his blue Nansic security shirt.

Momentarily distracted by the sight of his bare chest and back I blinked and picked up the bottle. "Augmentin? Why would she give you antibiotics?"

"She asked about my cough and I told her I had a sinus infection but didn't want to go to the doctor until I got insurance. She had part of a prescription left over."

"How sweet of her." Saltiness colored my voice.

He popped the lid off the bottle and dumped a horse pill into his palm. "Take these. I don't want your shoulder getting infected."

"They probably aren't the right antibiotic." I took the pill from him but held it in my palm.

He handed me a bottle of water. "They're better than nothing."

Grimacing, I took a sip of the water and swallowed the pill. "You know she's hoping you'll take her out again."

He rolled his eyes. "What have you been up to today?"

"I reached out to some friends. They're on board. Are you sure we can trust Dr. Nelson not to turn us in to Nansic?"

With the clean unicorn T-shirt on, he grabbed the car keys. "If he wanted to do that, he would have told them who I was yesterday."

The day before, Caleb came face-to-face with the good doctor in an elevator at Nansic. Instead of sounding the alarm, like Caleb expected, Nelson nodded once then glanced under his brow at the nearly invisible camera peering down at them. Maybe we had an ally in the doctor, but not turning us in was hardly in the same ballpark as helping us bring down the company.

"We can't drive the car," I said and motioned to the keys in his hand.

"I got some Bondo on the bullet holes, so they're covered, and I put plastic over the holes in the windows. It's not pretty but I don't think we'll get pulled over." He turned to the door. "We're lucky they didn't hit the engine."

CHAPTER THIRTY-NINE

We pulled to a stop down the street from the doctor's house and waited, watching for any surveillance. Lights inside the house told the story of a typical family evening in suburbia. The bullet holes did nothing to air out and improve the smell in the car. Now, I couldn't even roll my window down to get fresh air. I battled nausea while we waited. At the point I thought the bile would win, Caleb sent a text to the doctor's cell.

Finally, the phone chimed with Nelson's response. *Not here. Follow me.*

My cell phone rang and showed Professor March's number. I answered but didn't get a word out.

"Harper? Government agents are here," she hissed, her voice muffled like her hand was over her mouth. "They're shutting me down and taking all my research. Some crap about this being an EPA investigation now."

"What?" I sputtered, my grip turning to a vise on the phone. "Can they do that?"

"This is a cover-up. Someone sent them. What I want to know is who, and how they found out." She paused. Muffled voices told me she was talking to someone. "I've got to go." She disconnected.

"What is it?" Caleb asked.

"They shut down the research." I glared at the house in front of us. "He must have told them."

Caleb's mouth firmed. "We can ask him ourselves."

A couple minutes later the garage door opened, and his car pulled out. Caleb followed at a distance, still on alert for a tail.

We pulled into the parking lot of a small grocery store. The doctor got out of his car and looked around before walking in.

I got out of the car. A wave of vertigo swept over me, and I gripped the car door to remain upright. I'd dealt with weakness and dizziness since the shooting, but this carnival ride was new.

Caleb grabbed a cart and we headed inside, to the produce section, hardly the clandestine meeting place in the movies.

We caught up with the doctor over the mounds of apples. He picked through them, not looking up.

"Why are you contacting me again?" he hissed.

"Did you tell anyone about the geese?" I demanded.

His wide eyes darted to mine, then away. "No, why?"

"The EPA took over the research site. Only a few people know about the extent of the symptoms the geese are having and their connection to Nansic. You're one of them."

He rubbed his eyes. "The company has connections everywhere. I swear it wasn't me."

I eyed him for a moment, weighing his answer. He had no reason to lie. "It could have been the editor when the story was quashed."

"Is that why you're contacting me?" His face squished up like a bulldog. "Talking to you is dangerous for me, for my family."

I examined an apple for bruises. "We need your security badge."

A fruit avalanche tumbled down Nelson's side. He lunged forward to stop the produce from spilling to the floor. "You can't possibly take these people on. You're a college student. Not to mention your mental health history. They have all the details of your records."

I jerked back as if slapped. "That's private. How?" I gasped then stopped myself. With the tech help they had on payroll no information was private. "So, they'll make it look like I'm crazy."

"They'll use the breakdowns and paranoia to discredit you. This is a big kid game that you don't want to play."

My jaw firmed. "I had to grow up a long time ago. That's why we need to get inside the company. Then nothing they say will matter."

"They would know it was my badge. They'll kill me," he sputtered.

I met his gaze, my face stone, and wiggled the fingers of my bound arm in a morbid wave. "Trust me, I know."

He took in my injured shoulder, then glanced away, unable to meet my eyes. "I'm sorry, I didn't mean to—It's just, I can't risk my family." He blanched, likely realizing he was partially responsible for taking away mine.

I blinked back moisture in my eyes at the thought of Will.

"If you're sorry then help us make sure they can't hurt anyone else. The pesticide may not show up right away, but you know it's a death sentence for millions," Caleb said.

Nelson threw the apples into his cart without regard for bruising, then put his hands on his hips, his head hanging. After a moment of consideration, he shook his head. "Give me time to get my family safe. They leave to tour MIT in two days. I'll give you the badge the night they leave and report I lost it in the morning. Security will deactivate it immediately, so you'll have to do whatever you have planned that night. It's the best I can do."

"We also need a map of the lower level," I said.

He groaned, not even keeping up the appearance of secrecy. "I can't. It has the highest security clearance. My badge won't get you down there."

"You let us worry about that." My hand shook. The pound of apples in the bag was too heavy, so I set the bag in the cart.

"Fine. Text me an email address and I'll send you what I know of the basement."

"And we need any cash you've got on you," Caleb said.

Nelson didn't protest. He dug a wad of money out of his wallet and handed it to Caleb as he pushed past our cart.

As I watched him rush away, I struggled with a feeling of unease. It seemed like we'd been the ones strong-arming Nelson into our plan but something about his stance, straight and strong, didn't feel like a defeated man. I moved the feeling to the back of my mind and focused on the now.

The next day, Caleb went to work, and I finalized plans while trying not to worry about him. I continued to take Michelle's antibiotics. Being tired after being shot was expected but my body grew weaker each day, not stronger.

The chills hit me midafternoon. I bit my lip and took the bandage off my shoulder, dreading what lay underneath. The flesh around the stitches had puffed up, straining the thread. Placing my hand lightly over the wound, I let out a sigh. "Damn." The skin was warm to the touch.

If I told Caleb about the infection, he'd insist we put off our one chance of stopping Nansic. Not an option in my mind. I took an extra dose of the antibiotics and four ibuprofens to keep the fever down. I just needed to get through a day and a half. Then I'd either be dead or in the hospital.

While I rebandaged my shoulder, the door to the room opened. Caleb called, "Harper?"

"In the bathroom." I slapped the bandage over the angry flesh as his head appeared around the corner.

"Need some help?" he asked.

"You want to wrap it while I hold this in place?"

Picking up the clean bandage he stood behind me. "How's it looking?"

"Fine."

"And how are you feeling?" he pressed.

I held his gaze in the mirror and lied. "Tired but getting better."

He nodded. "Good. But keep taking those antibiotics just in case."

This time I wasn't lying. "I will."

After he finished with the bandage, he helped me with my shirt and sling, then wrapped his arms gently around my waist. His mouth nuzzled my neck with a feather touch. I relaxed into his embrace then turned to meet his lips with my own. Electricity zinged through my body at his touch, still so new yet familiar. A fresh warmth replaced my spiked temperature. I pressed into him.

One finger stroked my face. "Tomorrow night, if something goes wrong..."

I stopped his words with a kiss then drew away and said, "Whatever happens, I don't have any regrets." Then I pulled his lips to mine and didn't let go.

The next night, with a few last-minute essentials to pick up, Caleb got back to the motel late. I'd already done my part in obtaining the necessary tech tools. Thanks to some fundraising from threads I'd put out to Ren's and my hacker friends, we'd had enough untraceable currency to get what we needed. They'd been generous in their donations to bring Ren's killers to justice.

I took advantage of Caleb's delay and lay on the bed to garner my energy. Chills alternated with sweating throughout the day. The ibuprofen mellowed the fever but did nothing for the nausea and dizzy spells coming more and more frequently.

I closed my eyes and swallowed to keep the latest dose of antibiotics down. Obviously, they weren't the correct drug for the infection brewing in my shoulder but with no other option, I could only hope they would stave off the germs long enough to complete the plan.

The sound of the key sliding home in the lock jerked me awake. I forced myself to a sitting position and rubbed a hand over my face before Caleb walked in. His eyes darted around the parking lot before he closed the door and threw the bolt.

"How did everything go?" I asked.

"I got what we need. They aren't the prettiest, but they shoot straight." He set down the nondescript gym bag and pulled several Glock-17s and multiple magazines from inside, setting them on the table. The metal clatter was a ghostly familiar sound from my past. The usual expected bubble of fear didn't form in my gut. While I couldn't bring myself to pick up the guns, I could at least see them without setting off a panic attack.

I assessed the hardware. "They pack some punch. And get off, what, two rounds a second? They should do."

My calm voice earned a raised eyebrow from Caleb. "They aren't bothering you?"

I shook my head. "Not right now anyway."

With a nod, he unzipped a black duffle bag and put the

weapons inside, as well as extra ammo. "You leave the shooting to me and I'll leave the computer stuff to you."

"Deal. Did Nelson get you the card?"

"Yeah, he dropped it under the tire of the car, I guess so he can claim he lost it on his way home if anyone checks the security camera."

"Hopefully by tomorrow they'll have more to worry about," I commented.

With the bag packed and zipped, he put his hands on his hips. "Now, we wait."

Three tedious hours later the clock showed ten pm. I met Caleb's gaze and we stood without a word and walked to the door. All in black, I felt like a cat burglar headed to a heist. A cheerleader-esque giggle escaped my lips. Caleb paused, brows together.

I sobered. "Sorry. Nerves." Or fever-induced hallucinations starting.

He shook his head.

I sent a last glance back at the prescription bottle sitting on the table containing one lone anxiety pill. I left it. I'd do this without it.

We climbed into the car. Saltiness flooded my mouth at the noxious odor blended with the pine scent from the air freshener Caleb hung from the mirror to try and mask the stench. The mixture made the smell worse. I swallowed hard.

Ten minutes later we passed the nearly deserted parking lot of Nansic headquarters. A few cars from overnight security remained, as well as a shiny Lotus parked sideways across a reserved spot for company heads.

Caleb parked in a dark section of street, outside the view of security cameras. Being in the security office, he'd been able to map out a route of blind spots.

We tromped through the bushes and trees on the south side

of the campus. The terrain made the hike we'd taken to the test fields the week before look like a stroll through a park. Plus, I was handicapped with one arm strapped to my body. The other side of the campus, with the test fields, was heavily guarded now since our fiasco. Lucky for us, we knew the rotations.

Chill crept into my fingers from the moist spring air while sweat sprang from pores across my forehead.

The muscles in my legs shook with the strain of walking. By the time we reached the side door, I needed to lean against the brick of the building to rest. Caleb's attention focused on the locked door in front of us. I wiped the sweat from my lip and brow. He'd gone into full mission-mode the minute we stepped out of the car—muscles tense, laser focus, like I imagined him on an operation with his team. Only this time, I was his team, his backup. I couldn't let him down.

The smell of stale cigarettes from the many butts in a sand-filled bucket increased the pounding in my temples. This was a favorite smoke break spot for employees. The key card reader was one of the highest trafficked in the entire building which was why Caleb chose it for our entry point.

Key card in hand, he glanced my way. "Ready?"

"Let's do this," I said with strength I didn't feel.

Shoulders tense, he slid the mag-strip through the reader. He used his own card on this door. Security wouldn't think much of a card with a security ID opening a side door, but Nelson's would raise questions. While on duty, Caleb timed the walk from this door to the top floor. If we hurried it should take less than four minutes.

I steeled myself and ducked in behind Caleb. Cameras aimed down from their perch near the ceiling. In his uniform, with his cap pulled low, no one would see his face. Dressed in black and half-crouching behind Caleb's muscular bulk, I did my best impersonation of a shadow.

My quads screamed by the time we made it to the end of the hallway. Out of view of the first camera, we paused, and I straightened. I took a clip and wireless transmitter from my backpack and handed it to Caleb to attach to the back of the camera. With my new laptop, thanks to the donations, I hacked my way into security feeds of the entire building and set up the program I'd written for the cameras. It was a little more complicated than a simple loop on the recordings. Instead, it followed our projected path and looped the specific cameras at the times we would be within sight.

The program reduced the likelihood that security would notice us tampering with the feeds. But it also put a time constraint on each leg of our mission. Which sounded a lot easier yesterday when I didn't feel like I was about to pass out. The camera's power light would blink when the program was in effect as a signal it was safe to proceed, but the guys in the security booth would hopefully never know the difference.

I'd already accessed most of the other building systems, thanks to the water monitor installed in the holding pond. It was wi-fi enabled and sent current readings to computers in the labs. I'd piggybacked on the monitor's signal and gotten into the company computers, inspiration I'd taken from a famous Vegas casino hack involving a fish tank. But the security feeds were on a different system, and the water monitor didn't get me to the servers since they were in a signal-blocking bunker under the building.

Shaking muscles made me wish I'd insisted on looping each camera when we got to it, but the minute or two each hack would take made Caleb nervous. Running the program put us on a precise schedule but it also considerably reduced the likelihood of us being caught before we achieved our goal. A moving target is harder to catch.

Finger on the enter key, I glanced up at Caleb. "Ready?"

He nodded.

I hit the button, slapped the laptop shut and, clutching it with my free arm, ran to the stairwell behind Caleb. As we passed the first camera I glanced up and saw the flashing power light—it was on a loop. One flight up, my lungs burned along with my legs. Two flights up, Caleb pulled ahead by half a flight. By the fourth and final flight, my feet hit the risers with a slap and the concrete wobbled across my vision.

Caleb stood at the top of the stairs, shifting his weight from foot to foot, Nelson's security card in hand. Caleb's card wouldn't access the upper floors of the building, a designated Zone Three. We needed the doctor's card for two security doors.

His brow pulled together as I gasped my way to the landing. "Are you okay?"

Out of breath, I motioned to the thankfully still-blinking camera and went past him into the hallway. The next camera sat in view from just outside the stairwell door, though we were out of the camera shot. This was one of the three blind spots Caleb identified in his time spent in the observation room watching camera feeds. I opened my laptop, balanced on my bad arm, hit two keys to pause the program, then bent over to clear the spots from my vision.

"Harper," Caleb whispered from behind me, his hand gripping my arm. "You're not up to this."

I gasped. "This is our chance. I'm fine. Just tired." I forced myself to stand up straight. No one would ever have guessed Caleb was the one who'd recently died and been revived.

His eyes assessed me for a moment. "Are you sure?"

"Yes. We won't have this opportunity again. It has to be tonight. For Will." I knew bringing up my brother would stave off his questions. At least for now.

He shook his head, lips compressed. "If you get any worse, I'm carrying you out of here."

I rolled my eyes for his benefit then hit the enter key to restart the loop. The power light on the camera in front of us blinked the all clear. We crept around the corner and down the Berber carpeted hall of large wooden office doors, all closed. Rounding a corner, we paused to check that the power light on the next camera was blinking.

An open foyer lay before us with twin elevator doors. Ornately carved glossy tables with fresh flowers lined the opposite wall and huge potted palms sat on either side of the elevators. We crept forward. A voice from the hallway froze us in the middle of the foyer.

I shot Caleb wide eyes. There was no blind spot near us. Either we'd be discovered by whoever owned that voice or risk being seen by the cameras.

"I'll give the images the go-ahead for the campaign and then send you the additional ideas for a name." A man's voice carried down the hallway. "DX-200 has a nice ring to it, but I think we can attract consumers with something a bit catchier."

"We're going to be ready for this growing season. You have three days. We're kicking off sales next week and I'd hate to have to find another manager for the campaign."

"Don't we need to wait on FDA approval?" the first voice asked.

"Approval won't be a problem."

I recognized the voice from the recording I'd watched a million times. Marling.

When there was money to be made in poisoning the public, these people didn't waste time.

"Okay, I'll get right on it," the other man said, approaching our position.

Head darting from side to side, Caleb searched for a hiding

spot. Carpet-softened footsteps approached. Within seconds he'd see us. I took a stumbling step back.

Grabbing my good arm, Caleb jabbed the elevator call button and shoved me and his bag behind one of the palms, taking up a position in front of me. I steadied myself on the wall, my shoulder screaming in pain, palm leaves in my face. One of Caleb's hands reached behind his back and settled around the grip of the Glock seated in his waistband as the man rounded the corner.

CHAPTER FORTY

I slumped behind the plant, gritting my teeth against the agony in my shoulder, and curled into a ball, trying to make myself as small as possible. I bit my lip as a tsunami of tremors raged up my body and my knees gave out. Exhaustion and anxiety overwhelmed my senses. My free hand cradled my head, both to block out input to my overtaxed nerves and to cover my damnable red hair from view.

For a moment, I regretted not bringing my prescription bottle. My pocket felt empty without it. *You've got to do this for Will.* I held on to my anger and let it push out the fear.

Caleb spoke, steady and sure of himself, "Evening, sir. I held the elevator for you."

"Thank you," the other man said. Then continued in a hushed voice, "If you're on your way to see Marling, good luck. He's in a mood."

Caleb chuckled, completely relaxed. "Thanks for the heads up."

From between the palm leaves, I watched the elevator doors slide shut. Caleb spun and crouched in front of me, his hands covering mine.

"Harper. It's okay, he's gone," he whispered.

Make them pay, repeated over and over again in my head. I dropped my hand and shifted the computer to clamp it with my bound arm despite the pain.

"The camera." Caleb's voice penetrated my mantra.

My head snapped up to the security camera. The light still blinked. But not for long. With the delay, we had a second or two at most to clear the view and get to the next hallway or we'd be visible on the security monitors.

He pulled me to my feet by my good arm. I forced myself to move. We made it to the corner just as the camera stopped looping and went back to live feed.

Caleb peered down the wide hallway of the VIP wing. The door at the end of the hall sat ajar. The desk in front of the door lay empty, the secretary having gone home. There was only one camera left, aimed directly at us. The last section of hallway and offices were not under surveillance. A blinking power light greeted us, and we crept past, toward our goal.

My mantra changed as we progressed down the hall. *Complete the mission.*

We passed out of range of the last camera. I let out a breath, but the hard part wasn't over. It was just beginning.

Caleb put his back against the wall, and I followed suit. Eyes closed, I firmed my resolve then gave Caleb a nod.

The sound of shuffling papers and a drawer slamming carried out of the room. Caleb pulled the Glock from his waistband then held up three fingers. He silently counted down. On zero he sprang forward. One hand slapped the door back while the other raised the Glock into shooting position.

Close on his heels, I rounded the corner. A suit-clad man stood behind an oversized desk. The man on the video Will sent. This was the man behind it all. The one who wanted to poison the world with his damn pesticide.

His eyes wide, Marling stared at the gun aimed at his chest. "What do you want?"

Caleb spoke in a deadly calm voice. "You're going to come with us."

"You've got to be kidding," Marling sneered. "Do you know how much security we have in this building?"

"Thirty men inside, six more on the grounds and one in the basement," Caleb answered without hesitation.

Marling blinked.

I stepped from behind Caleb and glared. A mask slid over my features. Like the anger made me a different person. It felt better than fear. Way better.

Marling's confusion melted from his face as recognition set in. "You," he spat then laughed. The wicked witch had nothing on him as the evil sound reverberated around the large room. "I'm paying two dozen men to look for you and you're stupid enough to walk right in here."

Caleb's face remained stone, the gun trained on center mass.

I straightened as much as the agony in my shoulder would allow, attempting an imposing stance. "We're going to need your card, and your eye. Not necessarily the rest of you, so keep talking." I paused and tilted my head toward Caleb. "See what happens when you piss him off."

Unconsciously, Marling put his hands in his pockets, no more laughter in his voice. "Killing me won't stop the DX-200 from being released."

"Maybe not. But it would make me happy," I said in a saccharine voice.

Caleb pulled a new knife from the cargo pocket of his pants and snapped it open. It didn't compare to his old one, but it would get the job done. The blade shone in the light like a promise. "What will it be, Marling?"

With his gun in hand, Caleb stood behind Marling while we waited an eternity for the elevator. I couldn't help but glance at the camera for the tenth time to reassure myself the feed remained looped. The power light winked at me and I released the breath I'd been holding. I'd manually hacked the camera the second time, not knowing how hard it would be to get Marling out of his office.

Fresh blood dripped from a gash on Marling's forehead. A reminder from Caleb of who was in charge.

I chewed on my bottom lip. The elevator dinged and slid open.

"Hang on a second," I said, my gaze on the screen of the open laptop in my hand.

We waited in the foyer while Caleb pressed the down button to hold the elevator and I worked.

I switched the feed loop to the elevator. It took forty-five seconds to move the loop to the elevator camera, my fastest time yet. Not bad for a one-handed hack. I left ten seconds on the foyer camera to avoid security seeing us. Running my program wasn't an option after we picked up Marling, too many variables to contend with to accurately guess how long each camera needed to be looped.

"Got it," I said.

Caleb shoved Marling into the empty elevator, and I followed, adjusting the sling which was biting into my neck.

Marling looked up at the camera and saw the blinking light. His jaw muscle bulged, and he couldn't keep his mouth shut. "Even if you get me out of the building, it won't do you any good."

We'd tossed around the idea of taking the executive and forcing him to admit on camera that he'd ordered Will's death, and ours, as well as burying data showing DX-200 was dangerous to humans and animals.

"We aren't kidnapping you," I said. We needed irrefutable evidence, not a forced confession.

Caleb, gun still aimed at Marling, swiped the executive security card in the slot then punched the button for the basement. This was part of Zone Four, the most restricted area in the building. Only Marling, his special security team, and a handful of computer geeks had access. The elevator lurched into motion.

Caleb took up position behind the executive, the gun in his pocket. He spoke, his voice like steel, "You try anything stupid, you die."

My computer open, I furiously typed to move the loop to the next camera. The floors slid by too fast. I rushed to finish the hack, sweat dripping down my shirt. My finger hovered over the enter key and we slowed to a stop. I pressed the button as the doors slid open.

A single security guard sat behind a desk. The security camera over his shoulder blinked. He sprang to his feet when he saw Marling. "Sir."

Marling's mouth worked like he was chewing gum, but he nodded to the security guard.

"What can I do for you, sir?" the guard asked, his eyes sliding over Caleb then me, taking in my flushed cheeks and hovering over my bound arm.

"We need to get into the servers." Marling waved to the locked door. A card reader sat to the left of the door next to a biometric scanner which required a retinal scan along with the security card.

"Yes, sir." The guard stepped aside, and his gaze rested on Caleb.

Caleb nodded.

"A little late for an IT call, isn't it?" the guard asked, his eyes on me and my awkwardly balanced computer.

"Yes, it is." Marling's voice said more than his words.

The guard glanced toward Marling, his hand moving to the holster of his gun on his hip. "Sir, are you sure you're okay—"

Caleb leapt into motion, wrapping one forearm around the guard's neck while his other hand ripped the gun from the man's hand. The struggle took mere seconds. With the element of surprise and his larger size, Caleb easily disarmed and subdued the guard.

Marling bolted to the elevator but stopped short when Caleb fired a warning shot inches from his nose. A high-pitched squeak escaped Marling's lips and he skidded to a stop.

I flinched at the sound of the gunshot, which would likely have had me curled in a ball in the corner mere weeks before.

Caleb aimed the gun again, one arm still around the guard's neck. The man struggled to breathe for a few more seconds, then went limp. Caleb eased him to the floor without taking his eyes off Marling.

Setting the computer on the desk, I slipped two zip ties from my pocket and got the unconscious guard's hands behind his back with my free arm while Caleb kept his gun on Marling. Without two working hands, I secured the zip tie with my free hand and teeth, ignoring the pain erupting in my shoulder with each movement, then repeated the process on his ankles. Finished, I pulled out one more zip tie and faced Marling to do the same.

His glare told me exactly what he thought of me. I smiled and gave the zip tie an extra tug, to be sure it was tight.

After he pulled the guard's unconscious form behind the desk, Caleb shoved Marling to the retinal reader and forced his head to the panel after he slid the security card through the slot.

The light flipped from red to green and a heavy metallic *thunk* resonated through the cement wall.

I strained to open the reinforced door and paused in the doorway. Servers lined the walls to my left and workstations lined the walls to the right. Overhead, the air conditioning clicked on and cold air blew over the already chilled room. To my fever-heated skin, it was like stepping onto Antarctica in a swimsuit. I took a moment to lean my blazing forehead against the cool wall while Caleb hustled Marling inside. The smell of computer hardware with a side of concrete hit me. Behind us, the heavy door swung shut.

Shivering, I hurried to a workstation and plugged in while Caleb forced Marling onto his knees. My fingers flew over the keys. "Your access code," I demanded.

He made a face and pressed his lips together.

Caleb pushed the muzzle of the Glock into Marling's forehead. "Don't make her ask twice."

I turned from the computer to glare.

"If you kill me, you'll never get the code," he said triumphantly.

"You're right," Caleb agreed and moved the gun to aim at Marling's foot. Without another word or warning, he fired. The sound of the blast reverberated and amplified off the cement walls. Along with Marling's screams.

CHAPTER FORTY-ONE

Blood dribbled out of Marling's shoe onto the bare floor while he doubled over into a ball, still screaming. This far down we didn't need to worry about anyone hearing, unless another guard came.

My ears rang with the sound of the shot, and my gaze focused on the bloody wound. My vision shimmered in front of my eyes. I swallowed and held on to the desk until the dizziness passed. It was getting hard to even sit up in the chair.

Writhing on the floor, Marling continued to shriek, "You shot me. I'll have you killed for this."

"Go ahead and try. Again." Caleb smirked. "Now, what is your access code?" He aimed the gun at Marling's other foot.

Marling held up a hand and cried out, "No, no, I'll give it to you."

Caleb kept the gun steadily aimed until Marling rattled off the ten-digit code and I entered it. I nodded when the display changed to a navigation screen. I blazed through the internal server, downloading everything about DX-200. I pushed a thumb drive into the jack and backed up each document. Files flashed over the screen, the words blurring together.

274   EMILY BYBEE

Adrenaline was the only thing keeping me upright. The room faded around me, as it often did when I focused on my computer. File after file, memo after memo, all went to the laptop and flash drive. To be thorough, I copied all of Dr. Nelson's and Marling's emails, active and deleted alike.

"Who is working with you in the government?" I demanded. I needed to be sure I entered all the pertinent queries into the search.

"Go to hell," Marling snarled.

"That's not how you talk to a lady," Caleb chided and put his boot over Marling's wounded foot then leaned his weight onto the wound.

Fresh cries echoed off the walls. Caleb applied more pressure. The pitch of Marling's screams kicked up an octave.

"Patton...Patton in the FDA," Marling screamed.

Caleb stepped harder on Marling's foot. "Who else?"

"Congressmen Briarwood, McCray, and Jones. That's it, I swear."

Caleb stepped off the injured foot. Marling's screams subsided to groans and he lay still on the concrete.

I entered the names and copied the documents, glancing over them as they came up. "Five hundred thousand dollars? That's all you gave them?"

Marling gasped, "Politicians are cheap. Especially when they know they'll get a cut of the profits."

I shook my head and continued to download onto the flash drive.

"How's it coming?" Caleb asked almost an hour later.

"I think I've almost got everything." I paused as an order for tests from Nelson's lab came up. I was no expert, but I'd picked up a bit over the last days. I scrunched my brow and dove into the trail of paperwork. This wasn't right. Why would Nelson have been testing estrogen and testosterone levels? And the dates were before the side effects started showing.

Caleb glanced at his watch. "It's almost zero-one-hundred. The next shift will be coming in fifteen minutes. We've got maybe five minutes."

His use of military time was comfortable, the language of my childhood. "Just give me a few more minutes. I want to make sure we get as much as possible."

"You okay?" Caleb asked, apparently hearing the shift in my voice.

"I'll explain later. No time."

"Copy. Three minutes, then we are out of here no matter what."

I nodded and focused on the screen. My fingers flew over the keys. What seemed like mere seconds later Caleb said, "Time's up, Harper."

I pulled up and saved one last document, a memo from Marling to what looked like his boss from the solicitous language used in the message. One sentence caught my eye and I froze then read it aloud, "The side effects of DX-200 are projected to affect ten percent of the population, or thirty-three million individuals, and not for twenty to twenty-five years. Projected profits over those years are expected to equate to between thirty and fifty billion. By setting aside one percent of profits, the company should be ready to deal with any potential settlements and lawsuits. Thus, there is no reason to hold up production of DX-200."

I turned in the chair and focused my slitted eyes on the pathetic man at my feet. My hands closed into fists, itching to beat him to a pulp. "No reason? Thirty-three million people getting dementia is no reason to hold up production?"

His bleary gaze focused on me. "It's just business. Shareholders want profits. That's what I do."

I shook my head, unable to comprehend his logic.

"Harper, we have to go. Now," Caleb ordered.

I spun and unplugged my computer, tucking the flash drive into my pocket. Caleb shoved Marling away from the doorway. Fresh yells erupted.

"Shut up or I start shooting knees."

Seeing the menace in Caleb's eyes, Marling swallowed his screams. "At least untie me. I'm obviously not going to run."

Caleb sneered. "Nice try. You're going to have some time to yourself to contemplate your decisions."

Marling's brows drew together. "You can't leave me locked in here."

Ignoring his further protests, I checked the camera outside the door to be sure it was still on the loop. I pulled the door open. Caleb followed close on my heels, giving Marling a wave as he closed the door on his screams. The now conscious but immobilized guard shouted, "You'll never make it out of the building."

Punching the elevator call button, Caleb glanced at his watch again. "Cutting it close."

The elevator crept toward us, seeming to take forever. I finished getting the camera program I'd written for our exit path ready and waited. A wave of dizziness rocked me almost off my feet. I leaned against the wall to keep upright but gasped when my inflamed shoulder touched the solid surface.

"Harper," Caleb said and grabbed my arm. His brow crinkled and he touched my face. "God, you're burning up. You need a hospital."

I pushed off the wall and swayed, my energy reserves empty. "We can worry about that once we're out of here."

The elevator dinged and the door slid open. I pressed the button to start the program. We were on a timer for our exit strategy. Caleb supported my good arm while I stepped in. He pushed the button for the first floor and glanced at his watch again. He'd planned this mission down to the second, just like he would have on a mission with his team. We were behind schedule.

With his gun in hand, he stepped in front of me and raised the weapon to aim out where the doors opened. The metal door slid aside, and Caleb scanned the area for security. Silently, he waved me forward. I crept around him into the hallway. The main foyer spread before us, several stories tall with four wide hallways branching off the main area. The wide glass doors of the main entrance lay a hundred feet to our right, like fresh bait on a fishhook.

Off to one side of the main doors, and just out of sight from the elevators, a security guard manned a desk to watch the front door twenty-four hours a day. I prayed the guard wouldn't bother to investigate the ding of the elevator so late at night.

The main contingent of the security force was stationed in the surveillance office, which was around a corner and down the corridor. A guard would walk down the hallway to the elevator in mere minutes to relieve the guard we'd left bound in the basement.

The most direct exit was straight past the lone guard and out the front door, but to reduce the chance of casualties, Caleb and I planned on a less-traveled side exit.

Ten more minutes and we'd be home free.

I took a step toward the hallway to my left and glanced behind us at the hallway to the security office. Behind Caleb, a large, uniformed man strode around the corner, heading for the elevator. He was early. His surprised gaze met mine.

"Caleb," I yelled as the guard reached for his gun.

Caleb didn't hesitate. He spun on his heel, dropping to his knees at the same time into a crouched position, and fired. The guard dropped his half-drawn weapon. It clattered against the tiled floor. He stumbled backward, holding his shoulder.

Footsteps pounded down the hallway from the security office and from the desk at the entrance. A siren sounded overhead, its piercing scream sharp in my already pounding skull.

"Shit," Caleb swore. In seconds, armed guards would swarm our indefensible position. He grabbed me around the waist and swung me back into the still open elevator.

Crouched in the corner, I flipped open the laptop and punched in a series of buttons. So much for stealth. I hit enter and activated a backup program written by a friend of Ren's. With the mission blown, I didn't need to worry about subtlety.

The program hijacked the entire security system including cameras, motion sensors, and elevators. Because the security doors were on their own separate system, I couldn't unlock any of them. With a few keystrokes, the security guards were blind, and I was the only one with access to the security feeds. I locked every elevator except the one we were currently riding to the third floor.

A ding announced our arrival and the doors slid open. Caleb cleared the room and waved me out. I followed, laptop balanced in my hand and cameras brought up to show me the guards pounding up the stairs and converging on our position. The camera in the hallway to the right showed five guards racing toward us.

"Go left," I said.

Caleb didn't question me and started down the hallway to the left, gun leading. I flipped through different cameras and feeds, searching for a clear path to our secondary exit strategy, a stairwell at the south corner of the building.

Flipping through camera feeds as fast as I could, I almost missed two guards heading our way. They were directly in our path and blocking our secondary exit in the stairwell. I tapped Caleb's arm and held the computer out.

His brows pulled together, but he nodded. We hugged the wall and crept to the corner. The sound of door handles being checked and boots scuffing the carpet was all the noise that carried to us. Caleb watched my screen, waiting to see if the guards would turn down the perpendicular hallway and out of our path.

No such luck. The guards made their way past the hallway, approaching our position. In moments, they would round the corner.

One guard turned so his face was visible on the camera feed. Caleb silently swore. He'd wanted to avoid bloodshed as much as possible. Most of the guards were veterans, just like him, trying to work after their service was up. Except for the mercenaries on the special security team. They were killers.

The guards left us with no choice. Caleb raised his Glock and then spun around the corner, firing in rapid succession. Knowing the position of the guards from the camera feed gave him an advantage. The first dropped to the ground without getting a shot off, his gun arm limp at his side and a wound in his thigh.

A bullet hole was visible through the blue uniform shirt, just outside the edge of his bulletproof vest. They were risky, more difficult shots, but hopefully not lethal.

The second guard got one shot off before Caleb dropped him in the same fashion. The bullet hit the wall over Caleb's shoulder. The guard rolled on the Berber carpet, putting pressure on the wound at his shoulder. Recognition replaced the anguished look on the man's face. "Walker?" He used Caleb's fake name.

"Sorry, Baker," Caleb responded.

Baker's face twisted in rage. "What are you? A fucking thief?"

Caleb busied himself by kicking their weapons away, then met Baker's gaze. "No. You'll understand once everyone knows the truth."

He looked like he wanted to say more.

I gripped his forearm. "We have to keep moving."

The gunfire gave away our location. We raced toward the stairwell. I did my best to monitor the security team's movements. Two more turns and we would be at the stairwell.

Guards racing down a hallway stopped my scroll through the security feeds. "Damn. Caleb, three are coming from the north, two from the south. They've boxed us in."

He nodded and ducked down an interior hallway and quietly checked one door after another. The last one, a set of double doors, clicked open. He cracked the door and we slid inside, closing it behind us. I leaned against the wall and gasped in air to combat the dizziness.

Before us was a familiar room. I recognized the guest lounge from the tour where we'd had snacks. The long tables sat empty and outside the wall of dark windows the test fields and runoff pond were visible under the floodlights. On the opposite side of the room, in a small alcove, a kitchenette lined the wall.

Caleb rushed to the other side of the room to check the door leading to the factory where the tour had been. A simple traditional locking mechanism graced the door, obviously not a sensitive area. The handle refused to turn. He stepped back and fired a shot into the metal then cracked the door and scanned the area.

A quick succession of bullets greeted him. Slamming the door, he didn't return fire, conserving our ammo. We were cornered.

CHAPTER FORTY-TWO

Caleb wedged a table under the broken door handle. It wouldn't stop anyone from entering, but it would slow the process.

"Fuck," he spat and pointed the gun at the floor while he paced.

I furiously scrolled through feeds looking for a way to the south stairwell. At least five well-armed men blocked every path.

"We don't have much time before they find us. These guys are all ex-military and know how to clear a building," he said.

The hallway we'd just exited flashed on the screen. Three men crept down the carpeted hall, testing doors. None of them were dressed in the guard uniform. Instead, they wore street clothes with Kevlar vests.

My gaze remained glued to the first man. His close-shaved head and thick neck brought goosebumps to my skin. He was missing the bandage from his meeting with the frying pan, but I recognized the behemoth I'd brained. Bruises from his fight with Caleb had faded to yellow around his nose and eyes and his split lip was mostly healed.

His two companions looked familiar as well. One was the

merc who'd chased us through the alleys. The other was the shooter from the SUV outside the hospital. He'd shot John.

Caleb waved me to the edge of the kitchenette. He put me in a corner behind him and took up a position off to the side, behind the cement wall bump out.

His brow pulled together and he checked the magazine and inserted a full one out of reflex, preparing for what he knew was coming. "Embrace the suck."

I recognized the term from years of listening to military men.

We're going to die. Caleb knew it. I knew it. I grabbed his arm and pulled until he ripped his gaze away from the door and glanced back at me.

I couldn't die without telling him. "Caleb, I love you."

His face softened, and emotion flooded his eyes. "I love you too, Harper," he whispered in a choked voice. His hand covered mine, then the military training firmed his features, and he returned his attention to the door. "And I'm not letting you die here."

Unable to do anything, I watched the mercs approach the door. My heart pounded so loudly in my ears it seemed everyone in the building should be able to hear. I wiped my sweaty palm on my pants and gripped the computer. Even though I was watching the mercenary on the screen reach for the handle, I jumped at the soft metallic sound echoing off the tile floor.

Caleb waited, hidden behind the wall, his face like stone. He glanced at the computer screen. The behemoth waved the other two through the door first. As the two crossed the threshold of the room, Caleb took one deep breath. With no hesitation, he dropped to one knee while leaning just outside the shield of the cement and fired three shots in quick succession.

I watched a split screen, one showing the hallway and the other from the camera in the room with us on the opposite wall. I could see the mercs leave the hallway and enter the room.

The first merc fell to the floor. The man who'd shot John lay dead, a single bullet wound in his forehead.

Caleb fired another three shots. The second merc got a shot off. The bullet buried deep in the cement column next to Caleb's head. Caleb's second shot grazed the man's neck and the third hit him in the shoulder. His gun fell from his grip as he clutched his throat. Blood poured from the wound.

It was almost like watching an action movie. Only with this movie, I heard the impact of the bullets and felt the spray of cement dust over me. In this movie, Caleb and I would likely die.

The behemoth lunged back around the corner and returned fire. Caleb ducked behind the safety of the cement and replaced the empty magazine.

On the far side of the door, the second mercenary stopped moving. The pool of crimson blood flooded my brain with images from my nightmares. The volleys continued with no hits. Caleb swore. "He's keeping us pinned down until reinforcements get here."

Flipping through the screens, I saw multiple units converging on our location. "They'll be here in less than three minutes."

Once they broke through our makeshift blockade on the second door, we'd be exposed with no cover.

"Get ready to jump out the window," Caleb said between shots.

"What?" I managed, my mouth hanging open. "How does jumping out a third-floor window help us?"

He met my wide-eyed gaze. "Harper, there's no other way out."

I protested, but the gunfire drowned out my voice. Caleb dropped the Glock and pulled his backup from the bag.

"Grab a baggie for the flash drive," he ordered.

Staring out the darkened window, understanding dawned. I glanced over my shoulder and snatched a plastic baggie from the box on the counter in the kitchenette. With the flash drive sealed inside, I pushed it to the bottom of my pocket.

On the computer screen the guards pounded closer, closing us in. I looked up to meet Caleb's gaze.

"Ready?" he asked.

The forty feet to the windows might as well have been a mile with the bullets heading our way. Adjusting the sling around my neck, I crouched on weak knees, but nodded. We had to get the information out to the world and to do that we had to get out of this building.

Caleb reached into the duffle bag and grabbed a metal cylinder. With a flip of his thumb, he released the pin then tossed the smoke grenade into the open doorway. Spinning on his heel, he fired three bullets in a wide triangle into the large pane glass window. The bullets penetrated the glass with a distinctive *clink,* but the rest of the pane stayed in place.

"Go," he whispered.

I leapt to my feet, nearly falling to the floor when my legs buckled, but forced myself forward, Caleb close on my heels. He fired the gun back through the smoke to give us cover. A bullet whistled past my ear, hitting the glass window. Out of reflex I ducked. An arc of bullets sprayed around us through the air, narrowly missing their targets.

The impact of Caleb's body into my back sent me crashing to the floor as a fresh spray of bullets whizzed through the air we'd just inhabited. I gasped, pain lancing through my body, taking away my ability to cry out.

Caleb rolled over and returned fire. The telltale clink of an empty gun turned my head.

"Keep going," he said and climbed to his feet.

He turned and ran toward the smoke, crouched low. I struggled to my knees, my mouth open to protest.

Just before Caleb reached the white smoke, the behemoth emerged from the fumes, gun drawn. His gaze fixed on me, he missed Caleb coming in from his side. He repositioned the gun to aim at my chest, but before he got the shot off, Caleb hit him low in a football-style tackle.

Both of them went flying. The gun clattered to the ground and spun away across the tile, disappearing into the smoke. The two grappled, each trying for the upper hand. Caleb landed several punishing blows. The crunch of bone announced a broken nose. Caleb swung like a demon.

Caleb's opponent broke free and scrambled to his feet then reached to his belt, pulling a lethal eight-inch blade from a sheath. Close behind, Caleb pulled his own knife from his pocket and snapped it open. The blade was maybe half the size of the mercenary's. An evil sneer spread over the behemoth's face.

One arcing swipe came close enough to shave a few hairs off Caleb's face. He stepped to the side at the last moment and brought his own blade up. The merc adjusted and blocked the blow. Barely.

I'd seen this fight before. It was like watching a rerun of a bad TV show. Only this time, I didn't have a frying pan to help. My hands trembled, itching to do something, but captive to my paralyzed brain.

Caleb feigned to the right. The behemoth lunged. Caleb used the merc's momentum against him to twist his arm at the elbow. The large blade clattered across the floor. Caleb held on, maneuvering his own blade for a blow to the abdomen.

Just as hope dawned in my chest, the behemoth brought up his knee into Caleb's lower back. His incisions were mostly healed, but the fresh surgery site was a weak point. One the mercenary obviously remembered.

Caleb gasped. His half-cocked arm jerked to his body in a protective reflex. His knife dropped to the floor after a second blow to his back. The merc took the advantage, hitting the surgery site again, then flipped Caleb onto the floor, one beefy hand around his throat.

"Run," Caleb rasped.

Ice replaced my muscles. I stood, unable to leave him but knowing I was no match in a physical fight with a man who outweighed me by three times. More guards arrived, banging at the blocked door. In seconds, it would be over. Ren died for nothing. Will died for nothing.

The mercenary reached for his gun, just out of his grasp but now visible in the receding smoke.

I broke my frozen muscles free. I wasn't going to lose anyone else I loved. Without another thought, I dropped the laptop and dashed to the dead mercenary. His handgun was by his side on the tile, just outside the crimson pool of his blood.

I scooped up the dead mercenary's gun in my good hand. The familiar weight of the rough metal handle felt right against my skin.

The behemoth lunged for his gun, wrapping his fingers around the handle.

Calm swept over me. I took aim and breathed out, then paused my breath, just like Dad taught me. My finger squeezed the trigger in quick succession.

The behemoth jerked. His body stiffened as the bullets hit him in center mass. A gurgling sound bubbled from his lips and he slumped to the floor half on top of Caleb.

Caleb's wide eyes met mine over the dead man. He glanced

at the weapon still in my hand. I followed his gaze to my hand and lowered the weapon.

The pounding at the door grew louder and the metal legs of the table screeched on the tile as the guards gained a few inches of clearance on the door.

Knowing we were out of time, Caleb heaved the weight of the mercenary off himself and grabbed the gun from the man's limp hand. He waved me toward the window. "We need to go. Get as much distance as you can."

We bolted across the tiled floor. The door gave way a few feet before we hit the window. Caleb aimed back and sprayed cover fire to hold them off while I aimed my gun out the window. After two shots, one floodlight went black. Three shots later, I hit the other floodlight and the field and pond were cast into darkness.

I was definitely out of practice. Or maybe it was the fact I was wounded and feverish. I'd have taken them out in one shot, even running, when I was twelve. A pace in front of me, Caleb leapt into the holey pane of glass. It shattered against his weight. I leapt into the air. Small shimmering chunks cascaded around us. It was like jumping through a waterfall of glass.

For a second, I floated, not going up or down. Then gravity took over and I plummeted toward the ground. In the darkness, I couldn't see what lay below me. I could only pray I hit water instead of bone-breaking dirt. A splash announced Caleb hitting the water a second before I hit the surface of the holding pond.

CHAPTER FORTY-THREE

I remembered half of the dash across the darkened fields and through the trees. The rasping gasp of my breathing drowned out the sound of my chattering teeth. Partway through the trees, my legs gave out. Caleb threw me over his shoulder, my limbs dangling as he ran to our hidden car.

All the security officers were called inside when the alarm sounded to help in the building search. We had a head start, but it wouldn't last long. I was vaguely aware of Caleb laying me in the front seat of the car and cranking up the heat while a string of swear words flowed from his mouth. I insisted we go to the motel to upload the data before he took me to the hospital.

I alternated between body wrenching chills and sweat pouring from my pores. After he was sure no one followed us, Caleb pulled into the motel.

"Damn it, Harper. You should have told me it was infected."

I opened my eyes and focused on his wet and tousled hair, his wrinkled brow. "You wouldn't have let me go."

His gaze met mine. He knew I was right.

I fumbled with the pocket of my jeans and pulled out the

baggie, not releasing my breath until I saw the drive was dry inside. I shoved it to Caleb. "Get it uploaded."

"What? I don't know how."

I couldn't stay upright any longer. The chills turned to violent vibrations throughout my body. I lay back on the bed, trying not to think of the chemicals on my skin from the dip in the holding pond. "Bring me John's computer."

Caleb set the spare laptop on a pillow beside me so I could see the screen and pushed the flash drive into the slot. I was past feeling the pain in my shoulder. My body was numb.

Blackness crept in on the edges of my vision. I wasn't going to last long. But I needed to make sure they saw something. My brain struggled to remember what had been important—if I needed to send instructions. But my energy was extremely limited.

I typed in several email addresses and attached the files. Barely able to hold my hand over the keyboard I hit send. The email went out to five of Ren's and my closest hacker friends, all with their own specialties. They would know what to do with the information, I assured myself.

My eyes closed of their own accord, but I was at peace. No one could stop us now. They wouldn't get away with it, none of them would.

Caleb's voice sounded far away, calling me, then swearing profusely. But I couldn't answer.

The soft beeps of monitors and hiss of air stirred me into consciousness. I struggled to wake as if coming out of the depths of murky water. Cracking an eyelid took Herculean effort. Vague shapes formed into faces from my blurred vision. Caleb sprawled on a chair next to the bed, his mouth slack and his eyes closed. I rolled my lead-filled head to the other side and saw my mom, her head resting on my bed, her hand in mine.

A weak squeeze was all I could manage, but at the movement, her head jerked up. She gasped, "Harper. Oh, thank God."

"Mom?" I croaked. I seemed to have swallowed razorblades at some point.

Jumping to her feet, she stroked my face around the tube going up my nose. Tears spilled down her cheeks from her tired eyes. "It's okay, honey. You're going to be okay now."

Caleb stirred at the sound of our voices and let out a huge sigh. "I was beginning to think you were really gone."

"We need to wash off the water," I rasped.

"What?" Caleb and my mom shared a worried glance.

"Chemicals, holding pond." I stopped to catch my breath.

Understanding dawned, and Caleb took my hand. "Don't worry. You've been washed off."

I nodded. "The files."

A wide grin spread across Caleb's face which sported a full-on beard now, not the trimmed hair from our mission.

Silky soft fur rubbed against my cheek and the sound of motorboat purrs turned my head. Luna shoved her forehead against mine with the force of a punch.

"Luna," I gasped as a sob bubbled up and I closed my eyes to revel in the feel of her closeness. "I missed you so much."

"Meow," she answered and threw her small body against the side of my head.

"I'd say she missed you too," Caleb chuckled.

"You need to see this." Mom beamed and grabbed the remote control for the TV. "You did it. Your friends hijacked every major news outlet. Everyone knows what Nansic did and what they were planning." She turned on the news. "It's on almost every channel." Cameras showed Marling, his foot in a cast, being led into a courtroom. The headline read: *Nansic trials continue today.*

"There's still a lot to be done. Government officials being implicated has the country up in arms. There hasn't been a scandal like this since Watergate. But with the documents you leaked, the public is out for blood."

I stroked Luna as my brow pulled together. "How long?"

Mom gripped my hand. "You've been in a coma for six weeks. The infection in your shoulder spread. You were septic." She paused and sucked in a breath. "We nearly lost you."

I blinked several times, not sure what to say. Six weeks. My mouth opened but I couldn't formulate a coherent thought.

The door opened and a ghost strode into the room. I gasped, all oxygen gone from my straining lungs. The room spun. From my trauma or shock, I didn't know.

Will froze, his eyes wide as he stared.

I must have brain damage. This was a hallucination. But I didn't want it to end. I wanted my big brother back. If he wasn't real, then I didn't want to live in reality, anyway.

"Why didn't you call me?" Will asked.

Guilt flooded my constricting chest. *Was he asking about the phone calls I'd rejected?* "I—" was all I could manage.

"She just woke up," Caleb said. "I was going to call you in a minute."

I blinked. Caleb could see him too. My damaged neurons struggled to come up with an explanation.

Seeing my distress, Mom spoke, "Honey, Will got back a week after the break in."

"You're alive?" I choked out. "How?"

He crouched next to the bed, taking my hand in his strong fingers. "I got the jump on those bastards and left my dog tags on one of them before I set the fire. I didn't have any way of reaching you." He glanced to our mom. "I got a message to Mom with our old code, but no one knew where you were. I had to lay low and make it back to the States by not-so-legal means."

I gripped his hand like it was my safety rope over an abyss. "You're alive."

"Can't get rid of me that easy."

Sputtering neurons connected, and memory came flooding back. I gasped, "Nelson."

"He testified last week." Caleb grinned. "He told the court everything."

I struggled to sit up. "No, he..." My arms gave out and I slumped back to the bed.

"Honey," Mom jumped forward to help me. "Rest."

"No, we have to get Nelson." Luna purred louder, sensing my upset. Nausea washed over me that had nothing to do with nearly dying.

"What?" Will asked. "Why?"

"The tests. He ordered the tests." My sentences came out in huffs of breath. But I had to tell them. Everyone had to know the truth. We'd thought Nansic was the problem but in reality the danger was so much bigger. "The sex hormones are all wrong."

Caleb's brow scrunched. "Are you sure?"

"They lowered estrogen and testosterone production." I shook my head. "Infertility. It was his goal all along."

Three sets of wide eyes stared at me.

"Nelson left with his family after testifying," Caleb said, his blue eyes glaring at nothing out the window. He looked like he wanted to punch something. "He's gone."

I closed my eyes and shook my head. It wasn't possible. We'd caught one criminal and let an even worse one escape. I'd scream if I had the voice. I wanted to climb out of the bed and start searching for Nelson myself. "Who the hell was he working for?"

"We'll find him, Harper," Will assured me. "You need to rest now."

Unable to do anything but stew in my utter fury, I slumped back and let Luna's purr wash over me as I floated back into the darkness.

When I woke again, they were all huddled in the far corner, talking in hushed tones.

Will spotted that I was awake first and came over to the bed.

"You don't need to worry about Nelson. I reached out to Delta. We have a beef with this guy. Trust me, we'll find him." The lopsided grin that I loved so much spread over his face.

I pushed away my frustration and let the joy of my brother being here, alive, wash over me.

"In the meantime, Caleb told me everything. You did great, kiddo."

I glanced at Caleb. He'd told Will everything? Caleb held my gaze for a minute then looked at his shoes. Okay, maybe not everything.

"I underestimated you," Will continued. "I thought I needed to protect you but, well, it seems you can do that yourself." He raised his eyebrows. "So, tell me about this frying pan technique you've developed. I may need to include that in Delta training."

Caleb and I took turns telling the story of braining the merc. My body could only handle about ten minutes of talking at a time, it seemed. My head fell back to the pillow, exhaustion pulling me back under. But I fought to keep my eyes open, not willing to let Will out of my sight.

He held my hand. "It's okay. I'll be here when you wake up."

Will was there when I woke up again. Caleb and my mom went to the hotel to freshen up. The moment I opened my eyes, tears of relief flowed. Will wasn't a dream.

"You two make a good team," Will said, the sides of his lips pulling up.

"Who?"

"Come on, give me a break." He rolled his eyes. "You and Caleb."

I tugged the edge of the sheet higher. "Huh, I guess so. It was kind of necessary."

"He never left your side, you know. He showered here, refused to leave until today when he knew you were okay."

I nodded, unsure how to respond.

Will shook his head. "You don't have to pretend, Harper. I'm happy for you two. You couldn't have chosen a better guy."

Heat spread like fire over my cheeks. I glanced up to meet his gaze.

"And he couldn't have chosen a more amazing woman." Will smiled.

I gripped his hand. "I'm glad you're home."

His brows pulled together.

"What is it?" I asked.

"All this time, I thought I was keeping the country safe. Keeping you safe. When there was an even bigger threat right here at home."

I squeezed his hand tighter.

The door opened behind Will.

Caleb, freshly showered and shaved, walked in carrying a simple bouquet of daisies. He paused when he saw my flaming cheeks, his gaze darting from Will to me. "I can come back if you guys need some time."

Will jumped to his feet, grinning at the flowers. "No, I'll give you two some space."

Stepping past Caleb, he slid into the hallway and closed the door before we could protest.

Caleb contemplated the closed door for a moment, then turned to me, unsure of himself. "I brought you these." He thrust the flowers out in front of him like a shield. "You said they were your favorite."

A slow smile spread over my lips. He'd remembered. I reached for his hand and pulled him down close to my face. His blazing blue eyes held mine, and for once I didn't hesitate before I jumped in.

CHAPTER FORTY-FOUR

The smell of fresh flowers and paint fumes mixed into a heady scent. I wove through the crowded gallery, greeting the many smiling faces. My paintings graced every wall—one side darker, with the splashes of red and black of my nightmares, the other the tranquil landscapes of my dreams.

My art professor pulled me into a tight embrace, and I gritted my teeth against my still sore shoulder. Turns out infections like the one I'd let brew in the gunshot wound caused lasting effects. My shoulder joint would likely never be the same.

"I'm so proud of you," she gushed.

"Thank you for getting me the interview in the first place," I said. "I'm lucky he still wanted to show my pieces after I ran out of here."

My professor waved a hand. "No luck involved. He loved your talent."

My mom came up and linked her arm in mine. "I'm going to have to steal her for more pictures."

As we walked away, she whispered in my ear, "Are you holding up okay in this crowd?"

I put my hand over hers. "Mom, I'm fine." I met her gaze. "I'll let you know if I need any help."

She sighed and pushed a defiant flaming red curl back into place in my updo. "I'm sorry. I know you're fine. Old habits."

"It's okay." Although my anxiety would never be gone, for the first time in years I was in control. It wasn't controlling me. "Are they really asking for more pictures?"

With the international news coverage of the Nansic trial and my part in it, the opening was the largest and most well-covered showing the gallery ever hosted.

She shook her head. "I just thought you might need a break is all." She shooed me away. "You get back to your fans."

I smiled and moved on to the next excited face, turning my head to look for Ren's tall frame in the crowd before I caught myself. We'd talked about this day, my first gallery showing and how he'd be right there with me, so many times. Returning to a semi-normal life made my grief impossible to keep at bay. It crushed me when I let my guard down.

Instead of Ren's lean build, I spotted two muscular men moving through the crowd. Both made my heart rate kick up to a jackrabbit's pace, but for very different reasons.

"I didn't think you were going to come," I gasped and threw my good arm around Will. His formal uniform drew several stares from the surrounding women.

He held me, careful of my shoulder, then put me at arm's length and smiled. "I wouldn't miss my little sister's opening night, not even if they court martial me."

My brow shot up.

"He's kidding," Caleb said before I had a heart attack. "We're on leave pending the outcome of the newest sets of tests."

Both Caleb and Will tested positive for DX-200, though at vastly lower levels than many of the rest of men and women on their base due to the fact they were out on ops for most of the test period of the base food. But given the nature of their responsibilities as Delta Force members and the need to not be crazed rabid beasts, they were sent home while researchers worked to find a way to clean the chemical out of their systems—though it was not a likely possibility.

In addition to court martialing officers involved in the Nansic scandal, the Army quietly moved all exposed personnel home—some honorably discharged, others given desk jobs while they participated in close observation and testing. So far, only a handful of additional soldiers exhibited violent tendencies, but the long-term effects would take years to develop.

I pushed the possibility of Will and Caleb experiencing effects out of my mind and instead took in Caleb in his uniform. The dark suit jacket, decorated with an abundance of service ribbons and patches, gave him a serious air that his grin quickly dispelled. Got to love a man in uniform.

"Any news on where Nelson is hiding?" I asked in a hushed tone, all joy gone from my voice. Wondering where the bastard was holed up kept sleep at bay most nights now.

Will held up a hand. "Not tonight." He waved a finger as I opened my mouth to protest. "There are always going to be criminals in the world to catch, Harper. But I won't let him ruin your night."

I sighed. "Fine. But tomorrow—"

"Stop," Caleb interrupted me. "We came here to celebrate. So, let's get this party started." He pulled me in for a kiss that had me almost purring in his lap and Will clearing his throat.

"Okay," Will said. "I'm good with you two being a couple, but I don't want to see any of it."

Caleb laughed and held me tight to his side, beaming like he'd won the lotto, which, with his arm around me, was exactly how I felt.

EPILOGUE

Two months later
   Somewhere in South America

Dr. Nelson strolled around the brilliant white of his new lab, examining the shining equipment with a critical eye. Lab techs waited for orders as boxes of raw materials were unloaded and stored in the refrigerators and on the shelves. Outside the windows, the lush green of tropical trees swayed in the wind.

"It is to your liking, señor?" the company CEO asked.

"Yes, it is a very nice setup," Nelson responded. "Thank you for your generous offer." He turned to the man and held out a hand. "I think we will work very well together."

"Wonderful," the CEO nodded. "I will not keep you from your work any longer, then." With a nod, he left Nelson to the lab—twice the size of what he'd had at Nansic.

Nelson turned to the lab techs. "We will start the first trial with compound A." He walked to the cold boxes and extracted a vial. "Prepare the rats for the first dose please."

The phone in Dr. Nelson's pocket vibrated. "Yes, sir," he answered.

"I assume you have everything you need?" the cultured voice came from the other end of the line.

"Yes, thank you." Nelson straightened. "I appreciate your giving me another chance."

"This will be your last, doctor. Make sure we don't have to clean up another mess." The edge in the tone was unmistakable and shivers skittered up Nelson's spine like spiders. "Get the compound right this time."

"I assure you," Nelson rushed. "You and your investors will have a working compound within the year."

The line clicked, and Nelson turned to his desk. Time to get to work.

MEET THE AUTHOR

Emily grew up loving to escape to the fantasy world in books.

At the age of twelve, she began writing after having a series of extremely vivid dreams that begged to be made into a story.

In high school and college Emily focused on science and graduated with a degree in environmental biology.

After college she began writing again, but quickly realized she'd failed to take a single writing or grammar class. Luckily, she's a quick learner.

Emily now enjoys making up stories in genres from urban fantasy to romance to suspense and loves when she can add in a dash of science, just for fun.

OTHER TITLES FROM
5 PRINCE PUBLISHING

5PrinceBooks.com
Picking Pismo *Emi Hilton*
Spring Showers *Sarah Dressler*
Secret Admirer Pact *Bernadette Marie*
The Publicity Stunt *Bernadette Marie*
A Trace of Romance *Ann Swann*
Descendants of Atlantis *Courtney Davis*
Holiday Rebound *Emily Bybee*
Rewriting Christmas S.E. Reichert & Kerrie Flanagan
Butterfly Kisses *Courtney Davis*
Leaving Cloverton *Emi Hilton*
Beach Rose Path Barbara Matteson
Aristotle's Wolves *Courtney Davis*
Christmas Cove *Sarah Dressler*
A Twist of Hate *T.E. Lorenzo*
Composing Laney *S.E. Reichert*
Firewall Jessica Mehring
Vampires of Atlantis *Courtney Davis*
Liz's Roadtrip Bernadette Marie

Milton Keynes UK
Ingram Content Group UK Ltd.
UKHW031114080824
446563UK00001B/52